MAN FROM THE EAST

Dr. Mohsen El-Guindy

2nd Edition

Copyright © 2020 by Dr. Mohsen El-Guindy

ISBN: 978-1-953048-47-9 (Paperback)

All rights reserved. No part of this book may be used or reproduced by any means, graphic, electronic, or mechanical, including photocopying, recording, taping or by any information storage retrieval system without the written permission of the publisher except in the case of brief quotations embodied in critical articles and reviews.

The views expressed in this work are solely those of the author and do not necessarily reflect the views of the publisher, and the publisher hereby disclaims any responsibility for them.

Writers' Branding
1800-608-6550
www.writersbranding.com
orders@writersbranding.com

CHAPTER ONE

The wealthy egyptian, Selim abdel Razek, completed his law education at Cairo University. From the early 1940s until the 1950s, apart from being a lawyer of good repute, he invested a good deal of money in farming a vast piece of land that he inherited from his father. He also invested a considerable amount of money in the local agricultural trade and earned tremendous profits.

Due to the political turmoil that dominated the country and prohibited trade according to the mechanism of the free market, Selim decided to invest all his money abroad. He closed an agreement with an Arab client who imported agricultural products from Egypt. Selim lent him the money to cover importation costs, and the client deposited the equivalent amount in Selim's London bank account.

Selim also liquidated all his capital assets, and, through the same money transfer, was able to multiply his bank account several fold. Soon, London became his permanent residence, where he bought a decent house and established a law office to counsel his Arab clients and manage their business in Europe.

Selim offered legal and economic consultations to major companies dealing with the Arab world and eventually took advantage of his position as mediator to close substantial deals between the two worlds— deals that included trucks, airplanes, and oil tankers.

Ten years later, his wealth amounted to 600 million pounds sterling. As he gained his tremendous fortune, he lost his law skills except those related to gains, profits, losses, and money management.

While he lived in London, Selim left his wife, Safia, in Cairo to care for their son and daughter, Ali and Nadia, who were still in high school. Ali was one year older than his sister, and Selim planned to bring them to

London as soon as Ali graduated from high school. During their studies in Cairo, Selim traveled to Egypt frequently to see his family and ensure their needs were met.

After Ali's graduation, Selim brought his family to London with Saber, their servant, who cared for Ali since childhood. Selim always wanted Ali to continue studying business administration in an American university. Ali chose North Carolina University due to its wide reputation in that field. A nice apartment was rented for him in the Raleigh district near the university campus. Saber went with him to serve him, while Selim felt it was best if Nadia stayed with her mother and continue her education in London.

Before Ali left for the States, Selim spent time alone with him. "You're in your late teens now, and imagination frequently takes you away from reality. I want you to be alert and look after yourself well. Always remember that the wife a man chooses must be from his country, so they can understand each other better. Please be careful and use your brain in all things concerning your future."

"Yes, Father. Please pray for me."

Selim raised his hands to the sky and asked his Lord to protect his son and make his life in a different world successful.

Ali inherited many good characteristics from his father—a sweet, generous nature, admirable manners, and many sterling qualities and solid virtues. As a young man raised in the East, he was religious and observed his prayers. Compromise and hypocrisy weren't in him. As far as he was concerned, all people were as good-hearted as himself, entirely without conceit.

Ali was tall, his body molded by sports. He was remarkably handsome, erect, and lean, with dark eyes and strong, clean-cut features. He had a fine head of long, naturally wavy dark hair.

Nature stimulated his soul and made his relationship with the things he cared for absolutely romantic. A glance at the horizon, where the sea met the sky, captured his heart, while a glance at beautiful flowers decorating a green area made him soar into a world of golden rays. The flow of water between rocks and valleys made him feel that the universe played magic music heard only by those possessing tender souls and lively consciousness.

He always sought solitude to live in a world of his own, where he could swim among the stars and shelter in the moon's shade. Those thrilling moments stirred his senses with emotions that he expressed beautifully with tender words in a special notebook. His speech was sweet and smooth, like a flowing stream. He loved nature.

His athletic body reflected his tremendous interest in sports. During his high-school days, he won many medals in sprinting, swimming, and bodybuilding before his interests turned to karate, in which he won a black belt. That gave him strong self-confidence that he never demonstrated to others. His heroic achievements in karate, combined with his romantic character, gave him patience and self-determination. If anything annoyed him, he forgot it through robust exercise in karate or by jogging for hours. Then he sat quietly like a yogi, trying to develop physical and spiritual health through the withdrawal of the senses from external objects until he felt buoyed to the seventh heaven with gladness beyond reason.

After a seven-hour journey over the Atlantic, Ali and Saber reached North Carolina. As soon as he looked around his apartment and found it acceptable, Ali went down to the street to walk toward the university campus.

The main building was huge, while the flowering gardens were penetrated by roads that led to other buildings. Tennis courts sat near the swimming pool and gymnasium. Student residences overlooked the restaurant, and the central library, with its many floors, was some distance from various departments.

Ali felt the responsibility he carried and the challenge he faced. He would be studying in a different language, dealing with a different tradition in a different environment—even though his education in Egypt was conducted in English. He was ready to adjust and adapt to his new life.

His first day at the university was important and exciting. He was skeptical about what he would see, the acquaintances he would make, and exchanging memories. He saw cheerful boys laughing and neatly dressed girls looking at each other with an air of competition and superiority. The beautiful color of their dresses took him into a wonderland, then to a graceful garden furnished with colorful flowers. Suddenly, depression overwhelmed him as he saw the colors fade to that of autumn leaves, dramatizing his feeling of being a stranger in a different world. Instead of making acquaintances with his new colleagues, he hurried to the bookstore to buy textbooks and familiarize himself with the lectures he would soon attend as a freshman.

From his first day in the lecture room, Ali realized the importance of concentrating on his studies, because the professors explained only the main points, then asked the students to look up references in the central library. Ali went to the library to get the first set of reference books, which were six large volumes. He carried them in a pile, walking across the library pavement and trying to avoid being bumped, when he crashed into a girl, sending books flying.

She gave an outraged gasp, then tears came to her eyes. They fell down, and books scattered everywhere. He rushed to her to apologize, but embarrassment held his tongue when he saw tears rolling down her face. She lifted her face and looked at his intense, dark eyes for a moment, then she blushed and lowered her gaze, trying to collect her books.

Her beauty took away his breath, and his heart pounded so hard he feared she might hear its quick, uneven beats. *Oh, God, what a happy accident of nature*, he thought.

She had wide, gray eyes that held glints of sea waves and seashore sand. Thick, straight sheaths of silky blonde hair framed the face of an angel, and her skin was dazzlingly white and milky like satin. Her ivory neck, fine nose, and full rosy mouth endowed her with a decent pride that captured his soul. She was like a wonderful flower blossoming in his virgin heart.

From that moment, Ali forgot the feeling of being lonesome, because she would always be in the romantic worlds he fantasized. He kept looking at her, unable to talk, because he could scarcely breathe.

She looked into his eyes and felt his confusion. She said shyly, "It was my fault. I didn't look where I was going. My books weigh a ton today."

"Oh, no," he said. "It's my fault. Those tears in your eyes prove that. Please accept my sincere apology." He offered his handkerchief, and she wiped away her tears before returning it.

He held the handkerchief tightly, as if fearing to lose something precious. He helped her collect her books and saw they were similar to his. That meant he would probably see her often in the lecture room. As she walked away, he stared after her until she was out of sight.

Ali walked joyfully toward his apartment, jumping up and down despite the heavy books under his arm, thinking of the angel who captured his heart.

The following morning, Ali went to the lecture room and sat in the last row, pretending to arrange his papers while searching with hesitant eyes for the girl from the library. She wasn't there at first, but she soon arrived, chatting and laughing with a well-built boy. They sat together. Ali watched her from his seat as two other boys arrived, sitting beside her and her friend, participating in their laughter. His throat constricted when he realized she was surrounded by several competitors. The lecture began, and all present paid attention, because the professor only touched on topics, leaving the students to deduce details from their textbooks. He also regularly surprised them with exams and seminars on related topics.

After the lecture, Ali collected his papers and walked toward the door. When he passed the girl, she said, "Hi. Remember me?"

He smiled. "Yes. You're the girl from the library."

"Are you the guy who bumped into her yesterday and hurt her?" the well-built boy asked.

Surprised, Ali replied calmly, "I apologized to her. Besides, I didn't do it on purpose."

The boy looked at the girl. "You want me to beat him up?"

Obviously embarrassed, the girl said, "It was my fault. I apologized to him." She seemed annoyed as she explained, "John was a boxing champion in high school and likes to show off. I apologize for him."

"I accept your apology," Ali said in relief.

As Ali walked toward the door, one of the other two boys stopped him and asked, "Where do you come from?"

"From Egypt."

"Never heard of it."

Ali stood his ground. "In our country, we generously receive our guests and graciously entertain them." He quietly pushed his way to the door, refusing any further debate.

Ali sat on his apartment balcony, thinking. Peaceful by nature, he didn't like aggression or entanglement. Because he was a stranger, he decided to stay as far as he possibly could from any trouble until he achieved his goals.

The solution would be to stay away from that girl. It would be enough just to dream of her.

The following day, Ali went to the campus and had plenty of time for a walk in the surrounding park. The beautiful flowers brightened his heart and deepened his romantic sense of nature.

Suddenly, a beautiful call from behind stopped him. He turned and found himself face-to-face with the girl. He stood for a few seconds, fascinated by her. She was more beautiful than the greenery and colorful flowers in the park.

"Did you call?" he asked.

"Yes. What's your name?"

"Ali."

"That's a famous name in our country. No doubt you know of Mohammed Ali, the boxing champion. I came to apologize for what John, Peter, and Timmy said yesterday. John is a bit short-tempered, and his attitude may sometimes hurt other people's feelings. Peter and Timmy idolize him."

"You don't need to apologize for them. They should apologize of their own accord."

Feeling his annoyance, she said tenderly, "I also came to thank you for your patience concerning the pain they caused you—and for your decent response."

"Your attempt to comfort me made me forget what happened."

They entered the classroom together and sat down, listening to the professor. Ali looked to his left and saw John, Peter, and Timmy staring angrily at him.

After the lecture, Ali wanted to leave, but the girl asked, "Do you understand these lectures?"

"I think so."

"Can you extract the relevant material from the references?"

"Yes."

"Could we study together sometime?"

"I'd be delighted."

"You haven't even asked my name yet."

"I feared you might feel it was an intrusion."

"I'm Diana Stevenson," she replied, astonished by his sensitivity.

He smiled. "I'm Ali Abdel Razek."

"When and where can we study together?"

"There's a small garden about one mile from here, quiet and isolated, where we could read without interference. How about nine o'clock tomorrow morning?"

"OK."

At eight-thirty the following morning, Ali walked briskly toward the garden, his thoughts whirling. It was her idea to study together. Did that mean she liked him as much as he liked her?

He was on time, and she was waiting for him in a rosy dress that matched the tender beauty of her skin. Her thick blonde hair against the color of her dress added purity and harmony to the sunrise.

"Good morning," he said softly.

She looked up, smiled, and held out her hand. He took it, pressing it gently as he faced her, and holding her with his eyes.

After a while, he asked, "What should we start with?"

"How about economics?"

Ali began explaining in a strong voice. When he realized certain points were difficult for her to understand, he gave simple examples to demonstrate their meaning. Then they moved to taxation laws. She liked his logic and simple way of explaining things. Most of the time as he talked, he didn't look at her, but at the sky or the extended greenery, as if they inspired him. She looked at his profile and felt as if he were flying with her to a far, bright horizon.

After they had enough reading, they took a walk through the beautiful surroundings.

"Tell me about your country," she said.

"An ancient country with its history rooted in the deepness of time," he said dreamily. "It's the land of prophets. Its people are generous and kind, their bodies sprouting from the fertile soil and watered by the Nile. They work hard and ask the Lord to provide the necessities of life." She wanted to ask more but realized that he was far from her, thinking of his ancestors' roots. She excused herself and went on ahead. When she glanced back, she caught him eagerly watching her.

Ali went home at noon, and Saber served lunch. Saber noticed the happiness on Ali's face and the extreme joy that stimulated his appetite. Afterward, Ali sat on a bamboo seat on his balcony, recalling his morning with Diana. Saber, seeing Ali lost in thought, approached quietly and sat beside him.

"Ali?"

Ali didn't answer.

Saber called several times, until Ali finally said, "Yes, my friend?"

"Be frank with me. Is there something in the university that deserves all this introspection?"

"Yes. I met a girl. I think I'm deeply in love with her."

"Does she love you the same?"

"I don't know. Sometimes, she seems to."

"Listen carefully, my son. As far as I understand, the girls here behave naturally, without reservation, and their tenderness might be misunderstood by those of us raised in the East. You may think she loves you and carry on with such thoughts, which are, in fact, just an illusion that will collapse. You're still young and very romantic. I fear you may suffer from this experience."

Ali lowered his head, thinking of Saber's words. Ali knew his acquaintance with Diana was still at an elementary stage. It was too soon to judge the nature of such a relationship. She might love him one day. Until then, he'd be satisfied with the love he carried for her. He was too proud to admit his love, because he feared her reaction. If his love had no future, he could kill it within himself by forcing his body through the severe exercise of karate or yoga, and remain immersed in his soul to allow a full recovery from such a painful experience.

The first semester was almost over, and the approaching examinations forced Ali to devote more time to his studies. However, he and Diana met occasionally in quiet places to review their courses. She relied totally on him to explain the main points for each course.

At their meetings, he didn't dare tell her about the love he carried for her for fear of an answer that would shatter his hopes.

Diana felt the value of his friendship. He treated her elegantly and with extreme politeness. If she interrupted an explanation, he stopped immediately to listen to her, then asked permission to proceed.

When they took walks, he insisted on carrying her books. Gifts of sandwiches, hamburgers, peanuts, almonds, and pistachios demonstrated his extreme generosity. Sometimes they went for a boat ride with Ali rowing for hours in silence, his gaze on the blue sky, clear water, and the golden sunlight reflecting in her gray eyes and on her blonde hair.

One day, he felt sad, because his strong love waited to express itself to her.

When Diana noticed his long silence, she asked, "Where were you just now?"

He smiled. "I've always been here with you."

Finally, the examinations arrived, challenging both of them, but they passed. When the results appeared, indicating their success, their reason fled with joy, and they looked like two children receiving their first gifts from their parents. She offered to celebrate the happy occasion with him, and he wondered what they should do.

She told him she knew a place he would like and promised to pick him up at six o'clock the following morning in her car. He was astonished that such a celebration would take place too early in the day.

Laughing, she said, "Seeing the sunrise is worth it."

Diana arrived on time in her fancy yellow Buick. Ali slid into the passenger seat. "Seeing you driving gives me the impression that you've suddenly grown up."

She laughed. "Your comments are always unpredictable, but I like hearing them, anyway."

Five miles from the university, Diana parked the car on a hill looking down into a wonderful valley.

"My eyes can't resist the beautiful view," Ali said, fascinated. He looked at her with gratitude. It was clear she knew what impressed him.

They got out of the car and looked down at the valley.

Ali said thoughtfully, "There are certain things in this world that deeply impress me."

"I know you're a sentimentalist who loves beauty," she said sympathetically.

"How'd you know that?"

"A woman's the first to feel what passes into a man's heart."

"I haven't shown you any of my feelings."

"I watch the glimmering of your eyes whenever they settle on something beautiful."

Picnic basket in hand, they walked into the valley. Green grass covered the land, with trees lifting toward the sky. A lake shimmered in golden light, its banks speckled with bright flowers. Before them was a blue horizon with green land. The sun rose, shining joyfully on the lake, lighting up the valley through which they walked.

They sat near the lake, enjoying the silence until his words broke the holy calm. "Living in this world is meaningless unless you feel its beauty. This green carpet, stretching around the lake, and the sunrise, which shines on the valley every morning, are but an eternity that has existed since the beginning of time. I wonder how many times the sun rose on this place and how many times the valley received a new morning."

He took a deep breath of the fresh air, fragrant with the scent of grass, and continued in a voice filled with emotion. "I feel man is part of nature. When he stretches his hand to others, he becomes exactly like this lake, which waters the green. When he believes in truth and establishes it among people, he's like the sun when it rises on the valley and changes the darkness to light.

"If happiness creeps into his soul, he resembles the birds when they rise singing from the grass. Stormy waves on the angry seas are his pain and misery." He stopped for a moment, then said thoughtfully, "There's a difference between man and nature. Man is free to choose between the path of good or evil, while nature was created pure, thus unable to commit sin. Man, loaded with sin, can come here to purify himself in the lake's clear water."

Diana patted his shoulder. "Stop flying to heaven and come down to earth, so we can share sandwiches and orange juice."

Ali sat, holding his knees with his arms, watching sunlight dance on the lake's surface. Diana handed him a cup of orange juice and gave him a long, reflective look. An air of good nature showed in his appearance, and the glow of health was in his vigor, and these gave her confidence. His straightforwardness captivated her, and his spiritual brightness gave him sensibility. She examined the details of his face, appreciating his good looks.

Despite all that, Diana's thoughts were busy. He found his happiness among green fields, beautiful landscapes, and the peace of nature's solitude. He was a sentimentalist and mystic, but those traits didn't fit with the coarse texture of life in the materialistic world.

Pushing back a lock of straight, blonde hair, she said, "Tell me about your hopes, your future."

After a moment of silence, he said, "I haven't thought of that before."

"Why'd you join the college of business administration then?"

"It was my father's wish."

"What does he do for a living?"

"He works in trade."

"What kind of trade?"

"Several kinds."

"Perhaps, after graduation, he wants you to help him at work."

"We haven't discussed it."

Conversation with him didn't lead to clear answers, but why was she asking? Did she fear romanticism might affect him, or was she just curious about a man she cared for and felt comfortable with?

It was already noon, though neither of them was conscious of the passage of time. Ali walked to the lake. The clear water reflected a hundred different shades of turquoise. As a religious Muslim, he washed his face, arms, and feet, then stood to perform his prayers.

Diana watched, amazed by Ali's sacred inclinations and prostrations in adoration of the Creator. While sitting between two such prostrations, a small bird landed peacefully on Ali's right shoulder. A tremor went through Diana, and she thought, seeing the bird's tranquility, that the universe was praying with him.

Ali finished his prayers and stood to walk along the bank. Diana went to him, trying to hold onto the thrilling moment. She walked beside him, their shoulders touching; she took his hand in hers, and said smiling, "So that you don't fly away from me."

Amazed, he looked at her passionately, though he stopped himself before he could say, "I love you."

On the way back, Diana drove in silence. Both of them were lost in thought. He knew she was made only for him. No other girl, no matter how beautiful, would ever take Diana's place in his heart.

As for Diana, a mixture of fear and the desire to let her feelings pour out overwhelmed her. She knew her heart admired him, but she feared the consequences. To her, he was a man from the unknown, sunk in idealism and romanticism—traits that would get him in trouble if he entered her heart. She tried to keep from loving him, but his love quietly and persistently crept into her heart.

CHAPTER TWO

Republican Senator EDWARD Stevenson, a man of power and wealth in North Carolina, was Diana's father. He came from a wealthy, prosperous family. In recent Senate elections, he ran against Norman Patterson, a black candidate, but the Senator usually won because of his ability to spend millions of dollars on his campaign. Large donations to schools and universities during the elections were highly appreciated by society and the media, leading to even more votes.

Diana was his only daughter. Her mother died when she was two years old, and Mary, her governess, raised her as if she were her own daughter. The Senator never remarried, because he was totally submerged in politics. Besides being a famous politician, he was co-owner of the Stevenson and Robertson Company, a clothing and makeup firm. He was president and chairman of the board, because he owned two-thirds of the shares. His partner, Clark Robertson, owned the rest.

When the Senator had time to himself, he thought of Diana's future. All his fortune would be hers one day, but he feared she might not be able to bear the consequences. Fluctuations in the market necessitated quick and firm decisions to guarantee good returns and satisfactory profits. Diana was only eighteen. Because of the Senator's heart disease, he feared that, after he died, she'd be exposed to the influence of Clark and his son, James, who already ran the company during the Senator's involvement in politics.

It was about time for her to share in the running of the company. He taught her a lot about the facts of life. In any move or act, she had to see the benefit first. He convinced her that everything had a material value she could utilize, and what was needed to collect profit was imagination and planning. He told her that people in Brazil often sold pieces of ordinary stones, covered with colored, transparent papers, as souvenirs. In Switzerland, they filled bottles with water coming from between the rocks and sold it at high prices as a curative for diseases.

Diana was raised to be materialistic and logical. During childhood, she preferred toys that demanded mental effort and complicated calculations. In high school, she excelled in math. She felt success was achieving goals and using available opportunities.

Of her many suitors in high school, none appealed to her, because she concentrated on computers and their programming. She imagined that, with a well-programmed robot, she could escape the world and fly to another planet.

The Senator succeeded in guiding her in that direction. Her imagination turned toward science fiction. If they went on a journey, it must be scientific, so she could discover what was in ponds and hidden between rocks. It was natural for him to advise her to study business administration, so she could take over for him when he retired in five years or so.

He planned to see her through to the end and keep her chained to him. He had to find a good husband for her, and there was none better than James, his partner's son. James was older than Diana by ten years, spoiled, and spent most of his nights in casinos with friends, but he was clever and rich. Marriage between James and Diana would multiply their fortune, and the family responsibilities after marriage would help straighten James out and make him stop fooling around.

The Senator hid his intentions from Diana, because it was too early. He was pretty sure he could convince her when the time came, and why not? She already had a mind and spirit of her own, and there was steel in her.

The Senator took a step further in Diana's career by telling Clark his plans. Clark was utterly delighted when he realized the benefits. James would gain from such a marriage without effort, and it was about time he stopped drinking, gambling, and having affairs. The Senator, however, added the condition that Diana must complete her education to acquire the experience necessary to share running the company and bearing the family responsibilities with James.

Diana sat in her room, thinking about what was happening to her with Ali. He took her to a rosy world doing its best to bloom, sending out ripples of green and gifts of flowers. In that world, he was like a spirit wandering to the horizon to bring back something beautiful. She hadn't been herself since she met him. He was different from anyone she ever met.

With him, she was in a state for which she had no name, an infinitely peaceful feeling of being cherished. His thoughtful consideration of everything romantic delighted her and opened her heart to him. Their friendship had grown steadily deeper since the day they visited the valley.

She felt a tremor of alarm at how close they were. She feared her love for him had no future. Everyone else seemed to know what he wanted from life, but Ali took each day as it came, totally unconcerned with tomorrow. He did well in his studies, but he cared little about the future.

Was it possible for him to be so out of touch with reality? If he had no strength to fight or tact to win his way, he would lose. His unrealistic dreams would never materialize, and he'd be crushed by the materialistic world. She couldn't bear the thought of that.

There was another thing to consider—her father would never approve of her being involved with a stranger from the East, someone who might destroy his plans for his daughter.

All those differences would crush their love on the hard rocks of reality. It would be better, for the sake of her material future, to stay away from Ali and give her heart the chance to recover in peace. She'd treat him like the rest of her colleagues and would study with him as well as John, Peter, and Timmy. No lake or valley would unite them and keep them from the others. In the hope of being cured from this possessing love, she wouldn't let her feelings go.

The second semester began, with students attending lectures again. While Ali was filled with eager longing for Diana, she deliberately avoided him. In the classroom, she sat, whispered a quick, "Hello," then turned her full attention to the lecturer, scarcely acknowledging Ali. Even when they were alone, they talked of impersonal things. Sometimes she surprised him by saying she spent the previous day studying with John, while the following day, she had an appointment with Peter for the same thing.

Ali wondered why they were talking like strangers. Why was she speaking to him in that cool, detached way, with hardly a glance? Sadness in his eyes and the surprise in his face upset Diana beyond measure, but she felt it was better to wake up before going too far.

Ali met her between two lectures and stopped her. "Diana, what happened? Did I offend you?"

"No," she said hastily, "you're just imagining things." She hurried to John and chatted laughingly with him.

Watching, them, Ali felt suffocated.

Days passed while she continued avoiding him, and he nurtured a feeble hope she'd return. Sunk in love, he wandered the campus gardens aimlessly, barely conscious of his surroundings. He missed lectures for weeks and stayed in his apartment, drowning in the feeling that he didn't deserve such abandonment and cruelty. Diana, seeing his suffering, wanted to heal his wounds, but she withheld.

Saber noticed Ali's somber mood and long stays at his apartment and knew it stemmed from agitation and depression. "Has your girlfriend deserted you for others?"

Ali was astonished by Saber's sagacity but also comforted, because Saber had saved him from having to open a painful subject.

"She's there, free like a bird, and doesn't feel the fire kindled in your heart, while you're imprisoned here with your sorrow. If that's what happened, go back to her and pluck her from her admirers. Put off disappointment and go to the classroom to fulfill the task for which you came.

"You're a fine athlete. Stand and fight. Put on the karate suit with its black belt and strike failure and pain with your strong fists. She'll return to you, because the love you carry for her has already touched the depths of her heart."

Ali was silent, then nodded. "You always read my mind and know how to set me on the right path."

Ali awoke the following morning with his courage revived and spirits refreshed. His mind was alert and clear. Peace descended on his soul, and his dark eyes shone with determination to conquer weakness. Putting his karate suit into his sports bag, he lifted it to his back. Wearing a soft white shirt, flannel suit, rubber shoes, and with his wavy hair shaking on his forehead, he looked handsome and healthy.

In the classroom, Ali concentrated fully on the lecture, deliberately not looking at Diana. After the lecture, he went to the gymnasium, searching for the karate arena. The karate team sat on the floor, listening to their trainer's instructions.

With light, quick steps, Ali reached them and asked permission to join the team. The trainer inspected his long body thoroughly and inquired about his karate rank. When he learned Ali was a black belt, he felt certain he would be a significant addition to the team, so he ordered him to dress in his suit and come immediately to the arena to demonstrate his skill.

In the dressing room, Ali skillfully tied his uniform and put on his black belt. Looking at himself in the mirror, he felt confident enough to step forward and punch the air with a yell.

He returned to the arena and sat in silence with the rest of the team. The coach asked him to stand and demonstrate stances, punches, kicks, certain forms, self-defense, and sparring. The coach, overwhelmed by the boy's skill, realized that his hope of North Carolina University winning the gold cup in karate championship for all American universities was within his grasp.

After training, Ali felt different. Filled with patience and self-assurance, he could tolerate the pain of his love. Looking at his watch, he saw the next lecture was due to start, so he hurried to the classroom and looked for an empty seat. There was one beside Susan, a pretty, cheerful girl. Ali smiled as he sat down, and she nodded with an even bigger smile.

Susan was a cheerful, beautiful girl who got along easily with her friends. Her mother died when she was an infant, and her father, a poor laborer on a cattle ranch, remarried a widow with four boys. Susan's stepmother was an alcoholic and enslaved Susan to help raise her four boys. Susan had to be patient and accept the awkward situation until she had a chance to live her own life.

Susan was a brilliant student. After she finished high school, she applied for scholarships with several colleges. The only one that offered her a full scholarship, including books, room, and board, was North Carolina.

The kind of restless life she led made her pretend she came from a high-class family. She attracted the eyes of many boys with her sexy clothes and earned their surprise by seeking admiring words about her tall, beautiful body. She didn't know that Peter was watching her with the eyes of a wolf waiting for its prey.

The lecture was about different economic schools of thought and ways to overcome development problems. Afterward, the professor called the students' names and asked them to choose related topics for seminars. Ali chose a topic about the difference between the old and new economic schools and their contributions to the current world economy. He had to give his seminar in six weeks, something that required serious preparation for such an important event in a student's life.

He was ready to leave the classroom when Susan stopped him. Diana told her about Ali's remarkable ability to explain courses and draw conclusions from suppositions, and she asked if he could help her prepare for her seminar.

Ali shyly agreed, and Susan laughed as she left. Ali glanced at Diana, who sat beside John, and saw her watching reproachfully.

Days passed, and Ali sank into his karate exercises. Diana felt a sense of emptiness creeping into her life. It was torture that her love for Ali was so deeply rooted in her heart. At home, she felt bored and empty, counting the hours until she saw him again. Even in her dreams, he was always there, walking along the lake, looking at the horizon with sad, reproachful eyes.

Ali sat on a campus bench in one of the gardens, reading references related to his seminar. Diana passed through and was glad to find herself alone with him. At least they could talk again, and that would be an improvement. Ali's heart pounded when he saw her coming, and he hurried to meet her halfway.

Diana could barely hide her disappointment when Susan intercepted him, calling him aside. Diana had no choice but to change direction toward the lecture room and abandon the meeting.

Arriving an hour before class, Diana needed to sort out her feelings, to think over what she'd done. She hoped to kill the love she held for Ali, but her soul was filled from his as a cup was filled from a flagon. Keeping away from him gave Susan the opportunity to take him for herself. With Ali's shyness, he might respond to her enough to become deeply involved with her.

Ali and Susan met frequently. It was impossible to do otherwise. She was always looking for him to discuss lessons and points that would help with her seminar. She was grateful to him, because he was patient with her and always offered more lessons.

Diana watched them with a twinge of jealousy. It was true she was avoiding him, but there always seemed to be a girl with him, asking his advice. Her belief that Ali and Susan shared a strong bond grew, and that made her even more anxious over her own relationship with him. The situation grew worse rapidly, because John was so confused by Diana's company that he thought she was his sweetheart.

Peter, however, strengthened his relationship with Susan by finding new ways to approach her, such as borrowing a book or lecture notes, or by pretending he didn't understand certain topics and asking her for detailed explanations, during which he praised her shining beauty and expressed his admiration. Longing for words of praise, she became more attracted to him and accepted invitations with him to see movies or have dinner downtown.

Six weeks passed, and Ali had to present his seminar. He was tense, because he had the reputation of being an excellent student who had a tremendous ability to understand difficult points and simplify them for his classmates. Raised in the East, he looked at the economy from another perspective, so he thought it would be better to compare between past and present ideas of the West with those of the East.

The lecture room filled with students, and the professor sat in the audience, leaving the podium to Ali. As he mounted the low platform with teacher's chair and desk, he saw rows of attentive eyes watching. He silently asked his Lord to help him explain his views smoothly and well. Ali began by giving a general overview of the major economic ideas and doctrines from ancient days to the present, then he moved to the economists who contributed to the growth of capitalism, beginning with Niccolo Machiavelli, Jean Bordin, and Antonio Serra. He mentioned classic economists, such as Adam Smith and Thomas Robert Malthus, then he shifted to the ideas of the early socialists, Saint-Simone and Charles Fourier. He went on to Karl Marx's economics, philosophy of history, predictions, and his ideas after the revolution.

He also emphasized the reformulation of the classical doctrine by John Stuart Mill, as well as the attempt of Alfred Marshall to restate the whole body of economic thought. Ali explained in detail the role of John Maynard Keynes in formulating the general theory of employment, interest, and money, and how it provided a marvelous rationalization for policies when compared to his predecessors.

"What book did you refer to in presenting economic ideas from ancient days to the present?" his professor asked.

"George Souls Ideas of the Great Economists."

"It's a good reference for your topic. Continue."

"By going through the doctrines of the great economists, one can deduce certain important points. First, the present economic ideas include several of those of the past. The difference is that, today, we apply them in a more-realistic way due to progress in modern research methods.

"Second, the economic theories of the past had their uses. The great ideas were, in some degree at least, relevant to their times. They transmitted light that filtered through the climates of their periods.

"Third, in their scientific pretensions, economic doctrines haven't been so successful as in their logic-spinning. Given a small sample of human behavior, one can be less certain that this sample will be typical of the behavior of the community in general. Individual men, combined in societies of any magnitude, react very differently in different times and places.

"This fact makes it precarious to build intricate logical systems of economic thought on rough observations of a few simple instances of human behavior. The risk of error is compounded when the specific instances chosen aren't observed but are imagined. That's the case when men are presumed to be completely rational and motivated solely by a desire for wealth or to avoid loss.

"An even greater difficulty in gaining systematic and reliable knowledge of human behavior is that men continually change their patterns of action and thinking. New ways of action produce new situations, which, in turn, stimulate more change. Any social science worthy of the name must be the science of becoming, not merely a science of what would happen if conditions were fixed.

"The question is whether we can have an economic science capable of describing the process of social behavior accurately enough, so it will be useful in making the decisions that will affect the future."

"What's your impression about the economic ideas of the present?" the professor asked.

"Some of you may think that when I talked about the economic ideas of the past, I meant their immaturity or inability to cope with the needs of modern societies. The classical ideas contain morals and ethics not found in present economic doctrines. Most records of economic ideas in ancient times are embodied in religious teachings, codes of law, or moral exhortations.

"The Bible, reflecting the theocratic state of the ancient Jews, contains many injunctions against greed and extortion and against overemphasis on material wealth. Plato recognized that production is the basis of the state and showed aversion to the emphasis on gain seeking, which accompanied the rise of commerce. He outlined what he regarded as an ideal state, in which the rulers were to be educated for their responsibilities from childhood and chosen by competitive examination.

"Craftsmen were to be excluded from political rights, since their occupations would prevent them from devoting the necessary attention to the high duties of citizenship. That division implied no similar gulf in riches, since the ruling class was to possess no property beyond that necessary to support it. Common ownership of property was to be the general rule.

"Aristotle based his economic opinions on good management of the household. The necessities of life constitute the wealth, but nothing is wealth if it's in excess of the need, or if it wasn't created for such use. He approved the natural art of acquisition that is practiced by managers of households and statesmen but not commerce carried on for gain.

"On that ground, Aristotle reserved his hearty disapproval for currency and the lending of money at interest. Money may be a useful instrument of exchange, but, he thought, when it tempted people to pile up unused gains or accumulate wealth by lending, it became sterile or unproductive, and it promoted disparity in riches and financial irregularities.

"St. Thomas Aquinas, like other church authorities, condemned the charging of interest on borrowed money, or, as it was called, usury, because, as he and Aristotle thought, money was properly only a medium of exchange and didn't itself produce anything.

"The growth of capital accumulation by lending not only occasionally wiped out individual borrowers, who believed they were the victims of monopolists of money, but it also seemed to threaten the structure of a society producing not for gain but for use, in which each participant was supposed to receive his just share.

"The economic ideas of the ancient world and those of the medieval age emphasized themes that ought to be included in the economic ideas of the present. Among those are: 1) The warning of the scared books that 'Love of money is the root of evil,' 2) Economists still don't believe that money, in itself, constitutes riches or that money is useful except as a servant of desirable production and exchange, and 3) Economists still must, and do, have to deal with justice and moral codes.

"Then the emphasis shifted to the improvement of life on earth for its own sake. John Locke, the chief English philosopher of the Enlightenment, emphasized the natural rights of life and liberty, which underlay the movement for representative government. He added to them a natural right of property, since he contended that no natural product had value except by virtue of the labor expended on it, and every man had a right to the fruits of his own labor.

"Jean Jacques Rousseau was a mighty force in the surge of ideas that helped foment the French Revolution. His major works, *Le Contract Social* and *Emile*, like the writings of Locke, were familiar to Thomas Jefferson and the other authors of the American Declaration of Independence, which asserts the 'inalienable rights' bestowed upon man by 'nature and nature's God,' among which are 'life, liberty, and the pursuit of happiness.' Rousseau declared that, in the state of nature, men were good, free, and equal, and had become otherwise only through miseducation.

"I conclude from all that that the present economic doctrines should be strongly correlated with man's justice, morals, and dignity. The present economic doctrines must be based on production for use and not for mere accumulation."

"Your interpretation is good so far," the professor said, "but it would be more feasible if you set up some realistic examples that show the incorporation of these ideas into real life."

"In the East," Ali replied, "we apply the Economic Islamic Doctrine derived from our sacred book, the Koran, and from the words and acts of the prophet, the Sunnah. It's an ethical behavior God has ordered us to do. It supports the thought that money is, in itself, unproductive, and favored a society in which those who produced goods and services, rather than those who rigged markets and hoarded riches, should receive the rewards. The basic economic principles in Islam can be summarized by the following:

"The source of Islamic economics is God or Allah, the Almighty. Therefore, the economic policy is divine in its source and positivist in its practice, which also means it's simultaneously a stable and developing policy. It is a stable policy that cannot be changed in the sense of its economic foundations that are found in the Koran and the Sunnah. Moslems everywhere submit to it all the time, irrespective of the degree of development of their society. The economic principles and foundations are both general and specific. Islam has, therefore, been required to use the proper interpretation, *Iljtihad*, in their application at different moments in time and space.

"Interest in loans, for consumption or production, is Riba, or usury, and Riba, whether great or small, is forbidden. Banking services are not Riba.

"Need, in the sense of seeking a minimum but sufficiently good standard of living, is the first basis of distribution of wealth. Everybody must first have that minimum, then comes work and ownership.

"The real owner of property is Allah the Almighty, and people are only inheritors. As such, they must deal with what they've been left according to Islamic law. Otherwise, the state is allowed to intervene and place the property under an interdict. It isn't lawful, for example, to gamble, to produce alcohol, to do business with Riba, to forestall the market, to stop money from producing, to use it on what isn't needed, to harm the rights of others, or to increase prices.

"The economic law guarantees a good standard of living and not just the basic minimum for every individual. For that purpose, Islam created fourteen centuries ago the institution of almsgiving, Zakat, which in modern terminology is synonymous with Social Security. Alms are required by Islamic doctrine to be given annually to the poor. The proportion is generally one-fortieth, which is to be paid in kind, money, or other equivalent.

"Islam shows an advantageous way to development. In the production domain, it glorifies work and forbids all aspects of exploitation. In the domain of redistribution, it first guarantees the basic minimum to everybody and then advocates the system of 'to each according to his work' irrespective of his religion or nationality. There's no objection to someone who's rich, provided he's pious. In any case, Islam allows wealth and riches only after poverty and deprivation have been eliminated. It doesn't allow extravagance and secures the economic balance between individuals."

"In your comparison between different economic systems," the professor said, "you relied on the Koran and the Sunnah, and those aren't reliable scientific books but rather are spiritual. Holy books don't follow the scientific procedures applied in proving theories. That works against you, don't you think?"

"Islam isn't simply a religious faith," Ali replied. "It's also a political, social, and economic system. That's what's intended by the phrase that describes Islam as 'a religion and a code of life.'"

The professor commented, "Although Islamic economics dates back to the emergence of Islam fourteen centuries ago, its introduction into the teaching curricula isn't known to us."

Ali replied, "The study of Islamic economics knew its heyday in the early Islamic era to the extent that several old Islamic books are full of original ideas that compare favorably with the modern concepts and theories of economics. More than that, the first world scientifically oriented books of economics didn't appear until the seventh century by the Gregorian calendar, in the light of Islam and through the creativity of Arab writers.

"Because Islamic economics is a self-contained system with its own economic policy that encompasses all the different interests, private or public, material or spiritual, and because it takes into consideration variations in time and space, several foreign and international voices cry out to stress the fact that Islamic economics is the hope for the salvation of humanity from the extremist positions adopted by each of the two dominant systems—capitalism and socialism."

"I see that you're impressed by the essence of Islamic economics, and I hope I'll have the chance to read its principles. Tell me, are you quite convinced by the Islamic Economic Doctrine?" The professor asked.

Ali smiled. "If it was destined that I possess a fortune, I'd certainly abide by Islamic economic principles, because they're the right path to salvation."

The professor looked at the audience. "Ali did well in his seminar. He started by working through old economic ideas to the present and concluded that they must be correlated with ethics and justice to mankind. He also stated that money isn't a goal in itself if it doesn't serve production and achieve economic balance in society. He rejected the appropriation of national wealth by a minority. Islamic principles were also presented, thereby adding to our knowledge of a new economic doctrine. Although we aren't familiar with this, we consider it an addition that deserves our appreciation."

The professor began applauding and was quickly joined by the others.

CHAPTER THREE

Ali collected his papers and left the podium to walk toward the door. Susan stopped him to congratulate him, and several other students gathered around, asking questions until they finally dispersed.

During and after the lecture, diana could hardly take her eyes off him. He seemed to leave everyone he spoke to in a good mood. Nature gave him a voice that could make itself heard, whether lifted by excitement or deepened by emotion. His speech was as sweet and smooth as a flowing stream. His deep, sure voice, the way he looked, and the way he moved made her drown in the tenderness that washed over her.

He disapproved of many economic practices, because his principles were high, and he was prepared to stick to them at any cost. He was very different from the boys she knew before, but that didn't matter. Her soul melted in the warm, sweet glow of his love.

Ali, seeking privacy, went to the nearest garden to sit on the grass. He closed his eyes and thanked God for enabling him to express his views properly.

He awoke to a soft, tender voice calling, a voice he knew well— Diana's voice. She stood there, contemplating him with her lovely smile. "I came to congratulate you," she said softly. "You were great, and the seminar went smoothly."

He stood and looked at her with blazing eyes. "A single glance would've revived me. I don't want to burden you with anything that might be a bother. It's enough just to feel you near me." He said with reproach.

"Don't make so much out of it. There are so many things I want to talk to you about, but I fear you'll misunderstand them."

"When and where will that be?"

"In the place you like most."

"The beautiful valley?"

"Yes, but don't rush things. What I want to discuss deserves reflection and consideration."

"I'll let you decide the date, but please make it soon."

They parted in the hope they'd be reunited.

Susan went with Peter to dine in a downtown restaurant. After dinner, he ordered a bottle of cognac and drank until he was tipsy. Susan shared several glasses with him and became befuddled. Drowsiness overcame her, so she asked Peter to take her home.

Instead of doing that, he drove down a deserted lane and stopped. Susan became frightened. He took her forcefully in his arms and murmured, "Gazing for a few seconds at your beautiful body lights a fire in my thirsty heart."

She reached for the door and managed to leave the car, but he caught up with her, threw her down, and sat on her. She kicked and fought with all her strength, but she was no match for him. She kept screaming, even when he covered her mouth with his hand. He socked her head several times until she was unconscious. After raping her, Peter left her alone in the dark.

Susan awoke feeling severe pain. She had to walk a long way in the dark to reach home, and, once she was in her room, she refused to leave it for days. She felt Peter must've already spread the news among his friends, but he kept the crime to himself, knowing she wouldn't dare humiliate herself by accusing him. He planned to threaten her if she made a fuss and didn't surrender to him again.

Soon it was time for Susan's seminar, but she didn't care. Her professor passed over her time slot and asked Diana to go ahead. Diana gave her presentation, then answered questions from the professor and students.

Ali watched sympathetically, seeing how easy and natural she was while trying to answer, explain, or admit that her knowledge couldn't stand before the storm of merciless questions. From the back row, Ali raised his hand in a victory sign, and she smiled, feeling secure.

Afterward, Ali congratulated her for her effort. She said laughing, "I felt like prey that fell into a hunter's net."

John and Peter came to offer their congratulations, and she thanked them, too.

"Do you know why Susan's been absent so long?" Ali asked Peter.

He shook his head. "I haven't seen her for days."

"Would you be willing to go to her room and see what's wrong?" Ali asked Diana.

Sharing his concern, she said she'd drop by on her way home.

When Diana saw Susan, she was shocked to find her face swollen and bruised. "What happened?"

Susan hugged her and burst into tears. Diana gently patted her back until she calmed down.

Susan confessed what happened, then burst into tears again.

"What will you do now?" Diana asked. "Will you stay imprisoned in your room with exams coming?"

"I've decided to go back home and find a job that keeps me away from people."

"No. You're going to continue classes as if nothing happened. No one else knows what happened between you and Peter. A horrible event like this shouldn't depress you and keep you from your studies. I'll tell everyone that you're sick and need a few more days to recover. When your wounds heal, return to class and catch up."

The following day, Diana told Ali Susan was ill but would return to class soon.

After several days without seeing Susan, Ali insisted on seeing her. He suggested he and Diana stop by her room.

Susan opened the door and found Ali and Diana staring at her in wonder. She felt relieved, as if she'd been waiting for them.

They entered her modest room and sat on the sofa, while Susan took a chair facing them, looking confused and embarrassed whenever she glanced at Ali.

"I've decided to quit the university and find a job," Susan announced.

"What's the matter with you?" Ali asked. "Where's the enthusiasm that glowed from you to others?"

Susan looked at Diana ironically. "Why don't you tell this noble man the sad truth?"

"What sad truth?" Ali asked.

"I'll tell you the whole story and save her the embarrassment," Susan said, "but promise not to tell me to go to the authorities."

"Not until I know why."

Susan told him what happened to her and looked into his eyes to gauge his response. Ali stared at the ceiling, trying to hide his disgust for Peter and hoping for a chance to break him in two. Susan, seeing sorrow and sympathy in Ali's eyes, turned pale and began crying.

Once she recovered, Ali said firmly and calmly, "You didn't do anything wrong, because you were the one who was raped. I'll stand by you and help you concentrate on the lessons you missed.

"What happened isn't the end of the world, and tomorrow brings new hope for the future. Tomorrow, I'll come here to escort you to class. We'll leave you now so you can get organized."

Ali set off at such a rapid pace that Diana had to run to keep up with him. He kept that up until she tired and took his hand to stop him. Anger showed in his eyes, and his sad gaze rejected what happened to Susan.

"She suffered a lot these past weeks, and no one stood beside her. She was like a beautiful flower, admired by all, then came this vagabond to deflower her in order to satisfy his mean desire."

"I didn't realize before that you get nervous when something offends you."

"If Peter harms her again, I'll break his bones."

"Your hand's cold and shaking. Please calm down. Let's spend a good time together. I'm glad to be alone with you."

Ali took her small hands in his. The warmth of his touch melted the tension that had been building as they walked. He looked at her good-humoredly. "I'm starving to death. Let's walk downtown and get lunch."

"Yes," she said softly. "At least I'll have you to myself for a while."

In the restaurant, they took a quiet corner table. During lunch, Diana said, "I'm amazed to see how quickly you convinced Susan to return to college. You have great influence over her."

"She felt the sincerity of my words."

"How long will you help her?"

"Until she catches up with the lessons she missed." Suddenly, he realized her meaning. "Does that bother you?"

"No, but don't go too far with her."

Feeling her jealousy, he took her hand and pressed it gently. "When will our date at the lake be?"

"When I decide," she said obstinately.

"Why did you walk out on me recently?"

"There are a million things I want to say to you, but not now."

"Then don't walk out on me until we meet again."

"That depends on your behavior with Susan."

He ate lunch in silence, his thoughts whirling. Diana was very nice to him, but did she feel as strongly as he did? He thought of John and wondered if he and Diana shared a strong bond.

She noticed his silence. "What are you thinking of?"

"I sail in the gray depths of your eyes."

She laughed. "Always the romantic."

"You are like a calm, gray sea that flows tenderly into my heart and fills it with love. You don't know what your beauty has done to me."

Her heart beats pounded loudly in her ears. "What did you say?"

"I'll tell you there among the flowers and sweet-smelling herbs. When will our date be?"

She looked at her watch to hide her shyness and avoid fixing a date. "I'm already late. Will you walk me home? It's less than a mile."

They walked down the street until they reached a large, handsome mansion.

She looked at him from under her long, golden lashes and said, "I live here."

"You come from people exalted in dignity, then."

"My father is the Republican Senator Edward Stevenson."

"That house can accommodate many people. Do you have brothers?"

"No. I'm the only child. My mother died when I was two years-old. I live with Mary, my governess, and an old driver and gardener."

"In such a huge mansion, I doubt you see each other very often."

She laughed. "That's exactly what happens most of the time." Waving her hand, she said, "See you tomorrow at the university."

Early the following morning, Ali waited at Susan's door and cheerfully told her it was a beautiful day, waiting to receive her. She hesitated to go with him, but he urged her to dress and told her how beautiful she would be if she wore a long dress that covered the outlines of her sexy body.

"America is a free country," she countered.

"It's a special request."

She looked into his eyes for several seconds. "For your sake, I'll do whatever you want."

She felt secure while walking with him and began accepting the idea of confronting her colleagues. In the lecture room, she sat with Ali, feeling restless. Her pale, sweating face made him lean over to murmur, "You'll become accustomed to this after only a few minutes."

After a few more minutes, Diana arrived, kissed Susan, and said, "You look beautiful this morning."

Then John and Timmy entered. Other students followed, all wanting to shake Susan's hand and ask about her health. Peter, the last to arrive, saw the crowd around Susan and turned away, but John saw him and called, "Peter, you know who's here? It's Susan. Come say hello."

Peter, forced to confront her, controlled his anxiety by saying, "Hi. It's good to see you again. We've been worried about you. I hope you're fully recovered."

Susan didn't look at him but talked with other students, smiling to hide the hatred she felt for Peter. From the anger in Ali's eyes, Peter knew he knew the truth.

Over time, Susan began to regain her self-confidence. Ali suggested she should stay with Diana and other students she trusted, so she could avoid any confrontation that might reveal what happened between her and Peter. Susan's self-confidence was further enhanced by Ali's studying with her regularly, providing her with summaries of the lectures she missed. Diana was keen to attend those study meetings to benefit from Ali's concise summaries, and to ensure that Susan didn't try to go too far with Ali.

Diana and Susan noticed that Ali hadn't attended several of their study meetings lately. His excuse was that he was busy exercising in the gym, so they went to see him.

Diana saw John boxing with another player. "I hate boxing, because people get hurt." She said annoyed at the violent punches John was launching to his opponent.

Suddenly, Susan said, "Ali's here too, punching one of the players."

They went to the karate arena and sat with the other observers to watch. Diana stared in surprise. Ali's strong punches struck his opponent like whiplashes. His loud yells endowed his face with a firmness she'd never seen. He moved about like an active volcano, spewing rocks in all directions.

He was obviously a karate champion out for victory. He never told her he was involved in such a severe sport. She thought he knew nothing but to fly to heaven, and, if she wanted to bring him to reality, he'd escape to his dreams of paradise. How could dreaming romanticism be the cover for such extreme strength? How could his captivating tenderness be contained in a rock-solid body that never seemed to tire? How could he endure the punches he received without any sign of fatigue, let alone return them without oppression?

Was that the dreamer she feared might crash against the ground of reality? Was he the one she thought wouldn't be able to change the world? Could he share the material world with her and not just romantic objects and considerations?

In Ali's seminar, he said the love of money was the root of all evil, and nothing was wealth, if it was in excess of the need for it or wasn't made for use. How could he interact with the American economic system when he believed in philosophies that the free world had long since rejected? She had to talk with him soon to still her whirling thoughts.

After the end of training, the players stood in a row to salute the trainer with a bow.

Susan looked at Ali in admiration. "How beautiful he is in that white uniform. He reminds me of...."

Diana cut her short. "Susan, forget about Ali. We're in love with each other."

Susan was astonished. "I thought you loved John."

"No," she replied firmly. "We're just friends."

Ali, seeing them, waved.

Diana went to him. "We were fascinated by your strong performance."

"I'm sorry for the violence you saw that might hurt your feelings."

Diana, holding his hand, led him to the dressing room. Susan followed, her mind echoing with Diana's words about her love of Ali.

"Each day," Diana murmured, "I discover something new in you. Sometimes, I feel I don't understand you at all. Please explain this."

"I want to tell you many things, but examinations are approaching, as is the university karate championship. I must be ready."

Diana understood he just postponed a date she was eagerly anticipating.

Ali spent the next few weeks with hard karate training during the day and concentrating on his lessons at night. As he ran miles each morning, he looked as if he were trying to shorten the days so he could realize his life's dream sooner. When he studied hard, he seemed as if he were urging the nights to pass quickly, so he could win his sweetheart faster and make sure nothing took her from him.

The time of the karate championships arrived, and the preliminary rounds began. Competition was merciless. The pain of the fighting bodies was obvious in their wounds and swollen faces. Diana sympathetically watched Ali move from one victory to the next. Those victories didn't come easily since he was younger than the others and had to fight against their high skill levels.

Seeing his wounded hands and feet, she hoped his struggles would end soon, with Ali safe. In the valley, she'd take him to the lake to wash his wounds.

During the fights, Diana remained in the crowd, encouraging him, which made him even more determined to fight until the end. He kept winning until he reached the final round, facing a huge African-American player from Louisiana University.

The fight began with a quick attack from the black boy, who struck Ali's head with a strong punch, followed by a kick to the stomach. Pained, Ali fell to his knees. Despair weakened his will. Should he continue, or should he withdraw before such a devastating opponent?

He knew the blows he received were illegal and intended to weaken him and force him to quit. He looked at Diana, who stared back in concern. The crowd shouted, but he couldn't tell who they favored.

The referee came to help Ali stand.

"Those hits were illegal," Ali said softly.

"One of you must be the champion," the referee replied, then went to the black boy and told him, "Your hits must reach the target without affecting it."

Ali realized he had no chance of winning unless he gave his opponent the same rough treatment. The second round began with a yell from Ali, who attacked with a strong punch to the head, followed by a straight-out kick to the stomach. When the black boy doubled over, exposing his head, Ali gave him an elbow strike to the back of the head that sent him to his knees.

The two players were equal. The final round would decide the winner. The fight began with an exchange of punches, kicks, and blocks. Ali made sure his blows reached his opponent's body effectively while he skillfully blocked all the black boy's blows.

His opponent soon became exhausted, and his punches were futile. Ali took advantage of the situation with a right front kick to the chest and another to the knee. He stepped forward to deliver a head punch, and that final blow won the championship for him. His opponent fell over, unable to catch his breath.

Students cheered and applauded as the dean of North Carolina University presented the karate prize to Ali. More applause came as Ali bowed to the crowd, walking proudly around the arena with the trophy held over his head and tears in his eyes.

In boxing, John also reached the final round of the heavyweight division and faced a boy from Michigan State. Although competition was fierce, John won in the third round with a knockout punch. For the second time, and in the same championship, another student from North Carolina won first place. The crowd shouted with joy at the double victory.

In the dressing room, Ali prayed, thanking God for helping him win the karate championship. His suffering body hurt enough that he lay on his back for a few minutes to relax. He tried to forget the rising pain by closing his eyes and thinking of what he loved. Diana attended all his fights. Because of her encouragement, he was the victor. She cared for him, but when would she speak freely? She was a major element in his life. It was because of her that he loved the university and won the karate championship. He lived for her.

When Ali heard John's voice congratulating him, he stood and slapped John's shoulder, returning the congratulations.

"You're a great player," John said. "You impress everyone who watches you."

"You're a great player, too. I watched you in training."

"I didn't know you were that good in karate, maybe because you prefer to live alone."

"I didn't like how you treated me when we first met."

"Can't you take a joke?"

"Yes, but with good intentions."

"How about being friends?"

"Sure. It's OK with me."

They shook hands.

"See you outside after you're dressed," John said, walking away.

Outside the dressing room, a crowd gathered around John and Ali to congratulate them. They carried the two champions on their shoulders while singing the college anthem.

After the students' enthusiasm weakened, John and Ali descended and sought a calm place to rest. Diana wasn't with the crowd, so Ali looked for her. Finally, he saw her sitting alone in a quiet corner.

Feeling his gaze, she looked up at him. He returned her gaze with tenderness and love, and she held out her hand. He took it in his palms and sat beside her.

He was about to speak when he saw tears rolling down her cheeks. "What makes you cry?"

"You."

He looked at her with compassion and affection.

She wiped her eyes and said, "I saw you fighting today, patiently bearing your pain and wounds, then you won and had tears in your eyes. At that moment, my love for you became ardent longing. I felt my heart break with the violence of my love for you. When that crowd carried you off, I came here, waiting to admit that my love has become too intense for me to keep it to myself."

He lifted her hands to his lips and kissed them. When he returned them, they were wet with his tears.

She tenderly stroked his hair and asked, "What makes you weep?"

"You."

John, watching from afar, was astonished. Diana had never shown any sign of love for him, but she was still his girlfriend, and everyone knew it. What would he say to his friends if they knew that the university boxing champion couldn't protect his girl? How dare Ali insult him by stealing her like that? Just a few moments earlier, John suggested they become friends, and that was how Ali treated him?

He'd teach Ali a lesson he would always remember. The thrill of victory fading in his chest, John walked away.

The university gave a big party to celebrate the dual championship. The hall filled with students anxious to see the two champions, who were already the talk of the college. Diana wore a long green dress to set off her golden hair. When she entered the hall, all eyes went to her, as if a bird of paradise had flown in. She looked for Ali and finally saw him in a dim corner, watching her in fascination.

She walked to him, and he met her on the dance floor. Diana laid her head on his shoulder as he touched his lips to her hair, sending a shiver of delight down to her toes. She'd been waiting eagerly for that moment. When it came, she accepted it, letting herself feel the thrill of being in his arms.

"Darling, you shouldn't be so remarkably beautiful," he murmured. "Diana, I love you."

"Never stop telling me that. My name sounds beautiful when you say it, as if I'm hearing it for the first time. When you admit your love, I feel I was made only for you. I want to take you to our valley and hide you from the other girls."

"Maybe the boys are staring at your graceful beauty. They make me jealous."

"How handsome you are. All the other girls in this hall wish you were holding them, not me."

"Not to mention the men who'd like to have my place with you."

"The girls' eyes haven't left you since you entered the hall."

"In this hall, I see nothing but you. We were made for each other."

"Yes. You're my fate. With all that love, our hearts will never be separate. Promise me the days will never separate us."

"I promise you, my love."

Her breath hot on his face, he held her as they danced to slow music. Other dancers watched them in admiration, but they didn't notice.

The band finished its slow number and broke into a fast song. Without warning, Susan joined the throng of dancers, gyrating and hip-swinging until she made a spectacle of herself.

Ali and Diana moved to the sidelines and watched in astonishment. Susan wore a very short skirt that showed a considerable amount of leg. Her long black hair shook with the beat of the music. Other students gathered to watch, clapping and shouting. Susan stretched out her hands to the watchers, inviting them to join her, moving from one to the other until she found herself in Peter's arms.

Half-drunk, he held her tightly and asked, "Would you mind dancing with me, Baby? I miss my moments with you."

Her anger rising, she said, "Leave me alone."

"Oh, no. It's been too long since I saw you. Let me wrap my arms around you."

"I'll scream if you don't leave me alone."

He laughed. "That would work against you. I'll tell everyone what happened that night. You know something? You were superb and delicious."

Losing control, she slapped him. He returned the slap with a harder one that knocked her down. Ali, angered, leaped against Peter's chest, punching and kicking until he fell down. With one hand, Ali pulled Peter to his feet and slapped his face repeatedly.

Bleeding and unable to catch his breath, Peter ran from the party, trying to avoid people's eyes.

John watched the incident silently. Although he disapproved of Peter's villainy with Susan, he couldn't help shouting in Ali's face, "Peter's my friend. Whoever hurts him offends me, too. Susan is Peter's girl. What's between them is their own business, not yours.

"I offered you my friendship yesterday. I withdraw it. Tomorrow morning at nine, I'll be waiting at the baseball field to teach you a lesson."

The party, originally organized to celebrate twin championships, became a calamity leading to a fight between Ali and John.

CHAPTER FOUR

Ali and diana eScorted SuSan to her room.

"I haven't done anything wrong," Susan said. "You saw that."

"Oh, no," Ali said. "You have done wrong. You were nearly naked, and your vulgar dancing was a plain invitation to the watchers to take advantage of you. Peter simply availed himself of that opportunity. All that happened, because you were fishing for compliments."

Susan burst into tears. "Is it so wrong to want boys to like me? I know they're all liars, but their words make me feel good. I was tormented by my stepmother. You don't know what my life with her was like. It was hell. She made me slave away my whole life to raise her four kids."

"Stop seeing people for a while and stay in your room until you feel safe again," Ali said. "I've helped you through all the courses. You can study for finals without returning to class."

"Whatever you say, but don't deprive me of your friendship. You're the only one who helps me without asking for anything."

She watched Ali and Diana leave, then closed the door. Ali and Diana walked toward Diana's house lost in thought. Diana stopped and looked into his eyes. "I'm worried about you."

"You mean John? I have no fear of tomorrow's fight, because I didn't do anything wrong."

"I'm worried about you because of John and the others."

"What's that supposed to mean?"

She tried to sound cheerful despite her concern. "The age of knights has passed my beautiful cavalier."

"As long as there's purity to disperse the clouds and reason to combat futility, there must be a knight. Always remember that my love surrounds you with peace and security. Even when I'm away, I leave my heart and soul behind to protect you from life's iniquities and pain."

"Sometimes, you talk as if you're leaving me." "My love for you has no boundaries. It's not limited by time and space. It's a luminous light that comes from my heart and touches yours wherever you are."

The following day, Ali and John met at the baseball field. A crowd of students gathered to watch the fight. Diana, filled with fear and apprehension, was there, too.

The two opponents circled each other cautiously.

"This fight isn't for Peter," John said. "I met him after the party, and he told me what happened between him and Susan. I detest his shameful act and blamed him for it. This fight's because you stole Diana from me."

"Until this moment, "Ali snarled, "I wasn't angry with you, but now you can be certain I'll break your bones. Diana never belonged to you, and you know that perfectly well. Stop talking and start fighting."

They stood ready, preparing to deliver the first blows, when they heard the karate and boxing trainers arrive.

The karate trainer grabbed Ali's arms. "Is this what you've learned from karate?" he asked. "To fight your brother or to defend yourself and help the weak?"

The boxing trainer put his hand on John's shoulder. "The noble boxer never uses his fists outside the ring. You two champions must remain examples for others to follow. Go shake hands with him."

The two boys looked at each other for a moment, then Ali held out his hand, and John copied him. They shook hands and hugged.

The crowd applauded, and Diana walked up with a smile.

"Did you know this fight was about you, not Peter?" Ali asked her.

"I knew it from the start."

"Please explain."

"I'll explain at the end of term, at the place that witnessed the birth of our love, the green valley with its blue lake. I have several questions I need you to answer."

When she saw his confusion, she added, "It's enough right now for you to know that the fight was for our love. It was enough for me to see you safe and unharmed."

Except for Peter, who failed some of his classes, Ali, Diana, John, Timmy, and Susan all passed their exams at the end of the second semester. Their first year in college ended, and the events of that year showed the many facets of the personalities in Ali's group.

Ali's personality was revealed when he won the karate championship, in his ability to understand his lessons and simplify them for others, and his willingness to fight when necessary to protect the virtues in which he believed.

The date of their meeting finally came. Diana reached the valley half an hour before Ali, and parked her car at the top of the hill. She took a deep breath to fill her bosom with the fresh morning air. Her heart pounded strongly with love, so she ran into the valley while hugging herself, as if holding the whole universe.

She looked like a white butterfly flying over waves of grass with the sun weaving golden threads around her. Her love flowed with the water in the lake and mixed with the valley's fragrant zephyr. She felt she and nature were one. Her entire life was meaningless before she met Ali. It began the moment he said, "I love you."

Diana, looking up the hill, saw Ali watching. She held out her arms to him, and he ran to her through a vista of trees. He picked her up and whirled her around before she could catch her breath. She looked down at him, her tears raining on his eyes, her long hair kissing his face.

He set her down and held her tightly. The green valley witnessed their love, and in his arms she tested paradise. She realized that whatever happened, she couldn't love any other man that same way.

When the heat of their love ebbed, they sat on the grass overlooking the lake. She feared spoiling Ali's dream of paradise, but she had a lot to tell him.

"When we first came here, I felt our spirits touch and join," she said. "They would never be divided, but the force of my love frightened me, because your ideas are very different, shaped by a different background. How could we agree on a plan for our lives? That's why I decided to stop loving you."

"Is that why you walked away from me?"

"Yes."

"What does John have to do with this?"

"I tried to convince myself there was nothing between us by having him as a friend."

"I love you as you are."

"I couldn't stop loving you, because it was a fire that burned my heart. When I wanted to return to you, I found Susan had your attention, so I became angry and jealous."

"What are the consequences you fear from loving me?"

"I was afraid your dreamy romanticism might take you away from reality. Over time, I realized I was wrong."

"What made you change your mind?"

"I admired the way you gave to others, how you protected and supported Susan, and your insistence on getting me away from John. When you won the karate championship, I realized nothing would stop you from reaching your goals."

He said after a short pause, "People who put tenderness, imagination, and poetry into their work rise to exalted places and reach the heart of life. Materialism has deprived life of its beautiful spirit. It's the right of people to dream of a life based on love, goodness, and beauty. I want to live by those principles. I don't separate dreams and reality, because I can make my dreams come true. My love for you is my sweet reality. It's also a beautiful dream that's agreeable to the bottom of my heart."

They removed their shoes, stood hand-in-hand, and walked along the lake, lost in their thoughts. She thought of the way his words touched her heart. He was right. It would profit a man little if he gained the world only to lose his soul.

Noticing her drifting into deep thoughts, he asked, "What's on your mind now?"

"I was thinking of your ideas about money. Didn't you say in the seminar that money is the source of all evil and is only a medium of exchange? By itself, it doesn't produce anything?"

"I thought we finished that in the classroom."

"You have your own ideas, though, and I'm anxious to hear them."

"I think most of the world's problems are due to the nature of the current economic systems. It's true that those systems were developed by specialists and implemented by experts, but, over time, they failed in one or more aspects. Those who developed the systems didn't take into consideration humanity and compassion. They emphasized the individual right to possess a fortune without limitation or public ownership by the state, not the individual.

"That resulted in two economic systems, each of which claims idealism and superiority over the other. Although it was anticipated that both systems would help progress and respect humanity, they turned into a struggle to control the world."

"It's a reality we can't escape."

"We can change it by adopting another economic system that contains compassion, justice, social progress, and individual welfare."

"What system does that?"

"The one I mentioned in my seminar."

"Why do you always relate religion to science? You deviate from logic. The professor commented on that."

"Religion is a must, because law made by mankind will never be as ideal as those made by God, Who knows better what's good for His servants."

"I appreciate your being religious, but we must separate relationships with God from the material world."

"No. They're one and the same, because the path of God is the same to correct and construct the world. It's man who changes and guides development, and only he who can change and modify the modes and relations of production. It's a truism that individuals and nations can exist only with good morals and human relationships, not with wealth. I take for granted of course the importance of the material aspect, because unless people live comfortably and feel society is ready to help them in need, their faith can't be expected to be incorruptible nor their morals developed.

"I don't agree that it's only abundance that brings about welfare to human communities. Material welfare must be twinned with faith. Otherwise, it turns into a threat, the effects of which we see clearly in the developed world with the increase in immoral behavior. Material progress, without faith or control, is likely to make people miserable and crush society's solidarity. If the purpose of any society is to progress and improve morally, we have to understand that it's necessary for progress to be complete to rely on both economic and religious facets.

"Concern with one facet at the expense of the other will lead to disequilibrium and disorder in the lives of individuals and society. We have superpowers trying to preserve their whims for power, pleasure, and material growth, thus threatening the rights of the majority, crushing them with hunger, frustration, and suffering. That has led to what's referred to as consumed peace or balance, which is based on horror and which might lead the superpowers to annihilate all life on the planet." "Although you have this wonderful economic system, Muslim countries are underdeveloped. How do you explain that?"

"It was this full and ceaseless use of reason in combining human science and divine revelation that made the early Muslims so great. In those days, Islam faced two great powers, Sassamidal and Byzantium, which were eventually consumed by the same forces of disintegration and turmoil we see in the world right now. Despite that, Islam was able to give a feeling of genuine humanity and a sense of its secular life to millions of people. It gave them a new blissful life by setting them on the path to God, the One and Only to Whom we must return, and to Whom we shall be accountable.

"Islam appeared fourteen centuries ago in a primitive period, a time of slavery and underdevelopment as far as economics is concerned. As a divine legislation, Islam's principles go far beyond that primitive era. They are valid for all times and places.

"Islam established from the beginning true equality and guaranteed a limit to the wealth of each citizen. It determined an economic balance among members of society and confirmed the principle of dual ownership between private, free economics and the interference of the state in the economy for the benefit of the individual.

"Worship duties have been decreed by God to organize the relationship of subjects with their Creator in the realization of the significance of servitude to God on Earth. Those include prayers, fasting, pilgrimage, poor dues, and almsgiving. In all forms of worship, God has enjoined the performance of worship in accordance with the rules He laid down, not according to the passions and whims of mankind.

"Worship duties represent God's rights imposed on His servants, whether they are financial or physical. Constant observance of prayers strengthens the ties of brotherhood among believers, dispels grudges and hatred from hearts, appeases the soul, and breaks up arrogance. All foreheads are equal in submission to one God, to Whom every creature submits in servitude.

"Group prayer, when appearing also in one unity, signifies the bondage and strength of believers. Fasting makes the soul feel the value of God's favor when it's lost. That reminds man of the beneficent. It also creates a feeling of the state of the poor, and, therefore, the rich give a hand to the needy.

"Hatred and grudges thus disappear, and enmity diminishes. The poor dues are purification for riches, a recompense for the needy, a leveler of class distinction by means of periodic sums of money cut off from the rich and a realization of equality between the affluent and the needy.

"Almsgiving, including the poor dues, which is spending money in order to gain of what God has, is illumination in the heart, brightness on the face, increase of provision, and love in the hearts of mankind.

"Pilgrimage is emigration to God and His messenger, alienation from passion of the soul, riches, and sins, and shedding of garments that are a reminder to the soul of the day when man will leave this world, never to return. Besides, it's the day of gathering together of Muslims, rulers, and subjects from different environments, dialects, races, and colors, performing the same rites, mentioning the name of God on specific days, exchanging friendship and love, discussing their affairs, and returning as innocent as the newly born, pure of blunders and sins in the care of God, Who considers them among those with Him.

"Going back to the Islamic economic system, there's no doubt that the worst blow that Muslims gave to Islam was to close the door of interpretation, *Ijtihad*, after four hundred years of Islam. Since then, there's been no progress in Islamic studies. The application of Islamic law froze at that time and gave birth to the pretension that Islamic economics were primitive, not suitable for modern times, and an obstacle to progress. That stems from our neglect of interpretation and to the application of economic principles for a specific time and place."

"Do you think the Islamic economic system is applicable worldwide? You're talking about Utopia, the land of no place, where the highest degree of social and political organization is experienced. You're talking about ideal perfection, an impractical plan for improving society."

"It's only with the approach I just mentioned that we can end all forms of blind fanaticism and distortion and develop a better world."

"If you inherit a fortune, will you deal with it according to your ideas?"

"I'll abide by my principles, and I'll be one of those who construct the world. Who knows? You may see it yourself."

Although impressed by his words, she nonetheless wanted to hear from him that her economic system was the most suitable for mankind's progress.

They left the lake and sat under a tree, leaning against its huge trunk. She looked at him from the corner of her eye and imagined he came from a legendary world. Working alone, he'd never be able to reform the world, even if that was his intention. He would be crushed by those who possessed power and contradicted his views.

She couldn't imagine her future with someone else, but if he shared her fortune, would he deal with that, too, according to his idealistic plan? Was he just dreaming, gambling on something that would never happen?

The sun sank to the distant horizon, and the lake glittered with golden light. They climbed the hill and stood at the top, watching their paradise.

He murmured in her ear, "The valley is my heart, and in it, you can find my love in the sweet zephyr and the fragrant odors of the beautiful flowers."

"Is that imagination again?"

He contemplated the valley without answering.

Diana sat behind the wheel, waiting for him to get in, but he said he preferred to walk and relive every moment they spent together.

She departed in a car crowded with her thoughts and his. She was no longer worried, because she loved him deeply, and he loved her sincerely. Love would satisfy both despite their differences.

That night, surrounded by love and security, she slept deeply.

The following day, a telegram came from Ali's father asking him to spend the summer vacation with the family in London. Diana gave Ali and Saber a ride to the airport. That was her first meeting with Saber, though Ali told her of his honesty and loyalty. She greeted Saber courteously and liked him, because he cared for her beloved.

CHAPTER FIVE

Days passed slowly while ali was away in London. Diana felt lonesome in the huge mansion, doing nothing but wandering in the garden or reading. She seldom saw her father, because of his obligations in congress and commitments with his electors. Since the senator was always busy, he depended on his partner, Clark Robertson, to run the business. As their profits rose, his appreciation of Clark increased, and the idea of Diana marrying James grew.

The Senator, noticing Diana sought isolation in her room, realized something was on her mind. At breakfast, he said, "I was pleased by your high grades in the second semester."

"I got help from a colleague who simplifies the lessons and explains them clearly."

"Someone I know?"

"No. He's an Egyptian, called Ali."

He looked up in surprise. "I haven't seen him with you."

"We studied outdoors. We both love nature."

"Where is he now?"

"In London, vacationing with his family."

"What does his family do there?"

"They live there."

"Tell me about him."

"It's as if he comes from an ideal world shaped by truth and virtue. He wants to spread love among people by helping them. Sometimes, he flies to dreamy worlds of his own creation."

The Senator glanced at her twinkling eyes, which grew warm and dreamy, and asked, "How far has your relationship with him gone?"

"He's wonderful. He can give me the world. I love him, Dad."

Annoyed, he asked restlessly, "Does he feel the same?"

"Yes."

He finished breakfast hastily, claiming he had to leave due to previous commitments.

At his office, he gave orders not to interrupt him for anything. His materialistic mind acted like a computer, estimating the influence of such an unexpected love on his plans for Diana. He had to kill their love before it grew and destroyed his daughter's future. It amazed him that she had surrendered to such passion. How could she let herself fall in love with a stranger who was so totally different?

Diana was raised on reality and materialism. He always planned to focus her mind in that direction, though he knew women often defended their love by being unrealistic.

How could he have failed to see she might be as sentimental as her mother and wouldn't care about making a fortune? Her mother always ran after him, asking for a warm place to settle after their marriage, but he was too busy closing a deal or executing a project.

He remembered her dying words, *Let Diana live her own life and don't impose anything on her against her will.*

At the time, he couldn't see what she meant, but he finally understood.

"To hell with women," he said. "Their extreme sentimentality makes them out of touch with reality."

The only intention the stranger had was to dominate Diana's fortune. No, the Senator would manage her, so she wouldn't get hurt. He would stop the greedy stranger and never allow him to own a fortune he hadn't earned.

James was the solution. Diana must marry him to be safe, but plans must be made very carefully and without any pressure that might force Diana to accept a marriage she didn't like.

First, he must find a way to make James and Diana see each other more often. Second, he must devote more time to her and talk to her about the great future that awaited her. Third, he must awaken her sense of logic and reason. Fourth, he knew that the heart disorder that affected him would crush her with grief, so he'd use that to make her accept James as a husband. Fifth, as a man of power in North Carolina, he had every means available to stop the stranger from influencing his daughter.

He repeated with his daughter what he did with her mother. He decided to execute all his practical decisions altogether. As a man whose heart was fed by figures, he didn't realize that the only way to help the world was through true love in the hearts of people. Man loves with his heart, not with the figures in his mind.

When Diana passed her examinations, the Senator gave a big dinner party in the mansion's garden. Congressmen, businessmen, and their wives were invited. At the top of the list were Clark and James Robertson. Delicious food was set out on tables around a swimming pool illuminated with underwater lights. In a corner was a bar that offered all varieties of liquor, served by barmaids dressed in white. On the terrace, an orchestra played while waiters passed trays of hors d'oeuvres and glasses of champagne. Light from the house and swimming pool mingled, reflecting on flowers and bushes, turning the grounds into a background of twinkling stars.

Diana wore a simple black dress, her blonde hair falling softly against her shoulders. She looked ravishing. She stood with her father at the entrance to the garden to receive their guests, who arrived in a long line until Clark and James came. James, examining her with experienced eyes, realized that the child of the past had become an exquisite young woman. He held her hand, bent over it, and kissed it politely.

Shyness overcame her, and she blushed.

"It's James Robertson," her father said. "Remember him?"

"Yes. He visited us with his father."

"This intellectual young man and his daddy watch over your father's business when he's busy with politics. Your father's an old man now. It's about time for James to take you to the factory, so you can get an idea about how your share is managed."

"I'm at her service in anything she asks," James said politely.

Diana, smiling and looking at him thankfully, didn't answer.

After dinner, an old congressman came to the Senator's table and asked Diana to begin the dancing. They danced together, and, within minutes, the marble circle was filled with couples. Although the old man had an elegant face, his fat, aged body didn't match Diana's beauty and loveliness.

With a glass of Scotch in hand, James stood alone in the dark, watching Diana in admiration. He'd known several women, but she was different.

She was a mature fruit, ready for reaping. She could entertain him instead of spending boring nights with cheap women he met at bars.

He asked for another double, swallowed it in one gulp, and walked up to tap Diana's shoulder and ask, "Have you a dance left for me?"

The old congressman laughed and said cheerfully, "We've finally found a perfect match for you."

James was a good dancer. As they moved across the floor, he said, "I remember you as a child. I never thought you'd turn into such an exquisite beauty."

She laughed shyly. "Thank you for the compliment."

"How about my taking you to the company tomorrow?"

"Why not? It's what father wants."

"Elements of success are not in the lessons you learn at the university," he said confidently. "You learn to succeed from work itself. I haven't completed my academic education, but my experience in business management is unmatched."

Sensing his inferiority complex, she said, "It seems I'll learn a lot from you."

The Senator was very pleased to see that his solution was working. He approached the couple and patted their backs. "You're made for each other. Together, you make a wonderful couple."

The following morning, Diana sat beside James in his black Cadillac. Although the factory was ten miles from her home, he showed his driving skill by reaching it in a few minutes. At the factory, he gave her a quick tour of the production lines for dresses and makeup. He invited her to his office to brief her about the company's status.

She realized in an instant that his office was the key place from which the factory was controlled. The spacious, high-ceilinged room had equipment for communication with the various divisions and with markets both in the States and abroad. A leather sofa and two chairs faced his desk. The floors were covered with expensive Oriental carpets, and the walls were lined with wood bookshelves, one shelf of which was empty to provide space for a bar. Bottles of liquor were neatly arranged on glass shelves, and clean, bright, crystal glasses sat in a cocktail cabinet under the shelves.

Diana sat on the sofa facing James' desk. He offered her a cigarette from a gold box, but she thanked him and declined. "I don't smoke."

James took a cigar from a large wooden box on his elegant desk and lit it. "How about a drink to start the morning? I have all kinds of liquor."

"No, thank you. I don't drink."

He walked to the bar to fetch himself a brandy. "What do you prefer?"

"Lime juice."

He laughed. "I have plenty of that, too, because I usually mix it with gin."

James returned to his luxurious desk and asked his secretary to send in a glass of lime juice. He enjoyed sipping his brandy and glancing at Diana, as he explained the company's financial status.

"Our parents' fortune is estimated at twenty-two million dollars. Capital assets in the form of the factory and machinery are around fourteen million, and the net profits range from six to seven percent of the value of the capital assets. The limiting factor to increasing profits depends on our ability to win local and international markets. Our production always faces severe competition in local markets, which compels us to open new markets in Japan, Europe, and the Middle East.

"That's what I've done recently. The new markets are consuming all our products and need more. That wonderful achievement revives my life dream—to expand our production lines even more."

"It seems the company's success runs from this office."

"Right you are. My father's old and sick, and the Senator is always busy with politics and has to rest by doctor's orders." Thoughtfully observing her extreme beauty through the cigar smoke, he surprised her by saying, "It's about time you share the management responsibilities with me."

"What's that supposed to mean?"

"It's your company, too. You must take part in management."

"My education is more important right now."

"You can assume your responsibilities during vacations. I feel this is a good opportunity for you, because you've been kept far from matters concerning business, and it's time to familiarize yourself with your father's company. You'll have the chance to compare the lessons you learn with what happens in the real world."

"I think no opportunity has seemed as good as this," she replied.

"I like your enthusiasm. How about starting tomorrow?"

"OK."

"I've worn you out already. Come on. I'll give you a ride home."

She laughed. "On one condition—don't drive too fast."

He smiled. "Your wish is my command."

CHAPTER SIX

Dana and James' friendship grew during the summer vacation. Each morning, she saw him in his office to receive instructions about her day's work, which ranged from accounting to discussion with the heads of production lines. James was clever at occupying her time by pretending he wanted to hear her opinions and questions during their discussion. When she said she wasn't experienced enough to answer, he said, "Even modest opinions can help solve big problems."

Thus, her modest answers were praised and considered as highly intelligent. Diana liked her new work and appreciated James' keen interest in training her in every business activity. Over time, she respected him more, particularly when she realized that he was behind the business' successes.

The Senator spent more time with Diana by having breakfast and dinner with her. At night in the drawing room, resting in a comfortable chair, he asked her how things were going at the factory. She replied eagerly that she was very happy because of the immense experience she acquired from James.

After several more days, at another dinner, he asked her opinion of James—if he was taking care of her—and with the same eagerness, she said his excellent management was the reason the company was flourishing. The Senator couldn't have been more pleased by the growing friendship.

He proceeded with his plan. He had already succeeded in bringing James and Diana close together and directing her thoughts toward work and progress. The most-important goal was to have James accept her as his wife. The present situation was a good beginning for Diana to marry James. The Senator had to deal with her at a distance, without getting too close. Patience was needed.

From his office, Clark Robertson called his son and demanded he come over to discuss an important matter. When he arrived, Clark said, "I think it's time you consider getting married instead of spending your nights with your lowlife friends."

"I'm free to do whatever I like with my life," James said sharply. "Please don't interfere in my private affairs."

Clark was not offended, because he was accustomed to James' attitude. He said calmly, "Maybe marriage is the only way to protect you from yourself. You drink too much. Your eyes are red and swollen."

"Don't you ever stop blaming me? Since my mother died, you dislike everything I do." James stood to leave.

"The Senator talked to me weeks ago about the possibility that you marry his daughter. I personally welcome the idea. How about you?"

Utterly surprised, James sat in the nearest chair, thinking.

"If you marry her, everything she owns will be yours," Clark continued. "If not, a stranger will share it with us."

James spoke slowly, trying to sort things out in his mind. "The idea of marriage hadn't crossed my mind before, but you're right. A stranger would jeopardize all my plans. In the past, she was just a little girl. Since she turned into an uncommon beauty, I wouldn't mind marrying her."

"The Senator insists she finish college first. That means you'll have to wait three years."

"What do you suggest?"

"If you promise not to drink, I might persuade him to lessen the time period to one or two years."

"What does drinking have to do with marriage?"

"Because a drunkard like you might get a bad reputation and ruin everything." Clark said. "Promise to give up drinking, or we'll forget the whole thing."

James nodded, knowing that he was but throwing words in the air, "I give you my word."

Later, James sat in his office, thinking. He hadn't known the Senator wanted him to marry Diana. James might gain her part of the fortune after all. Such a marriage would fulfill his dreams.

How many times had he demanded that the board of directors allocate large sums of money to expand production lines after he succeeded in opening new markets? The Senator always rejected the idea, preferring to invest in stocks and bonds. Marrying Diana would give him more influence on the Senator, and his plans for expansion would become real.

The new situation required drawing Diana closer to him. Their meetings needed to extend to romantic places, like fancy clubs and restaurants. He'd make her love him, because he was an experienced man who knew women's nature.

At the end of a working day, James invited Diana to dinner at a fancy restaurant famous for superb seafood. When she tried to decline, he said, "There are several important work issues that needed to be discussed, and dinner will be a good chance to exchange views."

Embarrassed, she accepted, though she felt resentful. The Senator expected her for dinner, but she had a commitment with James. Seeing the way she dressed for the evening, he was delighted.

James escorted her to a handsome restaurant with a beautiful garden illuminated by dim lights. They went upstairs and stopped before a thick wooden door. A waiter, recognizing James, led them to a special table. A beautiful waitress in a very short dress welcomed them with tender words and nodded to James with a broad smile while setting down the menu.

Diana realized from the woman's friendly manner that James must be a regular customer.

Pointing to the menu in Diana's hands, James asked, "Have you made your choice?"

"All the dishes are alike. I'll leave it to you."

James pointed at the waitress and said, "The usual."

Without waiting, she replied, "Fried fish with cooked vegetables, shrimp with mayonnaise, snails, and caviar with fresh salad."

"Good girl."

She walked a few steps, then paused to ask, "Champagne, as usual?"

"Yes. Of course." She returned within minutes wheeling a table carrying their dishes and a small bucket filled with ice and a bottle of champagne. James happily removed the cork, which popped out. He filled two glasses until the foam overflowed.

"But I don't drink," Diana said.

"You don't drink or smoke. Don't deprive yourself of life's pleasures. A little champagne refreshes the body after a hard day's work. Look at the bubbles. See how they twinkle in your glass? Go ahead and sip." He raised his glass to her. "Cheers."

She was forced to copy him. After she tasted it, she exclaimed, "It's like apple juice."

He laughed. "After you finish your glass, you'll realize that what you think is apple juice is, in fact, an indispensable magic liquid made especially for intimate lovers."

He brought the glass to his mouth and drained it, then poured another.

"This one glass is enough," Diana said.

"Right you are. I don't want the Senator blaming me for getting you drunk."

She sipped her champagne and observed him thoughtfully. He was older than she by at least ten years. He looked experienced and highly confident. He was practical and knew how to achieve his goals.

While they ate, James surprised her by explaining that their special meal, rich in protein and vitamins, was also suited to champagne. For the champagne to produce its effect, food had to be eaten in a certain sequence. It was preferable to begin with light food like snails and caviar, then move to heavier food, like shrimp with mayonnaise, then end with fried fish and cooked vegetables.

When Diana asked him about the idea behind that, he said that intoxication by liquor would be gradually equalized with this food sequence, and would keep them from becoming drunk.

"It seems you have a lot of experience with liquor and food," she commented.

"Yes. Liquor soothes me in my solitude."

"How could a man like you become lonesome?"

"I'm not now."

Understanding his meaning, she felt she had exceeded her limit. She didn't understand it was the liquor that made her feel relaxed and at ease.

As James finished his third glass, he said, "I was about to forget the matter I wanted to discuss with you."

"Yes?"

"We have many things in common, and the day will come when we inherit our parents' fortunes and be the only proprietors of the company. Because our decisions must be alike, we must see each other more often."

"I don't think we differ that much. I'm fond of your management style."

"Do you trust me that much?"

"Yes. I told my father that your skill running the company was unmatched."

"You're absurdly beautiful. Has anyone ever told you that?"

She was about to tell him that Ali praised her beauty, but she stopped. Suddenly thinking of Ali made her fall into deep silence. She felt being with James privately was being unfaithful to Ali.

Her heart contracted, and deep sadness entered her soul, magnified by the feeling that the purity she enjoyed with Ali had been contaminated by liquor with James. Closing her eyes for a moment, she felt the ache in her heart like a physical pain.

Diana looked at her watch. "I promised my father I wouldn't be late. I hope you don't mind leaving now."

He felt terribly annoyed. "But the evening hasn't even started yet."

"It seems I'm a bit dizzy. I want to rest."

"Can't we wait a bit?" he asked hopefully.

"I want to leave now," she insisted.

James had no choice but to obey. He nervously summoned the waitress and gave her money, then walked toward the exit with Diana. The waitress stopped him to return the change, which was almost one hundred dollars, but he told her to keep it.

On their way home, she examined him. He was short with sleek brown hair, jovial with a loud voice, and had shrewd eyes that watched and noticed everything. He was industrious, a good speaker, but a trifle pompous. He had rank and wealth and thought highly of himself. Women might feel secure with him, but she couldn't possibly feel romantic about someone like that.

It was natural to compare him with Ali. They were totally different. One talked only of figures and chased opportunities to achieve his goals, while the other hoped for a new system based on justice and compassion.

One enjoyed life's pleasures. The other gave without taking. His movements in life were motivated by goodness, truth, and beauty.

Those ethics didn't pay, and she resented any ideas that contradicted a system that had been effective for over a century, one that dominated the world and in which she hoped to play an important role. Although James represented the system she believed was the fittest, nothing he said could shake her.

Oh, Ali, what have I done to you? she wondered. *I'm away from you with another man, but I think only of you. You don't know what you've done to me. You aroused in me a perfect tenderness. You placed within my soul a love of the good and the beautiful. You have a heart of gold and you are kindness itself.*

It's impossible for our love to end, because we sipped the wine of life from the same glass. I'd go through fire with you as long as you are with me

She awoke from her thoughts when James announced they'd arrived. Thanking him for a lovely dinner, she left hastily and climbed the steps into the house.

In her room, she removed her clothes and got in bed, pulling the covers over her naked body before turning off the light. Closing her eyes, she murmured, "I miss my moments with you. Come and take me in your arms."

His spirit whispered tender, reproachful words. She felt his pain and whispered regretfully, "Forgive me, my love." Holding the pillow as if it were Ali, she slept and dreamed of him until dawn.

On the other side of the Atlantic, Ali chatted with his family about life in North Carolina.

Selim looked at his son in admiration and asked, "Do you still practice karate?"

"I won the championship of the American universities."

"Your grades are high in all courses for both semesters. I'm very proud of you. Tell me of your social life."

"I was hesitant at first, but, after a short period, I managed to conform to university society. As a whole, it's an open society that allows all to express views, claim rights, and perform duties. The widespread media observe the implementation of policies and also people's conduct.

"Even the president and his administration are subject to judicial investigation by the courts. The parameters of success are to make fortunes and collect money. As for technology, it is extremely advanced, and it's used very effectively in developing production to win international markets. Everything there is run according to mathematical and materialistic manners."

"What's your impression of their economic system?"

"Although it's successful in terms of money and power, I doubt its validity. The West spent $78 billion on nuclear weapons in 1984. Such a huge sum is enough to produce one million atomic bombs, each of which can kill 70,000 people. That means that the developed world and Russia can destroy twenty times the world's population in seconds. Such an advance in technology could be turned by a fanatic into a barbaric act that could destroy the civilized world."

"What's the civilized world, my son? Aren't they the ones who possess power and technology today?"

"No, Father. Civilization is the result of generations raised on the wisdom of centuries, generations racing to spread good among people, protect the weak, and give to the poor. It's the use of science to discover God's blessings and extend them to the people. Civilization hides people's vices and shows their virtues and laudable actions.

"According to our religion, we believe that we're to be admitted to heaven only through God's mercy because of our faith, and are to be rewarded in proportion to our good deeds. In Islam, there's no conflict between matter and soul, no separation between economy and religion, which guarantees success in this world and the hereafter. After all, this world is the proving ground for the next.

"Man is God's viceroy on earth, and the purpose of Islamic economics is to construct the world and endow it with life. The developing world is suffering because it is poor in means, whereas the capitalist world is dying, because it lacks ends. In the West, people think technology is the only bridge to power and happiness. However, if technology isn't directed for the good of mankind, it becomes a harmful tool.

"Who said technology is civilization? You may find true civilization in a simple man pasturing sheep in the desert. He serves God and worships Him with the purity of faith. He attends to his prayers and glorifies His name. He receives passersby with civility and offers them food and drink to help them on their journey.

"If hunger comes, a few morsels satisfy him, and he thanks God for making them available. He praises God if granted a favor and remains silent and steadfast during mishaps. In all his events, he worships God, Who provides him with food lest he go hungry and with security lest he should live in fear. Who knows? Maybe, after the coming war, life will begin again from the land from which we came, the land of the prophets."

Selim realized that living in the United States for one year hadn't changed Ali a bit. He seemed even more adherent to his morals and principles. He surprised his son by asking, "Have you any idea about your father's fortune?"

"I know only that you're extremely rich."

"It's more than £600 million Sterling. The day will come when you, your mother, and your sister will inherit it. I sent you to the United States to learn the Western economic system under which we invest our money. I'm pleased to see you abiding by the values of our faith. Those values can reach people if you adopt the correct means for that. The day will come when you'll use your fortune to spread real, true values among people, but you can't do that unless you realize that money is perishable if it doesn't serve the poor and needy. I long for the day of your final return, because I expect you to take over for me when I retire."

One evening, Selim spoke to Saber. "Ali obtained high grades in his courses and won the karate championship. Is there anything else I should know?"

"Yes, Sir. He's in love with an American girl studying at the same university."

"That's natural. Any man is sweet on a good-looking girl."

"It's a true love, and it seems strong. You know his emotions reflect on his behavior."

"You mean he's a romantic who can't separate imagination and reality."

"Something like that."

"That's why I sent him there. I wanted him to face the raging waves of life alone, so he can learn to separate what's real and what's imaginary. Anyway, his news is encouraging so far."

"His love for this girl is real."

"It may be as real as you say, but it will merge with a beautiful fantasy in his mind. If this love ends in failure, he'll have to bear the consequences. What's so special about her?"

"She's very beautiful and is extremely fond of him, too. She is also exalted in rank and wealth."

Selim's heart filled with worry, but he had no choice but to commit all his affairs to God and ask Him to protect his son while he lived in another world.

Ali spent lovely days with his family in London. His mother cooked special meals for him and served him herself. His father was content to look at him in admiration, while Nadia, his sister, was filled with joy, because he was her example and a man of renown.

Ali was in Hyde Park one day, contemplating the beauty of the blue lake for many hours. Suddenly, he heard Nadia saying, "All the family's waiting for you at lunch, and you're sitting here, staring at the lake!"

"Sorry. I lost track of time."

While they walked together, she said, "You were lost in thought. Have you got something on your mind?"

"You turned into a beautiful young lady while I was in the United States."

"Don't change the subject. Tell me what's bothering you."

"I'm deeply in love with an American girl."

Nadia stopped, took his hand, and led him to the nearest bench, where they sat down. "Tell me everything that happened to you since you left us."

He laughed. "What about lunch?"

"Forget lunch. Speak."

He told her his love story. She felt like a child hearing a fairytale filled with magical creatures and their adventures.

Finally, they walked off hand-in-hand.

"I want to return with you and see her," Nadia said. "Your being away kills me. You're my only brother."

"One day, you'll marry, and then you'll be away, too. Life is meeting and departure."

"You're leaving again. Whenever I think of that, melancholy overwhelms me."

"Wherever I go, I carry my love for you and my family with me."

Days before leaving, Selim called Ali and gave him an envelope filled with a large sum of money, a gift to express his happiness at Ali's high grades. Ali bent forward and kissed his father's hand thankfully.

When he was ready to leave the room, Selim stopped him and asked, "Don't you need a car for transportation in the United States?"

"Thank you, Father," Ali replied joyfully. "I need one badly, but I was embarrassed to ask, lest you disapprove."

"I'll write you a check so you can draw money from my bank account in the North Carolina bank. You can choose any American car you like."

"I'd prefer a European sports car."

"What kind would you like?"

"A Ferrari."

"That's an expensive car, but I'll buy it for you, anyway. All you have to do is take care of customs. I advise you to concentrate on your studies and stay away from life's pleasures."

"I'll do my best to fulfill your commands."

Once Ali was back in his own room, he opened the envelope and found £5,000 Sterling. The first thing that came to mind was to buy Diana a gift with it. He told Nadia of his decision, and she volunteered to accompany him to stores that carried items women liked.

In a jewelry shop, they bought a large, gold heart on a gold chain. Ali insisted on having it inscribed with his and Diana's initials.

Ali sent Diana a telegram announcing the date of their reunion in the valley. He counted the hours until he could see her again. The family bid Ali and Saber farewell at the airport. After a long trip, they finally arrived at their apartment in North Carolina.

CHAPTER SEVEN

The following morning, Ali hurried to the valley and hid behind some trees to watch Diana before she saw him. She bent over some flowers, inhaling their fragrance, looking as happy as a free bird. He stood for a while, meditating upon her, then he walked slowly toward her.

Hearing his approaching footsteps, she looked up and felt a shiver of delight as her heart raced. She wanted to control her feelings, but he was already upon her. He held out his hands, and she took them, then he drew her to his chest and held her close.

In a trembling voice, she said, "Your love is so dominating, I can't endure it alone."

"My life was poor while I was away from you."

"You don't know how much I love you. I can't express my feelings."

"You're shaking. Do you love me that much?"

"Your love is the reason for my existence."

Looking at the sparkle in his eyes, she realized passion kindled in his heart. Captivated by that, she couldn't withhold herself. "Take me to the land of dreams," she murmured.

He flew with her to meadows woven of love flowers and springs flowing with love wine, until both were lost in love's drunkenness.

They leaned back on the grass, and Ali put his arm around her shoulders. Sunlight streamed down through the trees. Green leaves whispered, and the two of them watched the trees. After a short time, she fell asleep in his arms, and he remained still, fearing to wake her.

Many beautiful moments passed until she opened her eyes and said, "Sorry I slept so long. I long to live all my moments with you."

"I watched your face while you slept. If beauty came to be compared with you, it would lower its head in shame."

"How beautiful to wake up to such sweet words."

He rose to his knees and removed a small red velvet box from his pocket. "For you, my love."

She'd never seen the like of the gold heart she found inside. His gesture overwhelmed her, and she stared at the heart through her tears, filled by Ali's sweetness.

"Now my heart is in your possession," he said. "Treat it tenderly, and conceal it in your bosom."

Her heart melted within her, and she couldn't think of anything but the desire that rose in her like a tidal wave. "Hold me tight. I want to vanish in your arms. Love me this one time."

He pushed a lock of her straight blonde hair back behind her ear. "I don't want to deflower you before you become my wife. My love for you isn't for a moment. It's for an age to live together."

Seeing the sympathy and tender regret in his eyes, she asked lovingly, "Is there such purity in our world?"

"I can't imagine you with anything but a pure heart. I'll ask your father for your hand in marriage once we graduate."

"I long to bring you children who will be as noble and gracious as you." It was dusk, and the sun sank toward the distant horizon. Small birds lurked under the leaves as the couple walked along the lakeshore, holding each other tenderly. She felt embedded in his soul, flowing with his blood, and her name was written in gold letters upon his heart. She was everything he saw, touched, and breathed. Diana was as happy as a queen, captivated by his strong love. She found him irresistible, and their love melted the differences between them, while the future was colored with endless happiness.

Their second year of college began, and Ali's friendship extended to other colleagues who sought him out due to his reputation as a sportsman and an intelligent student who knew how to explain courses to others. Ali's group became Diana, Susan, John, and Timmy. They were together in classes, at the swimming pool, on the tennis courts, or at the gym. They took trips to the county borders, where green fields and beautiful lakes awaited them.

Ali's Ferrari arrived, and he stared at it in wonder and admiration. The white convertible was obviously classy and perfectly designed. It was unique in quality, distinction, and comfort. Its sporty design was based on racing cars.

On the outside, its flowing lines were striking. The two seats were a happy compromise between softness and support. Ali, sitting down, felt excited. The car was fully equipped to provide an exceptional ride— fog lamps, tinted and heated door mirrors with electrical adjusters, headlights, light alloy wheels, power windows, an alarm system, and a fully automatic air conditioner.

Ali's friends and acquaintances admired the car. Diana enjoyed driving it with him. One day, she asked him how he came to possess such an expensive car, and he said, "It was a gift from my father for doing so well in my exams."

She often wanted to ask about his father's financial status, but she never did, and the situation suddenly became more mysterious. That increased her love.

In the office at the factory, the Senator spoke with Clark and James. "James, I'm pleased to see you training Diana on the different activities of the firm."

"I told her everything she needed to know. I also had her participate in discussion with the heads of the production lines. She even made some valuable suggestions for certain problems."

"I raised her to be prepared for a practical life, and it's high time to encourage that. Training during summer vacation isn't enough. I want her to join you even while she's in college."

"I'll have a permanent office prepared for her."

"That's a good idea. That would link her to work, particularly when she can share in the benefits and the problems."

"She can start anytime. Her office will be ready in three days."

"Senator, didn't you suggest that they marry?" Clark asked. "James welcomes the idea. I see no reason for a delay."

The Senator paced the room, his hands clasped behind him, as he thought hard. "It's not that simple. She's strongly attracted to an Egyptian student, so I've decided to remove him from her life. James, you're clever and efficient. Give her a real challenge. I'll bet she rises to it. A permanent job would use up all her crazy energy on something that will give her a sense of accomplishment.

"Listen carefully, James. I know she doesn't feel romantic about you, but she can love you with her mind if she realizes the benefits. That requires you to be more fully present in her life. If we don't do it soon, there's no knowing what she might do. I'm sure you can help her when nobody else can."

"I'll do whatever you say, Senator," James said. "I'm determined to save her at any price."

The Senator lit a cigar. "She's fond of your management style. Do you know what that means? It's the first sign of a logical love. All you have to do is invest in it."

After a few days, Diana received a letter informing her she'd been appointed deputy director of the firm, with a monthly salary of $3,000. Enchanted by the idea of a job, she showed the letter to her father at dinner that night, who read it carefully, admiring James' clever approach.

"It's a good step on the right road," he said.

"You knew about this, of course?"

"Nothing happens in the company without my knowledge. I'm getting old, and you must take over."

"I'm afraid the job will interrupt my studies."

"It's too good an opportunity for you to refuse. You can go to the office each day after your classes. When exams are near, you can stop going to the office to study."

"I can manage that," she said thoughtfully. "Most students have to work. When do I start?"

"That's up to you."

Weeks passed. Diana went to the office three or four days a week. Although that reduced her time with Ali, the world of business responsibility pleased her very much.

James provided many opportunities for her to improve her talents and competence. He taught her the essence of administration and ways to convince customers and employees. He put her in the middle of real problems and asked her to submit reports demonstrating the negative and positive sides of a solution.

Some of her ideas were useful, due to her mental gifts, and James always demanded those be given immediate implementation. When good results were achieved, he showed her the fruits of her labor right away, which always made her happy. They celebrated by having splendid dinners at fancy restaurants, where they continued chatting out their dreams for expansion of the production lines.

Ali, seeing Diana's sudden diligence in her new work, encouraged her, because it was rare that students their age were given the opportunity to merge theory and practice. She told him how James was training her to assume large responsibilities in the future, and how her efforts had already increased the company's profits.

Ali listened to her enthusiastic words with the feeling she'd suddenly grown several years older, and she was leaping ahead of the most-beautiful years of her youth without noticing.

On the first Monday morning in September, Diana invited Ali to the company to see how she was managing her responsibilities. They went in his car and parked in a space reserved for a department head.

Diana sat proudly at her desk, and Ali smiled as he sat before her and asked, "Is it proper to start practical work as a deputy director? You've risen to a high position in one step."

"Management of the company is my father's right," she said proudly.

"It would be more appropriate if you learned management in three or four years. Start your work and forget about me."

Diana gave her secretary some instructions, then she suggested taking Ali for a tour. They left her room hand-in-hand and met James while walking toward his office. Diana introduced them, and James greeted Ali indifferently. Seeing them together irritated and angered him, but he tried to drive away the jealous thoughts filling his mind.

"I'm taking him on a quick tour," she told James. "We'll be back in an hour."

James nodded and went to his office to sit and think. Diana had to be burdened with enough work to keep her away from Ali. Over the past few weeks, James made her realize the importance of his existence in her life. All that remained was more patience and planning.

After the tour, Diana and Ali met James at his office. The moment they sat down, James gave her a file of customer orders for dresses and asked her to investigate the capacity of their production lines to see if they could meet the demand.

"Couldn't it wait until tomorrow?" she asked.

"This is urgent. I expect your answer in an hour."

Diana gave Ali a regretful look. "I'll wait for you in my office after you finish with James."

Once alone with James, Ali asked, "Do you mind if I look at your books?"

"Go ahead."

"It seems you have a good collection on economics." Ali studied the floor-to-ceiling bookshelves.

"I tried to read some of them, but I don't have the patience to read more than a few pages in a book. What's the use of reading when you already know the path to success? I run a large company with three hundred employees. My net profits are in the millions."

James went to the cocktail cabinet and poured a shot of bourbon. "Do you need a drink?"

"I never touch alcohol."

James finished his bourbon in one gulp, lit a cigar, and scrutinized Ali. He looked handsome and strong, a calm, quiet man.

James was filled with the need to humiliate Ali, so he said, "If you need a job, I wouldn't mind hiring you. We need laborers here."

Still examining the books, Ali said, "I don't need money to complete my education."

After he finished with the books, Ali sat in a leather chair facing James' desk and said calmly, "Diana's fond of your style of management and talks a lot about your skills."

"She's a good girl with an inquisitive mind." James poured another drink. "What's your plan for the future?"

"Nothing specific."

"It's strange to see a man your age without any plans."

"I know what I want to do, but there's no haste. Concentrating on my studies is a good investment for the future."

"Life, my dear friend, wants those who grasp opportunities and turn them to their advantage, not those who wait for them to become available without making any effort."

"I'd prefer to finish my academic education first before going into practical work. In the East, we feel that the future is in God's hands. Man has to work hard to gain His goodness. Whatever brings gain is due to God's goodness, not just our labor. It's what we call surrendering to God and having confidence in Him. You may work hard and plan well for the future without receiving the comforts, blessings, or benefits unless you believe in the Benefactor and resign yourself to Him completely. Praise be to God for His benefits."

James laughed derisively. "Oh, good grief. I thought you were a man of good sense. You mean a man waits for his chance to come without making any effort?"

"I mean exactly what I said. Whatever you plan for the future isn't sufficient to predict anything, because the future is in God's hands. Let me give you an example. A few moments ago, you asked Diana to investigate whether the production lines can meet customer demand.

"Can you guarantee the adequate delivery of products in due time? Can you be certain that those demands will increase, decrease, or remain constant? Fashions may change, thus influencing the rate of purchase. Can you predict the trend of prices in general or in detail?

"With all this technology, investors are still unable to accurately forecast when monetary cycles will expand or contract in local or international markets. The famous American economist, Wesley Mitchell, devoted his entire life to trying to explain disturbances that affect business cycles. In the end, he couldn't explain what caused the disturbances but instead introduced a type of theory that's merely descriptive. It doesn't lead to the logical analysis that would make possible the discovery and elimination of the root cause.

"His analysis showed that an economic system of interrelated parts develops internal stresses during expansion, and those stresses bring on recession. Uneven contractions in various parts pave the way for revivals. Mitchell posited no normal or equilibrium state for an economy, and he found none in its behavior.

"This lack of human understanding indicates that the future is in God's hands and occurs only according to His will. What man needs to do is tactfully plan for tomorrow, work hard during the day, and surrender to God concerning the future. Mitchell's finding that uneven contractions pave the way for revivals coincides with the verse from the Koran that states, 'With hardship comes ease.'"

James looked at him in astonishment. "Where'd you learn all that?" "From the books you haven't read in your library."

After a while, Diana entered the room and handed James the results of her investigation, then she took Ali's hand. They rushed to the door laughing as they walked to his white Ferrari.

From his office window, James stared at the car's elegant lines and realized that Ali was a strong competitor for Diana's love.

As they drove back, Diana asked, "What's your opinion of James?"

"He's a successful, ambitious man. You've seen that yourself."

"That's exactly what I expected you to say."

"He's surrounded by several factors that might destroy him if he's not careful."

"What do you mean?" she asked in amazement.

"There are many. He drinks too much, even at work. If wine enslaves him, he might lose his insight and motivation for his work. He's sure of himself, relying on his own experience without considering fundamental economics. Man usually follows the road to success, but road marks are subject to change over time. Those who tread that road need a good economic background based on the experience of specialists, and James has none. He even went so far as to ask, 'What's the use of reading if you already know the path to success?' In my opinion, that's fatal flaw."

Although she'd seen those things in James, Diana hadn't really thought about them before. She knew Ali was right, but she still wanted to argue with him. "Is it true that your religion forbids wine?"

"Yes."

"In our country, we think a few glasses of wine after a hard day's work refresh the body and enable it to continue working. As for economic science, what good does that do if it doesn't lead to wealth and prosperity?"

Ali felt her deep appreciation of James and thought for a moment. "Many good people in your country don't drink wine, and you don't, either. Don't underestimate science, because it serves to choose the right path to success. The day will come when you complement with science James' deficiency."

"What else did you notice about him?"

"He didn't like me from the very start. I found it difficult to get along with him."

"I didn't expect that!"

"Listen carefully, Diana. Beware of James, and beware of drinking wine. It's the source of all kinds of problems. Wine makes people lose intellectual faculties."

"You're jealous, aren't you? Do you love me that much?"

He put his hand over hers as he drove, his touch warm on her cool fingers. She closed her eyes and sank into her seat, hoping the moment would last forever.

Final exams for their second year approached, as did the karate championship. Ali had to devote more time to fulfilling all his duties. He exercised more with the karate team and ran for hours every morning. In his classes, he listened carefully to his professors talk about topics that might appear on the exams.

His friends strove for his concise, comprehensive summaries, because he was always ahead of them in his studies, and they had to catch up.

The excitement of the karate championship arrived, and Ali successfully passed the preliminaries until he was in the finals. He felt he was invincible, because Diana was in the crowd to encourage him. A TV station decided to record the final matches, and Diana told her father that Ali hadn't lost a match yet, so it would be a good chance for him to see Ali's final bout that night.

The Senator called James over to watch with him. When Ali won the cup, the students roared their approval and exchanged hugs and proud smiles. The two men looked at each other in silence, realizing the good-looking karate champion had all the qualities that would capture a young woman's heart.

In the newspapers the following day, James read every word describing the outstanding ability of the Egyptian student who won every single fight during the contest. The article also mentioned his high grades and intellectual abilities.

He threw the newspaper into the trash and went to a cocktail cabinet for some Scotch. He sat and thought hard. Things weren't going according to plan. The strong love between Diana and Ali might defeat his plans.

He thought Ali was just an ordinary student, but he was obviously very well educated and a fine athlete. His fancy Ferrari meant he was well off. Perhaps his father was an Arabian sheik.

Diana had to know James wasn't just training her. He wanted her for his wife, too. When good planning produced its effect, and Ali had been driven away, Diana would accept James for her husband. Time was on his side. The Senator approved the match.

When James told the Senator his conclusion, the Senator agreed and added that influencing Diana must be done gently through awakening her sense of logic.

North Carolina University celebrated Ali's second championship, but John wasn't as lucky. He lost in the semifinals. The TV studio gave a dinner dance, and Ali appeared there with Diana standing happily beside him.

As time passed, Ali and his friends passed their exams. He stayed with Diana for several days, wandering about drunk with love. When Ali left for London to spend his vacation with his family, Diana felt as if the world went with him.

During Ali's absence, James occupied Diana with important and trifling work and spent hours with her discussing possible solutions to various problems. The Senator appreciated James' efforts, and, to make Diana more attracted to her work, he sent her an invitation to attend the next meeting of the board of directors.

As president of the board, the Senator addressed the members, saying, "Today, we celebrate the addition of my daughter, Diana Stevenson, to the board. James' success in reorganizing the company and making it prosperous will be further strengthened by her participation in management. This meeting is an affirmation of her appointment as deputy director of the company due to her considerable share in its capital. I'd like to take this opportunity to thank James for all his work in training her in business administration."

In a very short time, Diana found herself responsible for several activities within the company. As time passed, she became an effective manager and solved several difficult problems. That pleased her father and made James admire her talents even more, though his admiration had become an obsession. Diana was remarkably beautiful, wealthy, and the daughter of the most-powerful man in the state. Marrying her would satisfy James' ambition to dominate the company and achieve his lifelong dream.

The only problem was her love for Ali, and that was a challenge he was happy to accept. He feared nothing. He had a plan for controlling Ali.

At breakfast one day, the Senator suggested to Diana that they spend the day fishing. Surprised to hear her father offer an entire day outdoors for relaxation, she cheerfully welcomed the idea and prepared the station wagon and fishing equipment.

Diana drove to a lake rich in fish, and it was their lucky day. They caught three large fish that she cooked with some potatoes. Both of them enjoyed the meal immensely.

Remembering the old days, the Senator asked, "Do you remember when we came here to discover things under the water and the strange creatures hiding behind the rocks?"

She didn't answer. She felt that the beauty of nature was meaningless except with her absent lover. His words came tenderly to her ears like a dreamy melody; *Nature was created pure and unable to commit sin. Man, loaded with sin, can come here to purify himself in the lake's clear water.*

Feeling a longing for Ali's sweet words, she stood to walk along the lake and dream of him. The Senator saw her drowning in romantic thoughts.

With a smile, he went to her. "I'm really pleased to see you interested in your work. I feared James would dominate the company and become its only boss."

"Don't worry about me. James wants to see me succeed. He consults me in every business matter."

"I don't fear him, but I own two-thirds of the company, and someone of my blood should represent me there. I should have a son working with me, but you, Diana, have a mind and spirit of your own. There's steel in you.

"Over the past few months, I managed to win the primaries. Now I'm preparing for the final election against the Democratic candidate, Norman Patterson. Politics takes up most of my time, and it's not easy to juggle my private business and political career. Thank God you're helping James manage the company."

"I'm doing well. With James' support, I can get things moving."

"He's a promising man. He has achieved good profits for us during the past few years. A few days ago, he asked for your hand in marriage. How do you like that?"

Surprised, she stared at her father. "Does he think of me as a wife?"

Pretending to be pleased, he said, "Yes. It's natural."

"What was your answer?"

"I said I'd talk to you about it."

"But I love Ali. I can't imagine living with someone else."

"Oh, that Egyptian you talked about? My dear child, there are things in life that need wisdom and prudence. Marriage is a whole life to live, not just a few moments of folly that usually don't last."

"Ali is a perfect man. He has all the qualities you're looking for."

"He's different from us in culture and tradition. What's he got to do with the company? Don't let him occupy the central place in your life. Think of yourself. I've been a Senator for many years. It would be embarrassing for you to marry such a stranger. I don't want a scandal to jeopardize my political career.

"This love, a combination of East and West, just won't work. James would never accept Ali as a partner, and the harmony between you and James will turn into a mess.

"I don't have to remind you that I taught you to brace yourself against the world, where everything is tough. All you have to do is prove yourself and work with James in an agreeable manner. Believe me, My Child, it's a matter of business and profit."

"Love doesn't submit to such materialistic measures."

"It does, and I'll tell you how. You're a millionaire's daughter, and you'll remain that. I'm not well. My heart may give out at any moment. As a father, I want to make sure that you're emotionally and financially safe."

"You're making this tough for me, father. You're stepping on my feelings, cutting out my heart."

"You want to be taken care of, and I know what's best for you. You're a darling and have grown into a beauty. James is the most-suitable man for you. Just think how much you'd benefit from marrying him."

A long silence passed. Diana suffered as he watched the influence of his words on her. What mattered to him was that she starts thinking of James not as an instructor but as a husband. "I'm your father, and I love you, but you must leave your feelings behind and try to see your way to marry James. Think of your own good."

"Is it possible for a man to love with his brain?"

"Yes, My Child. The brain is the seat of thought and guidance. The responsibilities you already have need a brain to think, not a loving heart."

"I couldn't possibly feel romantic about him."

"A woman can easily become accustomed to her man after marriage. It's like eating. The more you eat, the more your appetite for food increases."

Diana found herself torn between two men—one chosen by her heart, the other compelled by reason.

CHAPTER EIGHT

The third university year coincided with the Senate election. The Senator was running against Democratic candidate Norman Peterson, and the fever of the upcoming election expanded to the university. Many students supported the Senator, while a minority backed Peterson.

After the end of one working day, the Senator brought Diana and James to his office to discuss his election campaign. His words surprised them.

"You both know that I won the primary, but the battle with Patterson will be very difficult. I want you, James, to run my campaign. Diana will provide you with the necessary money."

James was astonished. "I've never assumed such a responsibility before."

"Don't worry. It's another form of management, and you're talented in that. Just use the money wisely. I'll give the speeches on TV and in public places, because I know what people want to hear. The campaign will take months, and, for things to work properly, I want you two to work closely."

He turned to Diana and handed her a checkbook. "You're delegated to cover all expenses James needs. I'll go over the expenditures with you each week."

James understood. It wasn't enough for the Senator to involve Diana in the company to place her near him. He also deliberately brought them together in his political campaign. It was James' big chance to show her his skill and thus capture her heart and make her accept him as her husband.

The Senator looked at his daughter. "Well, Diana? What do you think?"

Feeling important, she replied, "I agree, of course. James and I will form the perfect team."

With a challenge in his eyes, James said, "Sir, this time you'll win by a huge majority."

James launched a saturation campaign by buying newspaper space and time on radio and TV. He hired biographers to write accounts of the Senator's political life and his achievements for the state. He also hired eminent political editors to reshape the Senator's program by adding new plans and excellent ideas. He rented halls for public meetings for the Senator to meet with his supporters and discuss his comprehensive program.

The Senator had to work hard to cope with such an intensive program. He appeared frequently on TV, talked on the radio, and revised articles for the newspapers.

Months passed, and James never slowed. As the date of the election neared, he became increasingly agitated, looking for new ways to augment the Senator's chances. He produced T-shirts with the man's picture on them and gave them to schoolboys free. He produced household utensils and gave them to housewives as gifts. He contacted hotel owners and arranged to have signs promoting the Senator hung on the doorknobs of every room.

Ali listened to the candidates' speeches. The Senator talked about a rich, powerful America that had to be protected from attack. He demanded a serious effort toward the American dream of wealth and power by investing more money in giant projects. America was strong, because it faced big problems and knew how to solve them. He also mentioned the importance of reducing taxes on profits and private ownership.

Norman Patterson claimed that Americans allowed hatred, fear, and violence to thrive in their society, and he had ways to reform that. America, the richest and strongest country in the world, still suffered from inflation, idleness, insecurity, hungry children, and deficient hospitals. The economy threw all its weight on the shoulders of its laborers, and he wondered if it would ever be possible for the poor to shape their lives according to their desires, or if they'd always have to submit to influential people.

TV commentators began discussing the number of votes each candidate might receive, and it was clear that the Senator was far away of Patterson by a wide margin. Diana, fascinated by the campaign's result, expressed her admiration for James.

"He's the symbol of the state," James replied. "Winning will contribute to the welfare of the nation."

She was captivated by James' outstanding ability to direct the campaign. He was a man of practical experience who graduated from the school of real life. He knew how to influence people and gain their support. Such qualities couldn't be found in books or classrooms. They were natural gifts bestowed on someone who was destined to become a genius.

Her materialistic mind was fully awakened, and she found herself closely attached to James, obeying his orders and greatly appreciating all his views of the campaign. Because she was attentively engaged with James, she saw little of Ali. When she did, she talked of nothing but James' skill.

As the race neared its end, the Senator told James he felt fatigued, but James replied, "Victory is near. More effort at the end is critical."

The Senator spent the remaining days of his campaign with TV interviews and meetings of supporters until he was exhausted.

Three days before the final announcement of the election results, the Senator, James, and Diana watched TV in the hall of the mansion. Polls predicted a victory for the Senator.

Suddenly, the Senator turned white, clutched his chest, and gasped for air. He stood and walked a few steps before falling unconscious to the floor. Terrified, Diana threw herself on him and burst into tears. James calmly went to the phone and called the Senator's doctor.

"There, there," he said, reaching awkwardly for her and patting her hair.

At that moment, she felt he was the only shelter to protect her and her father from danger. Sobbing, she threw herself into his arms. He patted her back until she cried herself out. With his handkerchief, he wiped her tears and seated her on a chair. Happiness overwhelmed him, because gaining her as his wife was finally within his grasp.

"It's just a light heart attack," he said tenderly. "He has these on occasion. He'll be himself soon."

Suddenly, she looked grave. "We must call for a doctor."

"I already did that."

Her grief and anxiety lessened, and she looked at him gratefully. "I couldn't possibly manage without you. You're always ready."

"You know how I feel about you."

Blushing, she lowered her gaze without comment. She recalled her father's words at the lake. *My heart's weak, and my life is threatened at any moment. As a father, I want to make sure you're financially and emotionally safe. James is the most-suitable man for you, and you'd benefit from marrying him.*

She looked at her father, who lay unconscious on the floor, and realized for the first time he was right. He knew what was good for her, and he tried hard to provide it for her. What would happen to her if he died? She'd be alone in a merciless world that revolved like a wheel, alternating pleasure and pain.

She looked at James, who looked back with a confident smile. He was the strong chest on whom she could rely in times of pain and distress.

The doctor arrived and wanted to take the Senator to the hospital, but James insisted it was just a mild heart attack that could be treated at home. When Diana wanted to interfere, James said that if news of the Senator's heart attack was released to the media, her father might lose the election.

They carried the Senator to his room. The doctor examined him thoroughly before suggesting they hire a private nurse specialized in heart blockages. Again, James refused and demanded that Diana and Mary, under the doctor's supervision, nurse the Senator

The doctor had no choice but to call the hospital and have the necessary medicines and supplies sent over. He told Diana and Mary how to care for their charge. As the doctor left, James reminded him, "News of this must never reach the media. If it does, the hospital won't receive its yearly donation from the Senator."

Diana remained in the room with her father, praying to God that she would again see him mentally alert and able to speak.

James went to the living room and made a martini. Sitting in the Senator's chair, he thought hard. The Senator's image must be in the minds of the voters until the end, but how could they maintain with him sick in bed?

An idea came to him, and he quickly finished his martini before running out the door for the TV studio. In the montage laboratory, he ordered specialists to combine old pictures of the Senator to produce a succession of images showing him speaking to his supporters in different locations as if it were happening in the present. He demanded that pictures of the Senator saluting the voters after winning in previous elections be added at the end of the tape to show him still healthy, moving from town to town, thanking the voters who helped him win.

During the critical hours just before the announcement of the Senator's victory, his health improved. When Diana told him the good news, he rejoiced and asked for James so he could thank him. James, however, was busy at the door, dismissing people who wanted to congratulate the Senator in person.

"He has already left for Washington," James said.

After they left, James went to the Senator's room and shook his hand. Holding James' hand with one of his, the Senator held out his free hand to Diana, who gave hers to him.

He put their hands together and said with difficulty, "How much I hope, before I die, to see you two married."

Fearfully, she said, "Don't talk about death, Father. The doctor warned that you mustn't get excited."

James pressed Diana's hand in his and told the Senator, "Marrying her is my dream."

She looked at her father in sympathy. "Don't bother about that, Father. I'll seriously think about it."

"Take your time," James said with superficial tenderness. "We're in no hurry. I'll always be waiting for you."

Diana withdrew her hand and left the room. She walked to the front door and found her car outside as if inviting her for a drive. She drove aimlessly, trying to think. Her father's wish for her to marry James increased every day, and her refusal might kill him.

James represented security, expertise, and success, but she wasn't emotionally attached to him. Should she follow reason and choose him or follow her heart and choose Ali? How could it be that, when a girl was in love with one man, logic might insist she should marry another? What would it do to Ali?

She kept driving until she found herself in front of Ali's house. The Ferrari was there, which meant he was home. Saber welcomed her and showed her to the living room. Ali hurried in and immediately saw the sadness in her eyes. Distressed, she sat staring into space.

He tenderly put his hand on her shoulder, and she stood, looking into his eyes as if escaping confusion and distraction. All she saw in them was love, concern, and compassion, which made her burst into tears and throw herself into his arms. His chest was shelter against danger and fear.

He tenderly held her, kissed her hair, and gently patted her back. "Diana, what's up?"

She wanted to tell him, but she couldn't.

He lifted her head and said, "Don't say anything now. Come to a place where you can forget your pain. Don't you miss the valley?"

A faint smile came to her lips. "Let's go now."

In the valley, they sat beside each other on the grass and stared into the lake.

After a moment of silence, he said, "I used to come here alone when you were busy. I felt your soul flying over the streams and mixing with the flowers' scent."

"Did you suffer much?"

"Yes, but whenever I surrendered to pain, love invaded my heart and eased my restless soul."

"My beautiful angel, I can't live without you."

He was silent, then he asked suddenly, "Is it James?"

His question embarrassed her and made her cry again until her eyes felt sore. After she regained control, she told him what happened to her father, James' proposal, her father's support of the marriage, and how she feared to disobey lest he might die.

Her words caused him grave anxiety. He said, "I'm sorry about your father. He must've passed through a period of great emotional strain. Thank God he's safe. My sincere congratulations on his reelection."

He paused, then said, "When I met James, I had the feeling he wanted to split us apart. Our love will survive as long as you believe in it."

"I'll marry where my heart has chosen."

"I'll defend my love until the end. I trust in God. He won't abandon me." After a moment, he asked, "Examinations are approaching. Are you ready?"

"You're miles ahead of me. I have to catch up."

"Don't worry. I'll help you. Just let me see you."

"I promise."

"The karate championship is near, but I'm not ready yet."

"You'll always be the champion."

"Championship has no splendor if you aren't with me."

"I'll always be with you, my love."

Diana stopped work at the company for several weeks, because she studied with Ali and alternated nursing her father back to health with Mary. Ali gave her several lessons. She was grateful at his patience and self-assurance.

The fruit of their labor was mutual success in the examinations and the Senator's slight recovery. Ali didn't participate in the karate competition that year, because he felt James might carry Diana off if he was away from her. He kept her constantly with him.

Although she disapproved of his sacrifice, her emotional attachment to him increased, and they spent many days together, sharing the wine of paradise and wandering the gardens of heaven until the day when Ali had to return to London to be with his family. He left reluctantly, hoping time would pass quickly.

CHAPTER NINE

The Senator was still sick in bed, and Diana was with him, caring for him under the doctor's orders. When he saw grief in her eyes for fear of losing him, he insisted she marry James.

He said with a sad smile, "I'm proud of you, because of the way you took care of me these past weeks, but my happiness will never be complete unless you marry James."

Fear seized her. "Please, Father, save me the embarrassment. I don't want to cause you any complications."

"I'm your father and know what's good for you. Your future is with him, not someone else."

"Forget that now. Your health's more important."

"You must be engaged to him before I leave for Washington."

"You want me to marry him so soon?"

"I'm simply doing what I must. You won't give up your father for a stranger."

"You're talking about my life. I want to share it with Ail, not James. It's not fair that you slaughter my heart and throw it to a man I don't love."

"James formally proposed yesterday, and I accepted."

Enraged, she said, "It's my life to live, not yours! It's my right to choose my husband. I refuse to allow my marriage to be settled behind my back."

He pretended to have another heart attack and gasped, "I can hardly catch my breath. Hurry with the tranquilizer!"

Working past her tears, she hurried to the tray of drugs on the table beside the bed. With terrified, shaking hands, she gave him a pill and glass of water. He swallowed the pill and said after a moment, "I think I'm dying. Hold my hand. I want you near me in my last moments."

She knelt beside the bed, weeping violently, and kissing his hand, which became damp with her tears. "Forgive me, Father. I won't oppose your wishes any further. Just relax and get well. I'll do what you want and marry James."

"When do you think that will be?"

"As soon as you wish."

"Right after your graduation, which is six months away. Your wedding will be the talk of the town, I promise. Don't send the doctor to me. I feel better. You can go now."

She felt an urgent need to share her grief with Ali, but how could she tell him? How could she face him when she betrayed him? Perhaps she should try to convince him it happened against her wishes. Ali was considerate and wouldn't let her father die because of her. He must have a soft spot in his heart for an ill father.

She would put her heart on one scale and her reason on the other and prove to him that reason mattered more than love. She would use logic to convince him that life was filled with elements that were more important than love, like a better future, prosperity, and surrender to reality.

After that, she'd move to the next step and tell him that James was the most-suitable man for her, because their futures were strongly linked. Love was one thing, but marriage was something else—profit, advantage, security, and a brighter future.

In that manner, her thoughts began with love and ended with the desire for wealth. When she realized that, tears came to her eyes, because she knew that all her reasons were like bullets she was about to fire into Ali's chest. She felt compassionate toward him and wanted to escape to another world, but the fourth university year had begun, and she had to attend classes.

As soon as the Senator was better, he called James and announced that Diana agreed to marry him after graduation. James was very pleased by the news and said he'd visit them the following afternoon with two engagement rings.

Diana didn't argue with her father when he announced the sudden engagement, because melancholy and perplexity from the previous weeks left her unable to think. That evening, James slid an engagement ring on her finger, and she did the same carelessly, not knowing what she was doing.

Her expression was empty, and her heart filled with sadness. Events took place too quickly for her to stop them. No guests had been invited, lest something untoward happen to ruin the Senator's plan.

Diana, staring at her engagement ring, felt suffocated. Her stomach lurched, and she rushed to the bathroom and vomited until she was empty and exhausted. Then she went to her bedroom and threw herself on her bed to cry. She looked like a zombie.

Diana went to her classes with the new engagement ring shining on her finger. She wanted everyone to know from the beginning that she was engaged. Her separation from Ali had to occur sometime. It was better to get it over with.

She glimpsed Ali on a wooden seat in the university garden. She approached him while trying to collect her courage. Seeing him restored all the passion in her heart. In a trembling voice, she said, "Ali?"

He lifted attentive eyes to her and said sadly, "I haven't seen you for so long. I miss my moments with you."

Seeing the sadness in his eyes, she regretted what she had to say. "Maybe you'd better forget about me. I'm engaged to James."

His eyes darkened until they were almost black and lightless. Shock deepened the lines on his face.

He stood, stared into the distance, and asked, "Why didn't you wait until I proposed to your father?"

Grieved, she told him what happened and asked him to have mercy on her and try to understand her position. Her voice trailed off, as she swallowed.

Deathly silence fell. He lowered his eyes to hide his tears. Suddenly, he looked very dear to her. She wanted to press his face to her bosom, but she couldn't. Even saying his name was difficult. She forced herself not to cry.

She said, "Put sadness aside, Darling. I don't deserve it. I swear you'll find someone you can love and who'll give you what you deserve. You're strong enough to love again. You'll soon bear only memories."

His mouth twisted wryly as he said bitterly, "You say 'Darling.' You talk about loving someone else. That is ample punishment for loving you."

"What was between us is no longer. Everything changes. Everything ends. James wasn't my choice and was imposed on me by my father. My marriage is based on reason, not love."

"What reason do you mean? You love one person and marry another? You're wrong. Many things change or pass by, but not what we shared."

"Love isn't everything. James is the future. I'll share my life and fortune with him. There are other considerations that make a marriage succeed."

"What do you call what we had between us? Vanity? Absurdity? Or the beginning of a marriage based on love?"

"I call it beautiful moments that quickly passed."

"If I said I were richer than James, would you accept me as your husband?"

"I've said all I have to say. Remember, I possess a fortune that will be even greater if I marry James."

"Money again! Money gives semblance, not essence. It's medicine, not health; pleasure, not happiness; acquaintance, not friendship."

"Stop being so emotional, so we can at least part friends. Emotion will only lead to destruction."

"Man can achieve happiness when his emotions are fed with reason and logic."

"Reason implies the sacrifice of emotion to achieve goals."

"Diana, my love, what happened to you? You know it would profit a man little if he gained the world and lost his soul. I'm offering you my heart. You know what love is? It's the splendor that comes from the heart and enlightens the path of life. Don't sacrifice love. It's the most precious thing man can offer."

"Ali, please don't make our separation difficult. I'm sorry I had to leave you like this, but it was the only way I could. I passed through bitter moments, and my heart bled with pain. Please try to understand and forgive me."

"I love you, Diana. I love you very much. I know you've suffered, but I'm here to remove your pain."

She felt the beating of his heart, the agony of his soul, and his passionate love. Panicked, she tried to block those sensations, because she'd be lost if he became part of her life again. Troubled as she was, distressed by his unhappiness, dismayed by the trouble she brought him, she turned with her eyes full of tears and ran back the way she came, leaving him to stare after her in fear of their separation.

Diana avoided Ali after that. After lectures, she rushed home so she wouldn't have to talk to him. Days passed, but she was always present in his thoughts. Love possessed him so completely, it never occurred to him that any power on earth could take her from him.

His spirits were seriously affected, and the pain grew as time passed. Unable to sleep, he tossed and turned in bed as if on live coals. He spent his mornings wandering aimlessly. Agony wore him out, and his body, filled with ardent longing and sorrow, became thin.

He went to the valley seeking remembrance of beautiful days, but all he saw was desolate silence and withered flowers. He walked to the lake, hoping to see beauty, but all he found was a sea of darkness filled with snakes.

News of Diana's engagement spread rapidly throughout the university. All the students wondered what happened to Ali and Diana's love. She seemed constantly filled with anxiety, while Ali suffered from inner torture. When James came to pick her up, jealousy ate at him until the sickness and ecstasy of love became unbearable.

Susan watched Ali from afar. He stood beside her during her misfortune and always helped those who asked. He, the one who had all the advantages of life, loved in vain. She wished he could feel at peace again.

One day, she saw Ali aimlessly walking the streets and approached him, hoping to erase his pain. When she unexpectedly took his hand, he looked at her, hoping it was Diana, but he was disappointed.

He gave her a feeble smile without speaking. She led him to a quiet place, sat him down, and sat beside him, seeing the torment on his face. "Ali," she said tenderly, "you must rise above this pain and be yourself again."

"I've been ruined by estrangement, ardor, and sadness. I know nothing more shattering than to love with all my heart then not be able, no matter how I try, to break myself from it."

"You're a man of quality. How could you allow yourself to come to this? These things happen between lovers. Return from the dead and be cheerful again."

"I'm devoured by passion. All life has left me."

"Please, let me be with you. Our friendship can soften your pain over time. It will eventually revive hope in your heart."

He looked into her eyes a long time. "I don't want to hurt your feelings, but my heart will never be given to anyone else."

She looked away. "I'll take whatever you can give."

"I've always known you had a big heart."

She held his hand tenderly. "If you really seek salvation, return to school and sports. Those will keep you busy and help you forget the pain."

"I'm afraid I'm not interested in them anymore."

She laughed. "What's that supposed to mean? How can the other students and I succeed if you give up? We rely on your concise summaries."

As they walked back, they were silent until they reached her home.

As she said good-bye, she added, "Try to feel better. Smile, make your sun shine again. Your soul wasn't made for defeat. If you change your outlook, everything around you will change."

Although her words didn't heal his heart's wounds, they brought solace to his soul.

During the following weeks, Susan was like Ali's shadow, following him everywhere even when he wished to be left alone to cry out his desperate love. She refused to give up, forcing him to return to his studies under the pretense that she might fail if he didn't help her.

He tried to concentrate on his classes. Her strong insistence that he overcome his pain astonished him. He didn't understand that, deep in her heart, she felt her compassion turn into passionate love when she saw him suffering. She didn't tell him her feelings, because it was enough just to be near him and help him survive his misery. Besides, admitting her love at that time would've been useless, because his heart was already hurt by love.

She finally convinced him to return to karate, telling him the school suffered a great loss when he hadn't competed last year. When he said he was too weak to endure the physical stress, she insisted he stop escaping and practice with the team again. He slowly realized she was right and decided to endure patiently whatever the Lord decreed.

Susan watched him work out in the gym. At first, he was nervous and tense, and his blows strongly affected the players who sparred with him. She knew he wasn't practicing karate but was deliberately striking torment and despair. He was like a fire consuming itself when there was nothing else left to devour.

He ran for hours every day at dawn as if practicing for a merciless competition, but he was really chasing a mirage and the remnants of a vague hope. Hard exercise didn't help that much, because worry and anxiety cost him sleep every night. He feared if he slept, Diana would run off with James when he wasn't looking. His bowels burned with a dark, aching fire until he felt as if it would consume him.

He stopped attending classes for days. Susan came to see him and found him feverish and bedridden.

"Ali?"

He didn't reply.

Susan and Saber stayed at Ali's bedside for days, nursing and trying to cure him.

With tears overflowing, he said in anguish, "To whom shall I complain of this disjunction from my beloved and the flame that rages in my bosom? The worst of all vexations is the hostility of one's beloved."

Susan buried her face against his chest and said, "For heaven's sake, stop torturing yourself! She doesn't deserve it. She's with another man, and you're here, crying with the drunkenness of love."

Suddenly, his mind cleared. When he saw Susan watching him in grief, he smiled and held out his hand. "Diana, you came at last! This is my heart. Please take it. Our union will be paradise, and aversion is hell."

Weeping, she said, "I'm not Diana."

"Who are you, then? What are you doing here?"

Holding him, she cried bitterly. "Don't you know who I am? I'm Susan. I came to help. Please return to life again."

"I want my own love. I don't want anything else. I wish to have one glance at her, though death be my reward."

He got up to dress, but Saber and Susan dragged him back to bed. Seeing how sallow and slack his skin was, not to mention how emaciated, Susan decided to make a sacrifice. Ali had to recover enough to pass his exams by the end of the year.

Susan met Diana at the university and told her of Ali's condition, pleading with her to resume their relationship.

"What happened to the big love?" Susan asked. "Did it disappear when another man loaded with money showed up?"

"Stop being ridiculous, Susan. The pain that's tearing Ali apart is also killing me."

"You talk about pain? You look good to me, but you dragged his spirit down. You make his wounded eyes sleepless while you still sleep every night."

"I'm sorry to hear it. It seems I'm causing distress to many people, including Ali and my father."

"Do you really know what love is, or do you just know the word? You were born with a golden spoon in your mouth, but I wasn't. I know what pain is. It's synonymous with my life. That's why I can't stand to see people suffer, particularly Ali. He always helped others."

"His love still burns in my heart. You don't know the circumstances that made me accept James' engagement."

"If your love was true, you'd have sacrificed everything for it. Instead, you ruined Ali's body and soul while you chased a mirage that will disappear someday. His love is real, and true values last forever. He has to get back on his feet again, and you have the power to make that happen."

"I'm so sorry about his condition. What do you suggest?"

"Your separation must be gradual. Try to help him recover by giving him faith and love again. We must keep him busy with schoolwork and karate."

"I'm afraid if we do that, I will be attracted to him again, and I'm trying to forget him."

"Don't be alone with him, then. I'll be around until the crisis is over."

"What made you suddenly so interested in him?" Diana asked.

"Because I love him," Susan replied simply. "I don't want to see him hurt. Do you mind if I love him now, or do you want to keep him for your heart and the other one for your bright future?"

Her words struck a blow to Diana's already burdened heart. With tears in her eyes, she replied bitterly, "If you really love him, why push him at me?"

"It's a sacrifice from a girl in love. I'll control my feelings until he's well again. Maybe someday he'll feel the love I have for him. If not, I can at least return some of the help he gave others and me."

"Does he love you?"

"No. He loves only you, but I'm willing to take whatever he offers."

"I feel small beside you. I'll do as you wish. But I still love him, and his love will remain alive in my heart as long as I live."

As Ali recovered, Susan told him it was important to get out and see his friends again, because they were worried about him. When he asked about Diana, Susan said, against her own heart, that Diana wanted to see him, but that meant he had to get well.

Those words restored some of his health. As soon as he could, he returned to the university, dying to see Diana. Diana was horrified When she saw him. His charm had changed completely. His complexion was sallow, and his body was too skinny. She wept in pity. Her heart filled with sadness, she walked up to him and asked, "How are you, Ali? I haven't seen you for so long. Where have you been?'

"Didn't you realize that I need a fragrant breeze from your heart to wipe away the wounds in my soul?"

Tears came to her eyes. "Ali, I'm grieved for what happened to you, but it's all part of fate and destiny."

"I tried to forget you, but I couldn't. I can't stop thoughts of you coming to mind."

"Please, Ali, stop killing me."

"Do you remember the beautiful days we shared?"

She burst into tears.

"The silence in your eyes tortures my soul."

"Please be nice to me. You can see my heart is bleeding."

"A flame of fire has been kindled in my heart because of my love for you."

"Fair and softly, my love, my soul almost departed because of our separation."

"You say, 'my love.' Come, then, and murmur words of love."

"I love you. I love you with all my heart."

"Come to me, then, so we can fly above the clouds."

Weeping, she went to him, and he held her tightly. She was his heart, soul, torment, the cause of his distress, his beloved, and his true healer.

He felt more alive than he'd ever been. He felt as if he could walk on the mountaintops. They walked into the hills hand-in-hand and picked flowers. They visited the valley many times. It was more than a symbol of their life. They felt as if they were starting over as lovers, finding new delight in each other.

Over time, Ali's health returned, and he studied hard and practiced karate. He passed the exams at the end of the first semester, as did Diana and Susan, who kept studying with him to prepare for their final exams, after which they would earn their business administration degrees.

Ali practiced karate to participate in the upcoming championship, which was scheduled right before finals.

Susan saw that Diana didn't stick to their agreement. She forgot she was engaged to another man and let herself go with Ali. When Susan explained how that might have severe consequences, Diana begged her to leave her alone, because she was living the best moments of her life. Ali told her that, when his body was consumed with fever and he was so forlorn, he felt as if he'd been tied up and thrown to the bottom of the ocean. He couldn't enjoy the sight of the world unless he saw it through her eyes, nor did he feel delight except in her presence.

The two lovers, dominated by love, didn't notice that James watched them as they walked and laughed in the park one day. Trying to silence his jealous thoughts, he withdrew and formed a plan.

James told the Senator what he'd seen, and the Senator said it was time to print the invitation cards to the wedding and send them to their guests. Diana had to sober up from her feverish love, or all the Senator's plans would be ruined.

One evening while Ali and Diana studied quietly together in his apartment, someone knocked on the door. It was the Senator asking to enter. Saber showed him in.

The Senator glanced at his daughter. "It's a good chance for you to hear what I want to say to your friend."

He gave Ali a look of irritation. "You know perfectly well that she's engaged to another man, and her wedding will take place right after graduation. Her presence with you is an offense to her, to James, and to me. I'm a Senator, and I don't need to be ridiculed. I forbid you to see her again. If you disobey, I'll ruin your future and have you expelled from North Carolina."

"My love for her is pure," Ali said. "I take this opportunity to propose marriage. My circumstances might be better than those of James."

"Your marriage proposal is rejected. My daughter won't marry anyone but James, and their marriage preparations have already begun."

"She doesn't love him. He won't make her happy."

"Look here, Boy. You don't tell me how to deal with my own life. What you two call love is nothing but teenage absurdity."

"James is no better than I. I'm distinguished by my love for Diana."

"How dare you think of marrying my daughter? You're different. We know nothing about you. I won't allow a stranger to share in a fortune he didn't help create."

"Immense fortunes bring no happiness if there's no love between people."

"Stop talking nonsense. Get out of her life, and leave her alone." He looked sharply at Diana. "We've been over this a million times. This stranger has no place here. You won't give up James just to be nice to him. One way or another, you'll marry James. The date of your wedding is set, and until that day comes, you won't see this boy again unless you want to cause his ruin. Let's go home quietly before the situation gets worse."

Diana left with her father. Ali's world became dark, and misery consumed him again.

During a short meeting with Diana between lectures, Ali urged her to stand up to her father and reject James. He was frightened of her father's influence over her. He asked her to leave James and run away with him to Europe, but she knew that wouldn't work. Ali even accused her of being the cause of their misfortune, because it was up to her to either accept or reject James. Ali hated her tears after each meeting, because they represented defeat and surrender to her father.

The karate championship came, and Ali fought like a lion. He imagined each of his opponents was James or the Senator. In the preliminaries, he pummeled the other competitors savagely. In the final round, he became even more agitated and struck his opponent's eye with a fierce punch, then broke one of his ribs with a strong kick.

As Ali looked at the shouting crowd, he wanted them to shut up. When he was awarded the championship cup, he neither raised it to the crowd in salutation nor greeted them with a bow. Returning to the dressing room, he sat in a remote corner and wept ardently.

At the end of the college year, Ali, Diana, and Susan passed their exams. Hoping to escape his torment and painful memories, Ali decided to leave to his family in London immediately after the graduation ceremony. At the ceremony, Ali saw Diana, neatly dressed, walking hand-in-hand with James. Jealousy consumed him. He had to see her again.

After the end of the ceremony, Ali had a moment to be alone with Diana while James was busy talking with an acquaintance. He pleaded with her to meet him at a certain place, because he'd fly to London the following day and would leave the United States forever.

James saw them talking, excused himself, and went to the nearest phone. "I want it to go according to plan. Do your job, and I'll pay you well."

That evening, on a dark, narrow street, Diana arrived shaken and confused. Seeing Ali's sad expression, she said, "We can't go on like this. Can't we discuss this sensibly? Our love must end. I can't see you again. You'll never know how sorry I am."

"When you love someone, it's painful to think of her making love to someone else."

"Maybe it would be less painful to you if you find someone else."

"You sound like your father. Listen, my love. I'll take you to a nest in the mountains where we can be as happy as birds."

"Ali, please. It'll never work. Your words are nothing but a dream. They have nothing to do with real life."

He was about to continue blaming her when he saw four evil-looking men approaching. Realizing they were after him, he fell into a violent rage, murmuring, "Who sent them, your father or James? Stay where you are."

He walked toward them, glad to have men on whom he could release his anger. He wasn't about to surrender meekly to a pack of criminals. He fought like a furious lion, breaking bones and striking their faces, tearing their bodies until they bled. There had not elapsed more than a little while before the gang was routed. They ran away seeking their own safety.

Ali heard a movement behind him, he turned, and it was only a split of a second before a blade struck between his ribs. Blind with rage and maddened by pain, Ali grabbed the knife and threw it away as he stared at the man, who fled in fear.

"Diana, are you all right?" He asked.

Her heart leaped to her throat, and she shivered in a cold sweat. She ran up and found blood flowing from his mouth and chest. His eyes dimmed, and fire burned throughout his body. As he entered a world of darkness, he whispered, "Diana, take me in your arms."

She tried to hold him, but he staggered and almost fell. They sank to the ground as his blood flowed like a river.

"They got me," he whispered. "I'm done. Let me die in peace." He turned deathly white.

"I'll call an ambulance!" she said. "You'll be fine. I promise."

He trembled as if with fever and said, "Death is better than being alone, without you."

"Don't say that, my love. I'll live with you forever."

She continued crying and screaming until passersby gathered and called an ambulance. Paramedics took him from her, pulling him from her arms, then the police came to interrogate Diana. Crying hysterically, she was unable to answer them.

When they realized she was the Senator's daughter, they called him, and he and James arrived quickly. The Senator told the chief of police, who was a friend, that the victim was a karate champion and a schoolmate of Diana's at the university.

"He's just the kind of person who fights with thugs in some dark alley," the Senator said. "Diana must have been passing by and saw him lying on the ground in his own blood, so she called an ambulance.

There's no relationship between them. She's engaged to James. They're getting married on Sunday."

Before leaving he added, "Because of my position, I don't want you to mention her name in any investigation of this crime."

James looked astonished and innocent throughout the encounter.

The Senator and James escorted Diana home and decided to watch her carefully until the wedding. Alone in her room, Diana stood oblivious before the mirror as Mary, her governess, helped her undress. Seeing Ali's blood on her chest and face, Diana screamed and fainted.

At the hospital, doctors opened Ali's chest and stitched the torn flesh. They injected him with strong antibiotics to stop the wound from becoming infected and gave him a blood transfusion. He laid motionless, tubes up his nostrils and into his veins. A bottle of glucose hung from a frame near the bed. On the other side of the bed, a monitor revealed his pulse. After doing their best, the doctors left Ali to recover.

Saber learned what happened when the police came to search the apartment for evidence, while Susan read about it in the morning paper. They raced to the hospital to see what they could do, but the doctors said there was nothing to do but wait.

Ali remained unconscious for a week, during which time the wedding preparations continued. James tried to stop Diana's hysterical weeping with strong tranquilizers until she lost the power to think.

On her wedding day, she was taken to the church like a sacrifice being carried to the altar. The priest asked if she accepted James as her husband, and, intoxicated by drugs, she said, "Yes."

After the wedding, they rode to the airport in a fancy limousine and flew to Hawaii for their honeymoon.

In a narrow street near the church, passersby stepped over a large bloodstain on the pavement.

At the moment that Diana accepted James as her husband, Ali returned to consciousness for a few minutes.

Susan rushed to the bedside.

"Did she get married?" he asked.

"Yes."

He closed his eyes, rejecting life. A bell went off, indicating cessation of Ali's heartbeat. Doctors ran in and gave him several electroshocks to stimulate his heart, but it didn't work. They were ready to give up when suddenly, Ali's pulse, though weak, returned on the monitor. The staff smiled, while Susan and Saber sighed in relief.

As soon as Selim heard the news from Saber via the telephone, he rushed to the States. When he saw Ali lying unconscious in bed, his heart almost broke with fear that his only son might die. Saber and Susan were beside the bed, each one praying for Ali's life.

"What happened?" Selim asked Susan.

"I don't know."

He went to the police station, where the chief of police gave a brief account of the fight and said that Ali was found in a bloody puddle in the street. A girl, who'd been his colleague at the university, passed by and saw him, so she called an ambulance.

"What's her address?" Selim asked.

"You can't interfere in this case. It's under investigation."

Selim returned to the hospital, knowing someone tried to murder his son.

As days passed, Ali's condition worsened. Selim could do nothing but remain at the bedside and pray that God would save his son's life.

He spoke with the doctors and demanded a report on Ali's health. They came to an unexpected consensus—his body was cured, but they didn't know why he wouldn't regain consciousness.

Selim thought hard. Hadn't Saber told him that Ali had been in love with a rich girl? Was she the one sitting at his bedside, eagerly waiting for Ali to return to life, or was it the girl who called the ambulance?

He approached Susan, who looked at him sadly and said, "I share your grief. Your son is noble. He doesn't deserve this."

"Are you the girl he loves?"

"No. He loves another."

"Who?"

"Diana Stevenson, the daughter of Senator Stevenson."

"How can I see her?"

"I'm afraid you can't. She was married a few days ago and left with her husband for Hawaii for their honeymoon. It was in the morning paper."

"Can I see her father?"

"I think so."

"Why did she marry another man if she loved my son?"

"Her father chose what he thought was best for her—the son of his business partner."

"Why are you so interested in Ali?"

"He was my supporter and protector during a very difficult time. He is a rare person. I won't leave until he's well again."

"You're colleagues?"

"Yes."

"What's your name?"

"Susan."

"Susan, I'm very indebted to you. It seems like you're the only one around here who cares for my son's life"

That evening, Selim knocked on the Senator's door. Mary answered.

"May I see the Senator?" Selim asked.

She showed him to the drawing room. A few minutes later, the Senator came in and shook hands cautiously.

"What can I do for you?" he asked.

"I'm Ali's father. My son was your daughter's colleague at the university."

"I'm sorry about what happened to him. Violence happens in North Carolina sometimes."

"I know my son very well. He doesn't tend toward violence."

"He's a karate champion. Sometimes, such fights go beyond the university. I heard he fought against someone in a dark, narrow street."

"My son doesn't fight with knives. There's something strange about this case, don't you think?"

"I'm afraid I can't help you. If you have any remarks, you can tell the police. Like you, I was surprised when I heard the sad news."

"Why were you surprised, when the victim wasn't your own son? What surprised you was the presence of your daughter with him that night."

"What's that supposed to mean?" the Senator asked angrily. "Are you accusing me of something? If that's your intention, this meeting is over."

"I'm not here to accuse anyone," Selim said quietly. "The chief of police said there was a girl with Ali that night, and she, with the help of passersby, called an ambulance."

"Did he tell you it was my daughter?"

"No, but I think it was."

The Senator stood. "I'm sorry about what happened to your son. As a father, I understand your feelings. I hope Ali has a speedy recovery." He held out his hand. "I'm afraid I must go now. I have other obligations."

Selim stood and took the Senator's hand, holding it for a moment. Looking into his eyes, he asked calmly, "Why didn't you approve of the marriage of two people in love? Maybe my son is richer than the man you choose for your daughter."

"I chose the man most suitable for her."

"You know something? That was a wise decision. I once told Ali that the wife a man chooses must be from his own country, so she can accommodate his nature."

Selim shook the Senator's hand and walked toward the front door. Opening it, he turned and said, "I didn't come to raise problems but to find out what happened to my dying son. If he lives, I'll take him home in peace. If he dies, I won't leave this state before I know the cause of his death. I'll raise the matter before the court, which, of course, is my right."

With a smile, the Senator asked, "Is that a threat?"

"Instead of calling it that, pray with me that my son returns to life. Good evening."

Days passed slowly, each one carrying the possibility of sudden death. Selim had nothing to do but pray and wait beside Ali's bed, asking the Lord to keep him alive.

One day, while Selim prayed, he felt a weak, trembling hand touch his shoulder. His heart sank as he looked at his son.

"Father?" Ali murmured.

Selim buried his face against Ali's hand and cried violently. After controlling himself, he said, "Yes, my son. I'm your father. Come back to life. You're the spirit of my heart, the fruit and delight of my existence."

Susan rushed forward. Ali looked up at her and smiled faintly. She held him tenderly, laughing through her tears. Those hot tears striking Ali's cheeks showed her fidelity and compassionate heart.

Saber came up next, held Ali's palms, and kissed them as tears ran down his face.

The doctors changed Ali's glucose to light food, but he couldn't use his hands to eat. They thought weakness caused that, and movement would improve over time, but his hands didn't budge. Nurses fed him as patiently as a mother with a baby.

Making matters worse, Ali hadn't spoken since he returned to consciousness. He looked at the world like an innocent child. He smiled at his father, Susan, and Saber, while tears constantly poured from his eyes.

When orderlies tried to get Ali up out of bed for a little exercise, he fell to the floor. They pulled him up and gave him their shoulders to lean on, but his lower half didn't move. The only way he could get around was in a wheelchair. He looked at them like a crippled child, smiling and crying simultaneously.

Selim told the doctors what happened when Ali awoke, he had put his hand on his shoulder and called out his name, meaning that he could move and speak if he wished. "Could you reexamine him in light of that?"

After careful examination, the doctors arrived at a strange conclusion. Although Ali couldn't speak or move his limbs, his mind wasn't impaired, but it was mortally wounded, and had taken him back to his childhood, when he felt safe and happy. Physically, he was cured, but the anxiety he experienced and his massive wound left him with a deceptive paralysis. They concluded that his body wouldn't obey him again until he passed through another shock that would force him to destroy the barriers he erected in his own mind.

Sitting in the hospital garden, Ali seemed like a shadow staring into obscurity. Susan sat at his feet and put her head on his knees, waiting for a response that might show he felt life returning. If she felt a shiver, she learned he'd been awakened by a bird flying away or a colorful butterfly landing on a flower. His senses were attracted only to childish things.

Looking plaintively into his eyes, she spoke, assuming he didn't hear her. "I envy any girl for whom you carry all that love. How much I wish it was for me. Do you know that I love you with all my heart? You don't feel me, because your heart is with her. Who knows? Maybe someday, you'll feel the love I carry for you."

He smiled and cried as he listened to her.

She got on her knees and kissed away his tears. "Don't cry, my love. Just smile. Without tears, your eyes look like a pure spring that flows with kindness and compassion."

He smiled silently, then forgot about her and watched a bird flutter in a bush, listening ecstatically to its love song.

Nothing was left but to leave for London with the karate champion in a wheelchair. At the airport Susan shook hands with Selim and Saber.

"I thank you from the bottom of my heart for the way you cared for my son," Selim told Susan, giving her his card. "I hope someday you'll visit us in London."

Susan insisted on wheeling Ali to the plane.

She sank to her knees beside the wheelchair and took Ali's hands in hers, kissing them as the pain of separation filled her heart. Looking into his eyes, she said, "This is only a temporary cloud until the sun appears again. You'll be stronger and more glorious than ever. I'm sure I'll see you again, sowing goodness and harvesting love that reforms the world around you and spreads happiness among people.

"Didn't you do that when you stood by me during my time of distress? Didn't you fight hard to protect your love? You haven't been defeated. Periods of desperation often happen to those who seek goodness for the world. You won, my love, and I see it in your innocent smile, flowing tears, and sad expression.

"You know what those tears are for? You wanted to tell the world, 'Don't tear the love from my heart lest you kill a soul that wishes you goodness and excellence.' You know why you smile? Because love still fills your soul. You know why you won't talk? Because you're an open book that can be read only by good souls raised on giving."

He didn't smile. Bitterness showed on his face as he cried. She kissed his forehead and held him to her for a moment, then fled weeping.

He followed her with sad eyes until she disappeared. He felt tremendous sympathy for her. She was the only one who understood him and summarized his condition in words that traveled from heart to heart.

CHAPTER TEN

In Heathrow Airport, Safia received her son with sorrow and grief. She glanced at Selim and Saber and wailed to them with tear-filled eyes. "He left us strong and healthy, and now you bring him back crippled and torn apart. What happened to my son is more than I can endure. It's like an earthquake that has shattered my soul and consumed my being."

She bent to hold Ali's head and kiss him. Trying to hide her sadness, she said, "I still see my beautiful child in you. You're sitting in that chair only to rest. When God grants His favor, you'll rise to your feet and walk in the world again."

Nadia sat on her knees, taking Ali's hands in hers and kissing them as she wept. Through her tears, she said, "I won't despair of the Lord's favor. You'll survive and surmount this pain."

Safia expressed a wish that her husband buy an old mansion in a quiet district of London. Selim agreed without hesitation, because the new situation required more rooms for Ali and Saber and a large garden to separate the mansion from the intruding eyes of passersby.

Safia's wish was granted when Selim bought a two-story mansion. The ground floor was given to Ali and Saber, while the second floor housed the rest of the family. Safia bought expensive furniture for their new home, had the walls repainted, and carpenters modified the halls and corridors.

She and Saber pruned bushes, cut the grass, and planted beautiful flowers. Safia even replaced their old family car with a newer, moreexpensive one. Ali's room was carefully prepared to be simple, comfortable, and devoid of anything that might remind him of his agony.

Selim watched Safia from a distance, knowing she tried to forget about her son's condition by making herself so busy. He told her, "You're adding touches of beauty to our lives."

She replied, arranging flowers in a vase, "Beauty would be to see my son walk again, to take me in his arms, and to hear him ask how I'm feeling."

Ali said nothing to anyone. His mind was far from everyone, including his mother.

Two months passed. Ali's condition worsened. He stared at the ceiling, apparently lost in oblivion. Saber fed him by hand and carried him from the wheelchair to his bed and back.

Saber noticed that Ali often stared at the green lawn out the window, so he wheeled his chair out to the large, well-tended garden. Instead of staring at the ceiling, Ali was able to watch waves of green shining in the sunlight as branches waved in the soft wind. Daylight made his heart rejoice, while darkness filled it with sadness.

In his mind, phantoms came, whispering words of love, only to disappear as the words tortured his soul. Too many visions danced through his mind, and the image of a golden face with gray-green eyes appeared, which he quickly pushed away.

Winter passed, and spring came with flowers. Their scent penetrated his nostrils, and he remembered the tenderness of Diana's beauty and the charm of her eyes. As he heard the birds' delightful songs, her sweet voice vibrated in his ears, only to fade after a brief moment. Her words of separation to him burned in his mind like red-hot irons. The struggle in his soul grew. Sometimes, he longed to see her. At other times, he refused to recall her image.

Saber told Safia that taking Ali into the garden was useful, because his eyes moved attentively through the bushes and flowerbeds. Safia understood what was passing through her son's mind and ordered Saber to take him to Hyde Park, because the surroundings would give peace to his feverish heart, while the sun would soothe his weakened body.

In Hyde Park, Ali watched the speakers and listeners debating and interrupting each other. When he became bored, his gaze wandered across the lake and over the grass, away from the noise of people. Saber took him where his gaze went.

The lake attracted his attention, reminding him of beautiful days he wanted to forget and the silent pools of eyes that once were the mirrors of his heart. It was curious how her face haunted him. He tried to drive thoughts of her away without success. It was madness to love so deeply.

Silently, he pleaded, *Oh, God, I complain to You of the torment of my love and the complete exhaustion of my patience. Be merciful and indulgent, for my heart is breaking through the violence of my love for her.*

A chill came over him, and his breathing stopped. All he felt was the throbbing of his heart when the horrible image he'd been fighting for so long suddenly loomed up, almost blinding him. He saw James looming over her, sinking into her.

God, don't let me think of it anymore! He closed his eyes, but still he saw Diana's face. He'd never be free of the pain of knowing she gave her body to another man. He saw James' hands roving over her skin, his mouth teasing her, his body moving to take hers. Ali sighed as the torture continued.

Days passed, and the fine summer darkened into winter. In his room, Ali sat in his chair, facing the window toward Hyde Park. He wanted to bathe in the lake to wash away his suffering, but he was imprisoned in his chair. His spirit had been sinking for a long time, and his heart was almost dead. Her love made him dead to the world.

A year passed, and Ali was still locked in his misery. Hyde Park became his favorite place. With Saber nearby, Ali sat alone in the warm sun, taking companionship with his own thoughts. He dressed carelessly and neither knew nor thought about how he looked. His beard grew as it pleased, and his hair was long and spread down his back. Old people, sunning themselves, watched him in astonishment. Children, playing and jumping around, feared to approach him.

A small boy with big blue eyes and blond curls came along, holding his governess' hand. When he saw Ali in his chair, facing the sun and bathing in its light, the boy pulled back his hand and stared in amazement.

The governess examined Ali for a moment, then whispered to her young charge, "That cripple is a worthless bum. He's dangerous." She pulled the boy away.

A short distance away, the boy played with his ball, kicking it and running after it. One strong kick brought the ball under Ali's chair. The boy cautiously approached and glanced at Ali's eyes, fearing he might hurt him.

When he saw innocence and kindness in those eyes, the boy came closer until he was within Ali's reach. Instead of bending to lift his ball, he looked attentively into Ali's eyes.

Ali glanced at him. His blue eyes were like the water in the lake, and his blond hair covered his ears. He felt an urgent need to speak to the boy, because he was a reflection of beauty and the impulse of virgin nature. Ali smiled kindly at the boy, who stretched out his hand and touched the thick beard with tender fingers. Ali surrendered in silence to his curiosity as if he, too, were a child again.

The boy stopped playing with Ali's beard, then bent to retrieve his ball. In an adorable childish accent, he asked, "Could you play with me?"

Receiving no answer, he tossed the ball lightly to Ali. Striking his chest, it rolled to the ground.

"Why do you look so sad?" the boy asked.

He took a piece of chocolate from his pocket and put it in Ali's mouth. Ali chewed slowly and swallowed, sharing the sensations with the boy and rejoicing in his company.

The governess ran up, took the ball, and pulled the boy away, reproaching him. The boy wept, and Ali felt his weeping was a reflection of his own sorrows and expression of his grief.

In his room, Ali recalled the boy's face. His sweet smile showed the joy of life, and the brightness in his face reflected the freshness of youth. The boy's animation flowed through Ali's dying heart, making him want to be rid of his suffering.

He looked about in despair and found he had to shut his mind to images from the past and make his love die down. In his present life of exile and loneliness, far from her, he would endure the knowledge that she lived in another man's arms. What was to be done, and where could he go, chained to a chair that was hell?

He thought of his childhood, recalling vivid visions and memories. He remembered his home in Cairo with its broad, smooth lawn and the flowerbeds on the sunny side of the house that brought a fragrant scent through the open windows. Those memories carried his soul away on a flight similar to those in which he'd been uplifted as a boy. His spirit went into a dream world and rested.

On a sunny day, Nadia took Ali to Hyde Park and sat beside him in one of the garden seats set at intervals around the lake. She lay her head on his shoulder and rubbed his hair gently with her fingers until he slept. He could almost see Diana in James' arms, and a tremor woke him.

Nadia held him tenderly and patted his hair affectionately until he felt better. He continued looking for the boy. Nadia didn't understand his restless gaze at first, but, when she saw the big smile on Ali's face when the boy came to play with him, she rejoiced. At last there was someone who could stimulate his senses and energize his emotions.

The child, glancing at Nadia, asked permission to play with his friend. She smiled and nodded.

"Why is he always so sad?" the boy asked.

"He's lonesome and can't find someone to play with," she replied.

As before, the boy took out a piece of chocolate, broke it into pieces, and put them into Ali's mouth one at a time. Ali surrendered happily. Amazed, Nadia watched.

The governess came over and apologized for the intrusion, but Nadia said gently, "These two are dear friends. There's nothing to worry about."

The governess looked into Ali's eyes, saw his kind smile, and understood he was harmless. She walked away to sit nearby and watch.

The boy's joyful heart took Ali back to the time of his own enchanted childhood. He felt as if he had left his body and watched himself in the past. Why did he carry such love for the boy? Was it because of his innocent laughter, which made Ali's heart rejoice? Was it because the boy was still new to the world and didn't know what fate held for him?

The boy threw the ball to Ali, and it struck between his eyes. The boy laughed, and Ali's body shook with laughter, too. He kept throwing the ball. One time it struck Ali's forehead, sometimes his mouth. The boy continued laughing, as did Ali.

Sometimes, the ball rolled away to be caught by other children. They threw it to each other, refusing to return it. The boy ran after them, crying for his ball. Ali, unable to help, found himself weeping at the boy's disappointment.

A struggle took place in Ali. He was absorbed with sorrow and affliction, but his affection for the boy made him fight to rise above his disability and get rid of the chair, which was meant for feeble bodies preparing to depart from life forever.

Oh, Lord, Ali prayed, *I'm considering Your doings. I won't despair when I suffer affliction, for how many wondrous mercies have absorbed affliction?*

Nadia took Ali home and told her mother about the improvement in his condition when the small boy came to play with him. Their relationship stimulated Ali's response to life.

With confidence hiding her deep sadness, Safia said, "Your brother isn't as soft as you think. The world's waiting for him to return to it. I'm sure he'll recover from this crisis when God permits."

The friendship between Ali and the boy grew over the passing days. The governess left them together for hours after she understood Ali was harmless.

The boy stared at the lake and tossed in a stone. A ripple appeared. Every time he threw in a stone, the circles became larger, and he felt more enchanted, as if he discovered something new.

Ali watched peacefully, surrendering to the relaxation that took him into deep sleep.

Suddenly, he awoke to the boy's screams. He looked up and saw the boy crying and pointing at his ball, floating on the lake. Ali realized the boy must've kicked it there by accident, and the water slowly carried the ball out of reach.

The boy pulled Ali's hand, pleading for help, but he saw weakness and debility in his friend's eyes. Realizing his crippled friend couldn't help, he stared at his ball and cried.

Suddenly, the boy rushed toward the lake. Ali watched in fear. He looked around for help, but neither Saber nor the governess were there.

As the boy waded out deeper into the water, Ali became more frightened. He wanted to shout at him, to tell him to return to shore, but his disabled tongue refused to work. Ali could do nothing but pray to God to save the boy from drowning.

The water was up to the boy's chest. The ball was almost within reach, which tempted him to go farther until his feet slipped in a deep place, and the water came up to his chin.

"Help!" he shouted, knowing he was about to drown.

An inner voice resonated in Ali's ear:

You who are oppressed with anxiety should know that anxiety won't last. As happiness passes away, so does anxiety. Haven't you always searched for love and purity in people's hearts? You found that in the friendship of a boy whose heart is still pure and innocent. What are you waiting for when all that is dying before you? Get up from your slumber and wash out your heart with that purity! Get up to God's spacious world and drink from the spring of life.

As his entire body shook, Ali found himself praying to God. *In the name of God the Eternal, the Everlasting throughout all ages; in the name of God who begetteth not, and Who was not begotten, and unto Whom there is none like; in the name of God the Mighty and Powerful; in the name of the living God who dieth not, help me.*

His hand moved on the chair arm. His fingers contracted to squeeze his palm, and his right foot touched the ground, followed by his left. He tried to rise but fell to the ground. Crawling on his hands and knees, he moved toward the lake.

Every yard he crossed was a chain falling away from him, releasing his soul from its tortured prison. He shouted at the boy not to move until he could reach him. His tongue was released from its prison.

He reached the boy and carried him from the water, setting him on the shore before collapsing to his knees before him. Holding the boy tightly, Ali cried, letting his tears wash away his pain. The sun rose from behind the clouds, clearing away the darkness in his heart and sending hope to his awakening soul.

Saber and the governess arrived in time to see the rescue and felt as if they'd witnessed the power of God help the boy save Ali's soul, as Ali saved the boy's life.

Ali rose to his feet to rest against Saber's shoulder. Saber held him with one arm and walked forward slowly, pushing the wheelchair with his free hand.

Safia saw them approaching the mansion out the window and rushed downstairs, dashing through the garden to receive her son. Selim and Nadia followed, wondering what was happening.

Safia met Ali in the middle of the garden and held out her hands to him. He saw sympathy in her eyes—the limitless love of a mother. His love for her overflowed, and he spoke the sweet words she longed to hear since he came to London.

"Mother, how are you?"

She burst into tears and held him in her arms, raining kisses on his face. "I'm fine, my son. Welcome back after a long absence."

Selim held and kissed them both. Ali buried his face in his father's hands and kissed them, weeping, and Selim did the same. Smiling, with tears in her eyes, Nadia waited for her turn. Ali held her in his arms and remembered how they played as children in their villa garden in Cairo.

Ali spent many weeks afterward thinking over what happened. He'd gone through a bitter love experience that made him taste death. How long were those days in that wheelchair, how silent, how lifeless? The sun had gone out of his life, and he forgot how he was supposed to live fully until the end. He'd been in darkness while Diana enjoyed her life in the arms of another man she didn't love or care for. Wealth and social distinction were all she cared about.

He'd make his love for her diminish. His spirit could rise above agony. He had to grow up, and making choices was part of that process.

No, Diana, you don't deserve my heart. That island of love on which we lived has descended to the bottom of my tormented soul. My sadness, agitated with pain, has closed over it.

CHAPTER ELEVEN

One evening, the family gathered around the table for dinner. Safia and Selim were elegantly dressed.

"Where are you going?" Nadia asked.

Smiling, Safia said, "Your father and I will spend the night with some of our friends at the Ritz Club."

"I've never been there."

"It's magnificent, and it has an elite membership."

"Why don't you both go to the Casanova Club? It was a famous, aristocratic place once."

"The Ritz has an elegant air. I find comfort there." Safia looked at Ali, who ate in silence. "Don't you think it would be better if you became a member of one of the clubs?"

"I haven't thought of that," he said carelessly.

"You could make friends."

He fell into gloomy silence. After a moment, he said, "I need time to collect myself and enjoy a little quiet."

"Although you resemble your father," Safia joked, "you're much more handsome."

Selim looked at her and understood her meaning.

"Don't you think it's time to return to life?" Safia asked. "You're not a backward man. Have your hair cut and beard shaved. I want to fill my eyes with the beauty of your face."

Selim handed Ali a card. "This is the address of my tailor. Visit him and enjoy his skill in tailoring British, French, and Italian fashions."

"I'll think about it," Ali replied.

Ali returned to life. Why be desperate when he was only twenty-four? He had his hair cut, his beard shaved, and he regained his elegant appearance. He wore suits in the best styles. It was the first appearance in public of clothes worthy of the wearer and an honor to their tailor.

He drove his fancy Jaguar through busy streets. The car responded so beautifully to his touch that he was tempted to drive to the countryside and lose himself in the rush of speed and sound.

He joined the Ritz Club, where he played tennis and rode horses.

He made new acquaintances and connections. His dark Egyptian features and strong, beautiful body attracted almost all the women at the club, but somehow, he never fell in love. Perhaps he was too selfish or preoccupied with his thoughts—or perhaps there was a dream girl hidden in his sad heart.

He knew many attractive women, but he wasn't interested in them. His face, when not animated by conversation, was sad, and profound melancholy showed in the depths of his wide, dark eyes. He lived a life of luxury, but he was very serious, as if his months of silence added years of wisdom to his thoughts.

His generosity was the talk of his friends, who enjoyed daily invitations to dinner or lunch at fancy clubs and restaurants. He found privacy in the Rendezvous Club, which had a simple, informal style and character. It also had a view of Hyde Park to remind him of the day of his restoration to life.

Ali occupied himself with the beauty of nature. He drove around the countryside feeling the wonder of glorious creation. Beauty brought him back to the rosy dreams of his childhood. The English countryside was more beautiful than that of America except for the one place he liked most and tried so hard to forget—the valley of love.

He buried his love deep inside his heart. He thought of Diana when pain struck his chest after a severe cold, or rainy weather, or when her golden beauty came to his thoughts, reminding him of what he wanted to forget.

After a while, he longed for travel to break the boredom and monotony. He wanted to get a new look at life through a change of scene. Safia encouraged him to do that, and Selim said at the airport, while handing him traveler's checks worth thousands of dollars, "You'll get well, and the day will come when I ask you to help me manage my vast fortune."

Flying high in the sky brought solace to Ali's soul. The airplane flew smoothly through the white clouds, and the sun created a riot of rainbow color. After a while, sleep overcame him. The picture of Diana's beautiful face shone in his mind. He tried to shove it aside, but an inner voice told him that no harm would befall him if her image appeared to comfort his soul. Sighing deeply, he asked the Lord when his heart would recover from its pain.

During his stay in Denmark, he visited Kronburg castle, which was immortalized in Shakespeare's famous play, Hamlet. He watched the play being performed there by a British cast.

In a week in Holland, he enjoyed the magnificent art of Rembrandt and Hals, and in Elzemeer, he saw vast acres of tulips and pansies of various colors. The seen was magnificent and looked like a carpet decorated with a colorful brocade.

He stayed long in France, exploring the Savoi region with the Alps and its beautiful lakes. From the Savoi, he moved to the Cote d'Azur and spent days in Cannes, Antibes, Nice, and Grasse, enjoying the fragrance emanating from the wild plants. From the Cote d'Azur, he went to Monaco and spent days in the Hotel De Paris and weeks in the Hermitage.

In Switzerland, he enjoyed the beautiful Lake Lucerne and Liman, and in Vienna he listened to Strauss' music coming from every window and restaurant.

Finally, he reached Simmering. It was like a dreamland. He fell in love with it immediately. At the top, he watched the pleasant meadows beautified with lilies. The air was springlike, and the clouds sailed leisurely in a blue sky. The water in the springs was light blue, changing to wine color at sundown. In the morning, when sunshine lay on them, they looked like lines of gold.

Simmering was the most-beautiful, quietest place in the world. It became his special residence where he could retire into himself and find solitude. For months he stayed in a rented house, watching with pleasure the reawakening of his soul through its mysterious union with nature.

Nature also touched him with romance, so he walked among the trees, remembering days of love. He saw her tears in the running water of the silver brooks, her golden hair in the sunshine, and her beautiful face in charming, multicolored nature. No woman he'd seen so far could match her exquisite beauty.

Ali spent his mornings sightseeing and contented himself with sitting in cafés. From the window of his room, he stared out, watching the intensely white, clean snow set against a green background. Gray house roofs made an agreeable companion against the pale sky.

Springs were wonderfully calm and rich with the color of the setting sun. Winter inspired him with faint melancholy, and loneliness made him remember what he suffered. He made a real effort to banish Diana from his thoughts, but where could he escape when moments with her haunted him everywhere? Her love was still strong in his heart, and her picture was stamped in his mind until his dying day.

The day broke exceedingly cold, and the area was covered with snow. In the background, the dark-gray sky was solemn. Tiring of sights, he became restless with boredom. Change of air or scene failed to drive away thoughts of her. With his endless, silent staring into the distance, he saw her face everywhere.

Where could he go when she was embedded in his heart? He realized his spirit hadn't revived, nor had his soul returned to him, because he was still drowned in her soft fragrance, as soft as her cloud of golden hair and gray-green eyes.

He stared out the window as snow battered the rooftops. The desolate premises seemed vast and empty.

"It was a beautiful time when love filled our hearts," he muttered.

"What happened to us? Why'd you throw all this behind you? Do you know what you threw away? It was my heart, the most-precious thing I own. No, you aren't my love melody anymore, just an agony I suffer alone. You bled my heart dry with intolerable wounds, but it will never submit to such captivity again."

After seeing all the pleasures of Europe, he returned to London looking as if his two years abroad gave him the power to master his feelings. Something of him was missing, however, which made his identity incomplete. He didn't show any desire to work with his father and split his time between tennis, horseback riding, and inviting his friends to the most-luxurious places in Europe. His two-year trip gave him many adventures to relate to his friends. His eloquent speech allowed him to take them to the best pearls he'd seen in Europe. All who surrounded him were attracted by his charm, because he was respectable, modest, generous, and his father's son in wealth and good conduct.

One morning while Selim sat in his office, his secretary informed him a woman waited to see him. He told her to let her in.

When he saw who it was, he stood and smiled. It was Susan, Ali's colleague at the university. Selim welcomed her warmly and asked his secretary to bring her a glass of lime juice.

"Tell me your news," Selim said. "It's been nearly four years since I last saw you."

"I'm an accountant for a large firm in San Francisco. The work's interesting, and the salary is good. I arrived in London only yesterday with a tourist group. We're supposed to return to the States in five days. I've come to see Ali. How is he?"

"He's fine now. He stayed a cripple in his chair for a year and a half until God cured him. He divides his time between sports, visiting friends, and tourism. He just returned from a two-year tour of Europe. I'm sure he'll be glad to see you."

Selim called Safia and asked where Ali was.

"At this hour of the morning," she replied, "he's usually having breakfast at his favorite club, the Rendezvous."

Selim called Ali and asked him to his office. Ali was astonished, because his father never interfered with his private life. Ali also hadn't shown any desire to work with his father, so why the urgent call?

When Ali reached Selim's office, the secretary was astonished to know her employer had such an elegant, good-looking son. She opened the door, and Ali walked directly into the office, where his father sat behind his desk.

Selim smiled, stood, and shook his son's hand. "You know who's here?"

"No," Ali said in concern.

Selim pointed to the corner. Ali looked over and saw Susan seated in a leather chair, smiling at him. He was stunned. She looked like a beautiful dream from the past.

"Susan?" he whispered.

She rose and walked to him. Instead of shaking his hand, she hugged him and kissed his cheeks. Ali looked at his father in embarrassment.

Selim laughed. "Is there any other way to express a greeting than with a kiss?"

"Did I do something wrong?" Susan asked.

"No," Ali said quickly. "You're most welcome in London. I'm happy to see the heart that holds within it all the love of the world."

Ali was pleased to have Susan in London. Her warm, friendly heart always gave him confidence and reassurance. He suggested that she withdraw from her tourist group and stay in London a little longer, and he added she could stay at his parents' mansion.

She tried to excuse herself, but, with Ali's strong insistence, she gave in. Selim expressed his gratitude for accepting the invitation. "This is a good opportunity for Nadia and Safia to meet you."

As a distinguished guest, Susan stayed at the mansion for two weeks, during which time she became acquainted with Nadia and Safia. She became completely fond of them, and Safia loved her in return. She treated Susan like a daughter, because she knew how Susan had stayed with Ali during his difficult time. The hospitality from Nadia and Safia touched Susan's heart, and their strong family ties made her wish she had a family, too. She wanted to share with Ali and Nadia the limitless kindness and sympathy they received from their parents, something she never had.

Susan realized immediately that Ali's family was wealthy, though all of them performed prayers five times a day to thank God for His blessing. She loved the family and enjoyed its solidarity and the strong unity ties.

Ali made Susan share his days as he lived them. Early each morning, they had breakfast at the Rendezvous Club. Before noon, they went horseback riding or played tennis. Lunch was spent at the Ritz, and they ate superb dinners in luxurious restaurants each evening.

He took her out in his fancy Jaguar, showing her the city's landmarks, driving through Oxford, Piccadilly, and Bond Streets to see what kind of shopping she liked, though her only wish was to be with him and keep him company.

They spent days at the National Gallery, watching the opera and ballet. They went on sightseeing tours, spending days on England's warm, southern coast. In Scotland, they shared with the people of Edinburgh one of the country's popular festivals.

The beautiful days were, however, short. Susan soon had to leave for the States. Her last dinner with Ali was at the Ritz. He was neatly dressed, and she looked elegant in a dark silk dress. Candles on the table glowed with steady, soft light.

Fascinated, she studied him. The young man she'd known at the university had changed. His features showed masculine strength, though his spirit was delicate and tender. His face was very pleasing to the eye, filled with perfections that delighted her soul. She felt as if she were sitting with an Egyptian prince.

Happy and relaxed, she smiled as she looked at him.

"Your eyes are willing to talk," he said. "What's on your mind?"

"With you, I feel safe and secure, as well as other things I've missed in life."

"Do you know what you are to me, Susan? You're a heart that can heal the wounds of the world. That's how I always think of you."

"Don't you feel something else?"

He was silent for a moment. "You remember when I sat motionless in that wheelchair, and you spent hours with me, hoping I'd recover?"

"Those sad days are carved in my memory."

"You admitted your love for me with words of tenderness and sympathy. Those words revived my heart and pushed it toward salvation."

She was astonished. "I thought you were delirious, and I was talking only to myself!"

"Your words, mixed with tears, touched my heart and made me feel your loyalty and devotion. Susan, you're unmatched in the whole world."

"Has your heart responded to my words, or are you still in love with her?"

"What do you mean?"

"Aren't you the one who once said your heart would never love anyone else?"

His features contracted, and she understood his heart was still dominated by his love for Diana. She softened the conversation by adding, "I told you I wouldn't ask for anything you couldn't give."

Dinner was served. With a laugh, Susan said, "Let's enjoy this superb meal and good drink."

"I wish it were champagne, but here, they know my favorite is orange juice."

She laughed gaily, sipping her orange juice.

After a while, he said, "Love can take many forms. Strong friendship is a very exciting form of love."

Trying to hide her desperation, she said, "Sweetheart, women long only for love of the heart."

"Will you believe me if I say that our strong friendship surpasses the love of the heart? It's a priceless jewel that illuminates the road of my life when it becomes submerged in darkness."

He put his hand in his jacket pocket and took out a black velvet box. Opening it, he showed her a necklace of red rubies set with large diamonds. It was so beautiful she was stunned into silence.

"This modest present expresses our strong friendship," he said.

"It's a fortune, not a necklace!"

"It can't match the true fortunes that fill your heart."

"How I love to hear your words." He placed the necklace around her neck and admiringly she touched the beads with delicate fingers. Ali saw her happiness, realizing how dear she was to him.

Holding her hands in his, he pressed them gently. The warmth of his touch soothed her heart so much that she closed her eyes and said, "I love you." Opening her eyes, she saw him smiling at her. "Please let me say that. It comes from my heart."

"Say it as often as you wish. There's no doubt that I love you, too."

"You mean the love of friendship. I don't mind having that from you if that satisfies you."

On their way back home, she sat beside him in the car, fascinated by his handsome face. "You never told anyone you were that rich."

"Riches aren't something to be proud of."

"Your wealth might have gotten you what you longed for."

Sadness moved within him. "You mean Diana might have accepted me as her husband if she knew I was rich? I offered her the most-precious thing I own, my heart. She threw me over for money."

"Let me do her justice. Her father exerted a lot of pressure on her to accept James as her husband. He was seen as an element of her future success."

"She gave me her word she'd be faithful. Then, when she possessed my heart, she violated her covenant. I was faithful to my vow of love and never broke it. She could've refused James if she truly wished, but her materialistic thinking made her accept him. I almost died while defending my love."

"What did Diana have to do with your accident?"

"I have a hunch that the crime was carefully prepared by either James or the Senator."

"You have no proof of that."

"My heart tells me so. It has never failed me. Susan, please forget about Diana. I don't love her anymore, because she doesn't deserve my heart."

Susan stared at him, wishing with all her heart that he meant it.

The following morning, Susan said farewell to the family. With tears of gratitude in her eyes, she hugged Nadia and Safia, telling them how she came to love them in such a short time.

Ali took her to the airport, noting her sad silence and wandering eyes.

"When I'm with you," she said sadly, "I feel the beauty of the world. I don't want this feeling to end."

"Your presence has given me hope and revived my soul."

"Do you know I've lost all interest in men? Perhaps it's because of what I went through at the university. When I long for a man, your face comes to me and comforts my heart."

At the airport, when the boarding call came for Susan's flight, they held each other tightly for a long time. Looking into her wide, black eyes, he said, "I feel I'll see you often."

"That would be nice."

She walked to the gate, waving farewell. He stood looking at the long, black hair swirling down her back with her elegant quick steps. A sad yearning enveloped him. He felt a strong desire to fly with her to the place he wanted to forget—the valley of love.

CHAPTER TWELVE

The sad yearning Ali felt upon Susan's departure aroused enthusiasm in his soul. He wanted to do something useful with his life, and his reviving spirit became anxious to be released from its barriers. As he drove aimlessly down the streets of London, he found himself unintentionally stopping before his father's office. Working with his father still wasn't in his thoughts, but, with boredom eating at him, he went to Selim's office and asked if his father was alone.

"He's speaking with some Swiss businessmen," the secretary replied, pressing a button to tell Selim his son wished to see him.

"Let him in," Selim replied, surprised by the unexpected visit.

As Ali entered the room, Selim asked, "Do you need something?"

Ali waved his hand to indicate it wasn't important. He sat in a corner and amused himself by watching the conversation. The businessmen eyed him doubtfully even after Selim introduced the newcomer as his son.

There were four businessmen. The oldest spoke for the group and asked his colleagues to provide documents, which he handed to Selim, advising him to accept the deal. Selim read quickly. If he accepted, he would acquire a large amount of stock in a small company that specialized in producing electronic tools that helped manufacture computers. The company needed capital to buy modern machinery for its planned expansion.

"Within three years," the spokesman said, "the value of this stock will increase greatly. You have a guaranteed profit."

Selim paused, feeling uncertain. "I would like more time to consider this."

Suddenly, Ali spoke. "Aren't these stocks already on the market and available to speculators?"

"We haven't made them available yet," the man replied, "but we intend to do that in the near future. With your father buying a large block of stock at once, we'll be able to acquire our financing very quickly."

"What is the stock's value?"

"Three million dollars."

"That's quite a sum, which is why the expected profits from such an investment should be studied carefully. Is there any competition between your products and those of the Japanese? If so, you won't have much chance to compete."

"Our production specializes in European computers, which are made in Europe, not Japan. When those computers were further modernized, we were forced to finance more-advanced machinery to produce sophisticated electronics to fit the new versions."

"What's the exact status of your company? Do you have financing from any other source? If so, how much was it?"

"Four million dollars."

"Can I see the documents that show the cost of the new machines, their market value, and the interest rate? That would enable me to estimate the expected profits from this investment."

"We've already shown your father those documents, but we don't mind if you look. Here."

Ali went through them carefully, ascertaining their validity. "I would also like to know of any sudden changes in the interest rate. A sharp increase there would ruin the whole deal."

"Any investor faces such a risk," the businessman said.

"Risks must be estimated. I need a list of fluctuations of interest rates over the past six months."

"We don't have that right now, but we can get it from the bank very quickly."

Selim looked at Ali thankfully. His son had the instincts of a hardbargaining businessman. "Ali, this is your deal. Sit with our guests and discuss this with them. The decisions will be yours, and that depends on how you study the matter."

"But, Father…."

In Arabic, Selim said, "Your interest in doing business has lain dormant for more than three years. It's about time you took care of my money and yours."

Selim excused himself, saying he had to leave for an important business appointment. "I leave my son in charge of this deal. It's up to him to decide its worth."

He left the room and told his secretary to call his wife. "Tell her I'll come get her in a few minutes to have lunch at the Ritz with me."

At lunch, Selim told Safia what happened between Ali and the Swiss businessmen. "He seemed bored when he entered the office and sat carelessly in a corner with no apparent interest in the discussion. Suddenly, he began asking questions and showed he had good economic sense. I authorized him to make all decisions on the deal."

Her eyes glowing with happiness, Safia said, "Thank God. Ali's power for action is being renewed. I know my son. Once he sets on a course, he won't shift from it. How strange the world is. Things seem to happen by chance, but it is actually due to God's judicious planning and absolute wisdom."

The following day, Ali again met the Swiss businessmen and asked for additional information about the chances in the cost of labor and raw materials. Since the information was all at the company, Ali traveled to Switzerland to see it.

With his good economic sense, he was able to predict benefits from the investment and that the profits would cover all expenses and bring in reasonable revenue. When he told his father, Selim bought the stock in Ali's name and authorized him to close the deal. They would split any profit 50-50.

With the passage of time Ali became known as an intelligent businessman with a sense of modesty and a strong will to act. He went out on his own and Gradually built up an empire over which he had absolute control through owning the majority of his companies stocks. He possessed a remarkable instinct for sensing profit.

He began his investments by buying stock in small companies, then controlling, directing, and guiding their management until they prospered and their stock became profitable when sold on the market. He invested in selling Australian and European agricultural produce to the developing world. Market research through the collection and organization of data concerning preferences and the buying habits of consumers became his base for profitable trading worldwide.

He continued expanding his empire by buying companies that specialized in computer accessories, electronics for navigation, and jet planes. His fortune was diversely invested, and his appetite for excellence led him to establish a bank that gained a respectable reputation in trade circles for being highly capable.

The bank began by offering services for trade, insurance, finance, and managing investments and transactions. Five years later, Ali sensed the bank couldn't match the changes that resulted from the liberalization of the world's major stock markets, particularly the one in London.

He took several intelligent steps to harmonize the bank's policies with the changes. One of the most-important steps was the purchase of a British company specializing in buying and selling stock in international markets. That enabled him to diversify the bank's income resources, as well as its strong participation in joint ventures and venture capital.

The bank was the nerve center from which final decisions were made and orders issued from Ali. Everything he touched prospered, and he became an important, powerful man.

After ten years of hard work, Ali's fortune amounted to $700,000,000 pounds Sterling, in addition to his father's fortune which amounted to the same level.

Ali bought a jet plane and traveled the world, racing from one opportunity to another. He found physical solace in work at sites around the world, and his life became absorbed by his work. The only human contacts he had, besides his parents, were his employees and the heads of his several companies. Even those meetings were limited to what was necessary.

In his room, where he often sat alone, were dozens of business reports and technical journals scattered around. He didn't need much sleep and spent his nights reading until dawn. His money grew, and his strong will to expand his empire was like a sharp sword cutting through time to transform every minute into something of value.

His spirit enjoyed solitude, and he understood why. It wasn't only to relax his tired body, but also, there was a deeper emotion that reminded him of something he wanted to forget. He thought about Diana constantly. Even when his mind was on business, she was uppermost in his thoughts.

What was so special about her? Was it her beauty of movement or her enticing shape? All that and more existed in many of the charming ladies who moved around him like butterflies, hovering around the glow of gold.

He felt pain in his chest. He touched the place of the old wound, and restrained his soul from wandering too far into fancies of the past.

Ali had the opportunity to stay in London for many days. In the mornings, he threw off his absorption in business by playing tennis and surrendering to the pleasure of the game. In the evenings, he chatted with his father on business matters.

One evening, Selim asked, "What about your private life? Sometimes, you seem sad, and you seldom speak unless spoken to. That relaxed expression you always carry is hiding something. Haven't you thought of marriage?"

"I haven't."

"Your mother and I hope to live to see your wedding day."

"I'm very busy right now. I barely have time for myself. How could any woman accept that?"

"I want to see my grandsons before I die, Son."

"No woman will share her life with me unless I love her first."

"I just want to see you happy."

"Don't worry about me, Father. I'm leading a triumphant life, and it grows fuller every day. My life is running its course as I believe it should—easily, pleasantly, and decorously."

Selim was silent for a while, then changed the subject. "There's something important I wanted to discuss with you. It's about the way you're using your money in the light of Islam."

"I'm always ready to discuss that with you."

"Did you pay the Zakat (alms giving) of your wealth during all these years? Ten years have passed since you entered the business world, and you haven't purified your money by paying the Zakat to the poor and needy. You know Islam is built upon five pillars—testimony of belief in one God and Mohammed as His prophet, prayers, Zakat, fasting during Ramadan, and the pilgrimage to Mecca. Whatever good you send forth before you for your soul, you shall find it in God's presence, better and greater in reward."

"Zakat due on my savings amounts to millions. The problem is, I don't know how and where to spend it."

"Listen carefully, my son. A very important object of Zakat is the moral and psychological satisfaction of knowing that the person who pays is contributing to the building of his society and to making its members happy and content. By so doing, he becomes free from anxiety and confusion.

"If a man wants to extract the utmost joy from life, he should work for the joy of others. His joy depends on theirs. Their happiness is related to his. Zakat also frees men from the domination of money that sometimes leads to sickness or suicide. The amassing of money and miserliness are the first symptoms of such domination. One sign of this domination is when a man turns his back on an honorable way of life.

"He neglects his duties and the needs of his family, even the duties of his religion. The only active way to combat that is with generosity and charity. Zakat isn't charity in the sense the world uses it nowadays. It's a right of a poor person, who feels it's a kind of brotherhood. The good that emanates from it is too extensive to delineate, because it covers individual, community, and state.

"Why should it not, when it's a system defined by God Almighty and approved by Him in the last of religions? As for reward, that awaits all who render it. Thus Zakat, along with all Islamic rules, aims for the good of mankind in this world and its due and just recompense in the next. As for those who refrain from charity and who don't practice Zakat, their punishment is severe."

Selim was silent before adding, "Remember that Zakat is paid only to poor and needy Muslims. Charity however, can be given to Muslims and non-Muslims."

"All right, Father. From now on, I'll pay Zakat. I'll estimate its value over the past ten years and pay it to those who deserve it."

"Tell me about your bank. Is it usurious?"

"I'm afraid so. Usurious banks in the West play an important role in promoting world economy."

"All religions forbid usurious transactions. To Islam, usury is the root of many social evils. Usurious dealing inevitably corrupts an individual's conscience, behavior, and feelings toward his fellow citizens. It ruins society and mars mankind's happiness by introducing the evil spirits of greed and egotism, as well as encouraging fraud and gambling.

"It's a pity that today usury is the guiding force behind the use of capital, directing it toward immoral ways of investment. Thus, the capital borrowed at interest can secure profit, part of which is usurious interest, while the remainder is used to pay off creditors.

"The sole concern of the borrower at interest isn't establishing beneficial projects but those that bring in as much money as possible, even if it's obtained through the provocation of man's most-corrupt tendencies and instincts. It's a paradox to say that God prohibits something without which human life can't exist and develop.

"A believer should maintain that nothing malicious can be necessary for the continuance of life. Does it make sense that God, Glorified and All-Wise, should be heedless to what's good to the life of His worshippers? It's a fabrication that the world economic order could not, on any account, thrive without using the interest system. Still the fabrication survives, because it's promulgated by influential agencies that use it to dominate through wealth and power.

"However, where there's a will, there's a way. In prohibiting usury, Islam organizes all aspects of life in a way that isn't detrimental to social development. The Islamic community should aspire to free itself from the grasp of the usurious financier, with the intention of realizing social morality and happiness."

"How would an Islamic bank benefit from lending without interest?"

"There are common conceptions and principles that can be taken as guiding rules to Islamic banking in the investment field—the rule of sharing the loss as well as the profit. Participation, not the loan at interest, is the way to profit and to increase capital. Financing is ruled by the principle of security of capital and of obtaining profit. Expenditure is deducted from profit, not from capital. Financing working capital in projects at short-term financing is by participation, not by a loan at interest.

"Legal participation is a way to make money on the part of the money owner and work on the part of the participant. Each shares the profit. The bank may be a money owner or a participant. Financing by participation means that the bank shares in the capital of productive projects, and it becomes a partner in its ownership and management. It also shares in the profit or loss according to agreed-upon proportions.

"The bank can also sell its share to another and restore only the price agreed upon in the selling contract, whether it's less or more than its capital. There's no exploitation as in the case of a loan at interest, in which the lender obtains all his capital in all cases and also an increase equal to the amount of interest, whether the projects makes a loss or profit. The Islamic bank as a financier is a partner in the loss and gain. This participation obliges each of the two partners to do his best to make the investment-project thrive."

After that conversation, Ali converted his bank to one that was not usurious. As the bank was a specialized institution of financial expertise, it followed the technical means that make loss quite unlikely. The bank didn't invest in a project before its technical studies showed all probabilities of expense and profitability. As a further precaution, thebank didn't invest all its funds on one large project but in many smaller ones to reduce the possibility of loss. Moreover, it didn't content itself with quantitative distribution but resorted to geographic distribution, with the result that it was always safe from possible loss.

As for the Zakat, which amounted to millions of dollars each year, Ali spent it on poor Muslims and their charitable institutions. He went to Turkey after an earthquake, to Pakistan after a flood, or to Sudan or Somalia during a famine.

As for charity, he also contributed one million dollars to North Carolina University for its research fund in order to study the Islamic economic system in reference to other economic systems. He wrote a letter to his professor, who discussed his views in the seminar ten years earlier, hoping he would accept the responsibility for such a fund.

CHAPTER THIRTEEN

As for the happy bride and groom, their years together were purely American. They didn't waste time after marriage and flew directly to Hawaii for their honeymoon. During the first weeks of marriage, the bride had nightmares that caused her intense anxiety and feelings of oppression. The picture of Ali, sunk in blood and motionless in her arms, haunted Diana's dreams.

She hated the nights, because after each sleep, she awoke screaming, staring at her arms fearfully lest they were still stained with his blood. These incessant nightmares intensified the fact that she had married a man she didn't love. Fearing to see more of the murder attempt in her dreams, she passed her nights awake.

When a small nap overtook her, she awoke to James' hungry kisses after he'd been drinking in the hotel bar. When she pleaded with him for time to accept her new life, he took her roughly, without tenderness or love. The hate she felt for him made her suffer from his touch. Her weak body surrendered to him reluctantly, suffering his kisses like a block of stone.

In the morning, she watched him snoring with the smell of wine on his breath and realized the severity of the crime she committed against herself by marrying him.

Weeks passed, leaving James naked before her without adornment. She saw him in a more-realistic light. He had a sharpness about him, an edge to his voice, and he moved as if racing with the world. He also had a quick temper and severe mood swings. There was no middle ground. He was either totally happy or nervous and impatient. He was obstinate,ntoo. Once he made up his mind, nothing moved him. He didn't care about his wife's feelings, only about his own instincts. He gave her no pleasure and never brought warmth to her.

She wished he'd care for her and lighten the divine gladness in her soul, which, once in a lifetime, flamed in every woman's heart, but he ran over everything like a runaway train. The everlasting redness in his eyes showed that alcohol commanded him, and it was worthless to convince him to be patient with her. Nothing was left for her but to surrender to him and hate her wretched existence.

James longed for her to show she needed him, but she gave him only pity and made him feel a burden to her. Feeling her reluctance, he decided to dominate her body by exposing her to wine. He offered her a few drinks every day and night, claiming it would help remove her depression. She accepted only so she could tolerate his brutality.

Wine rendered her insensible to the pain James did to her body when his desire for her became violent at the sight of her lying drunk in bed, unable to reject or refuse. She soon acquired the habit of drinking wine to tolerate his egoism.

During the hours James spent in the bar drinking, Diana sat in her room, thinking of her life with him. It was impossible to avoid comparing him to Ali. James made love to her with his body, but Ali made love with his mind and heart. His mind was princely in its riches, presenting her with endless treasures.

Her marriage was looked upon as a success. She had to learn how to separate sex from love, to use it for gain, though she was constantly enslaved by her need for Ali, the only man she ever loved. She married James not for love but for the gain she would receive as his wife. He, in turn, married her, because she could do him the most good.

Their marriage was the talk of the town, and all present knew it would unite two fortunes. Her life with James had to succeed, and she had to accustom herself to see things as James wished. He would lead her to a wonderful life and would make it grow fuller. She was certain of it. He was always bright and ahead of his time. She'd survive, and life with James would flow pleasantly.

When they returned from their honeymoon, she put a merry smile on her lips and pretended happiness. She ignored her heart and considered her life with James a race toward the big dream of success and abundant wealth.

James moved with his wife into the Senator's mansion. Life went on between James and Diana as it usually did between businessmen - hard work during the day and long discussions at night about their big dream: expansion of production lines to fulfill the needs of the huge markets James opened within the States and abroad.

Often, the Senator shared discussions with his daughter and son in law until he tired and withdrew to his room. Glasses of whiskey, and warmth from the fireplace warmed James and Diana, as they talked about their dream until the early hours of the morning.

Profits flowed in. Dresses and cosmetics sold well in the hungry markets abroad. The accounts of the company owners accumulated in the bank, fixing James' big dream in Diana and her father's minds. Those profits made her feel that life with James wasn't a total loss.

The success of James in managing the company gave him the chance to school Diana to be controlled and dominated, so he could turn her in any direction he wished. He pushed her into the margin of his life and made all decisions without her. Over time, she forgot she was his partner and became his satellite, grasping after him.

When the next election arrived, James led the campaign to another success. The Senator achieved a great victory over his opponent. Diana was fascinated by James' ability, and the Senator appreciated him even more. James, taking advantage of that, asked for an assembly of the company board.

The board convened, and James began the meeting by saying, "During the past five years, I've managed to open new markets abroad. Local markets consume one-third of our production, while foreign markets consume two-thirds. We face severe competition in localmarkets, while foreign ones, particularly those in the Middle East, consume huge amounts of our products no matter the price.

"Our inability to fulfill this demand means our customers are shifting to other companies. In order to compete satisfactorily in international markets, we must expand. Before each of you is a project proposal to establish four new production lines. Objectives and costs are listed."

The Senator glanced at the proposal. "Twenty million dollars!" He said astonished. "That's nearly the value of all our capital assets. Where would we get such an amount?"

"As indicated in the budget, the equipment we need is expensive, as will be the wages we pay to the laborers. I suggest that the company issue stock valued at twenty million and submit them to the stock market. That will add to our capital."

"Who'll buy all those stocks?"

"I've already made arrangements with the bank for that."

"What's the interest rate? How long is the grace period?"

"The interest rate's high these days. It's 16%, and the grace period is seven years."

"Our company may not be able to fulfill the agreement with the bank at such high interest."

"As James told me before," Clark Robertson said, "the bank approved lending the money after it completed a risk-assessment study that showed that losses are very unlikely."

"I've also discussed the possibility of expansion with the head of our marketing division," James said. "He can brief us on his views." He nodded to the man.

"The average of our profit over the past five years is nearly three million dollars," the man said. "Taking into account revenues that would result from this proposed expansion, along with the sale of our high-priced products in foreign markets, our yearly net profit is expected to be more than seven million dollars. Over the next five years, that will cover wages, running costs, our obligation to the bank, as well as generate profits for the owners."

"I still say the interest rate's too high," the Senator said. "It might affect our obligation to the bank."

"We can't do anything about the interest rate," James said, "because that's determined by supply and demand on the stock market. Banks can't finance projects unless they have long-term deposits. If the depositors withdraw their money when they see the interest rates decline, banks will stop financing projects, and the whole investment process stops. Anyway, I convinced the bank to grant us a three-month grace period, during which no interest will be paid, as the new machines are installed."

The Senator surrendered. "It sounds risky, but a good businessman takes risks to make his dreams come true. Your father and I worked hard to bring the company to its present solid position. I hope you and Diana can turn the company into an example of the greatness of the American industry in local and international markets. I approve the project and wish you every success."

Clark Robertson smiled. "I'm an old man now. It's hard for me to work day and night as before. I put my shares in your hands, James, a long time ago. I rely on you to keep the company progressing. You have my blessing and hopes for success."

The board members left, congratulating each other. Diana stayed behind with James and looked up at him gladly.

"Although it's hard for me to keep up with you," she said, "I find it pleasant to live with you."

He roared with laughter. "How about celebrating with a dry martini?"

"Why not? It'll freshen me up."

He took a cigarette from a gold box and lit it. She demanded one, too. He gave her one, struck a match, and held it for her. She inhaled and coughed, unable to catch her breath. He patted her shoulder as he laughed, telling her, "You'll get used to it over time."

They went to his office, where she prepared two martinis. They drank and enjoyed James' ability to convince the board of his dream.

He looked at her for a long time. "Do you realize that you're very beautiful?"

"As if you were saying it for the first time."

"Maybe because my mind's always busy."

"Do you love me?"

"Of course. And you?"

"What do you think?"

"You seem satisfied living with me."

"I think I am."

"I don't see any difference between love and contentment. They're identical."

Instead of commenting, she raised her glass. "Cheers."

His eyes shining with victory, he did the same.

As planned, the company offered stock valued at twenty million dollars. The bank bought all of it under the agreed-upon conditions—the loan would be repaid after seven years at 16% yearly interest. James bought new machines, established four new production lines, and hired additional workers.

Production increased and covered the demands of local and international markets. Profits rose to 8 million dollars a year. Although annual interest was 3.2 million dollars, James was also paying the bank part of the loan in the amount of 2.8 million with the hope of paying it off before the grace period ended.

Although the cost of the loan and its interest consumed most of the profits, James increased production by motivating the laborers to work harder. When, due to price distortions in the markets, profits fell in some years, James insisted on fulfilling his commitment to the bank by paying part of the loan and its yearly interest from his and Diana's own accounts.

Diana and the Senator didn't mind, because they trusted his skill at running the company, and the situation was working out well. They relied on James completely to keep the company solvent and had already put all their shares in James' hands when the expansion began.

It was a hard day for James when he received a letter informing him that the interest rate had risen to 18%. He lit a cigarette and inhaled deeply, then he poured whiskey into a glass with a shaking hand and gulped it down with a frown. That meant the interest payment would be 3.6 million dollars a year, not 3.2. If he intended to also pay the yearly part of the loan, it would cost 6.4 million. What would happen if the interest rate rose high enough to exceed their profits? It would be a disaster.

Fighting back his anxiety, he decided to repay only the interest that year. At least the markets were steady, consuming all his products at a fair price.

When the lowering of oil prices in international markets reduced the revenues of the oil countries, the chain tightened around James' neck. Oil countries had to follow a policy of self-restraint and began reducing their foreign imports. The recession in international trade dramatically affected James' revenues, and two-thirds of his goods remained in the warehouses for three successive years.

He sent his appraisers to survey US markets, and they returned with the news that other, larger cosmetic and dressmaking companies could easily leave him behind. They were able to maintain their price-fixing cartels, make enormous profits, and continue to win.

During the recession, James couldn't pay the bank at the yearly interest rate. The bankers told him that his interest rate would become compound, computed from the principle plus accrued interest.

The company began running 75% short of normal profits. The losses were formidable, and prices slide downward. James shut himself in his office and calculated how long his small savings would allow him to survive.

"The bastards are going to shaft me," he muttered. "They want to push me out of business."

He had to do something, and he had to keep his mind clear. He reduced staff and workers to a minimum and eliminated 50% of operating costs. The workers demonstrated and sent a complaint to their union. When union representatives came to discuss the matter with James, he threw them out of his office.

As the recession worsened, James asked the bank to retabulate his debts until he could sell some of his capital assets. The bank agreed, only to have the retabulation show that debt had consumed all James paid for in interest and loans over the past few years.

The following morning, James had breakfast with Diana and was about to leave for work when he felt a sudden, strong pain in the right side of his belly. He rushed to the bathroom and vomited blood. When he screamed, Diana ran in and quickly took James to bed. She called the family doctor, who came to examine James.

"Is he still drinking too much?" the doctor asked.

"Yes," she admitted.

"Have him taken to the hospital immediately."

James remained at the hospital for one day. The results came back in a single report that the doctor read quickly before asking to speak with James and Diana together.

The results showed that alcohol inhibited the secretion of protein from the hepatic cells. Prolonged use resulted in the accumulation of protein. A poisonous product of alcohol metabolism, acetaldehyde, bound to the protein and inhibited enzymatic function, allowing acetaldehyde to accumulate until it caused a host of deleterious effects that would eventually lead to liver fibrosis.

Nutritional and vitamin deficiencies from poor food intake and faulty gastrointestinal function caused neurotic syndromes. Hepatic fibrosis showed in the congestion in James' stomach and intestine and in disturbance in his digestion and absorption of food. The analysis also revealed a swollen spleen and gastric bleeding from congested, lacerated veins below his gullet and above the stomach. The bleeding caused anemia and general emaciation.

Exhausted, James looked at the doctor and asked, "What do you suggest?"

"A few weeks in the hospital will put you to rights."

Diana felt an alarm ringing in her mind and glanced at James.

Suddenly, he looked older than his years.

With difficulty, James asked, "Exactly how long would I stay in the hospital?"

"At least two months."

"I can't leave the company that long, especially under the present circumstances."

"It's your life. That's more important than anything else."

James left the room quickly. "I'll think it over."

Diana wanted to catch up to him, but the doctor stopped her.

"His body's wearing out," the doctor warned. "I don't know what he's doing to himself. You'd better convince him to enter the hospital. If you don't, he'll be dead within three months."

Diana stared at him, her expression registering frustration, disbelief, and fear. "What about his child?" she snapped. "I'm two months pregnant."

"Does he know?" the doctor asked, astonished.

"I was waiting for the right moment to tell him, but he was always busy."

"Please tell him. There isn't enough time left to hide anything from him."

At home, in bed with a bottle of wine, James brooded over his fate. He'd been living in a dream of expansion from which he suddenly awakened to cold reality. At the office, he'd been brought to such a low state of mind that he shrank from meeting his staff, turning all against him.

He was exhausted by blood loss. Diana begged him to stop drinking. He obeyed for a few hours, but tremors and terrible headaches blasted his body, forcing him to drink copiously again.

Diana told him she was two months pregnant, but he didn't appear to hear her. He seemed more distant than ever before. Diana's world filled with misery. She'd been feeding on despair for three years. What happened to their dream? She became weak, as if all strength left her.

Days passed, and James' condition worsened. His belly and limbs became swollen. Bleeding and convulsions wracked him. His body broke down, leaving him in a coma.

At the hospital, doctors examined James' motionless body. Their differential diagnosis revealed high blood pressure. Hypertension caused serious neurological and mental disorders. Respiratory depression induced cardiovascular disorders that led to heart failure. Sudden death was expected.

Diana, the Senator, and Clark Robertson gathered around James' bed, watching sadly. They knew he was near death. He remainedunconscious for hours, then suddenly opened his eyes and, distracted, looked at the ceiling.

In a weak, trembling voice, he said, "I wonder about the young man you once loved. I tried to have him killed. It was an ambush. His image has remained in my memory ever since. I still remember his words, because everything he said has happened.

"He told me that whatever brings gain was primarily due to God's goodness, not just one's labor. Whatever one plans for tomorrow isn't sufficient to predict anything in the womb of the future, because that is in God's hand and occurs only according to His will. What man must do is plan for tomorrow, work hard during the day, and resign to God what may come. I planned for everything, but I didn't consider... consider...."

His eyes became dull, his voice stopped, and he took his last breath.

Diana looked into James' eyes. They were blank, cold, and dead. Instead of feeling sad, rage shook her from head to foot. She ran from the room with his words ringing in her ears and inflaming her blood. All she could think of was what James did to Ali.

How dare he try to kill her love? Why had he done it? What had he gained from such a murderous act? James was unromantic and of the earth. He'd been a brute and a fool with nothing to offer her but pain. She never cared for him, and her future with him was in vain. She depended on him for guidance, taking it along with doses of bitterness.

What had she gained? Nothing but a penniless orphaned child, nights of dreadful anxiety, mornings of blank pessimism, and days of infinite fatigue. He'd been nothing but a stormy wind that swept into her life, filling it with misery.

Diana took over the company after James' death, but she had nothing to run except debts. She asked the bank to reconcile and compromise her debts, but the bank feared she might ruin what was left of the company. They required a caretaker to protect their rights.

She spent nights of torture when the understanding of her ruin drove her to the edge of madness. How would she get through this horrible part of her life? She was like a sheep trying to avoid the butcher's hand.

As a last resort, she went to her father-in-law to ask his help, but she wouldn't see him. After James died, Clark refused to see anyone. Her father, the Senator, regretfully told her that James squandered all his savings.

She escaped her panic through drinking. Several drinks a day consoled her soul and helped her believe she could cope with the crisis. Her father asked her to stop drinking, but her blame-filled eyes and sad, withered expression made him shut up.

At the height of her hysteria, she decided to get rid of her baby. She didn't want anything to remind her of James. Motherhood was stronger than her hysterical wish when she felt the hard lump of life kicking inside her.

Her painful knot of rejection slowly dissolved, and warm joy flowed until it filled her. She consoled herself with the thought that, once the baby was born, he'd change her life for the better. She'd keep the baby, because he was the only thing she truly owned. The bank couldn't take that.

The full weight of the financial panic rested on the Senator. He gave up his political work and lived on the shady side of life. People abandoned him, because he lost money, influence, and power. His failing company made him blame himself for all the wrong plans he had for Diana. The fact that she was fragile, unable to digest the crisis and face her debts alone, made him crumble as if struck by an earthquake.

As months passed, the change in the Senator became drastic. His hair turned white, and his face became pale and lined. He moved slowly, tired easily, and had no patience with himself.

Nothing seemed as real to Diana as the approaching birth. She was overwhelmed by feelings that her baby would bring salvation. As the birth approached, Diana was seized with fear that someone would try to steal her baby. Hadn't they already taken everything she had? She was surrounded by enemies and deceivers, all trying to hurt her.

She escaped into drink, knowing she was a drunkard. The kicks of her baby deepened her sense she still had something to live for. It never occurred to her that the kicks might be the baby's rejection of the wine she poured into him while he was imprisoned in her womb, unable to defend himself.

When the date of the birth arrived, Diana gripped the hospital's bed linens convulsively. The intervals between her contractions became shorter, and the contractions grew in strength. The doctor waited until the next contraction passed, then reached into her and touched the baby's shoulder and head. He brought the head toward the birth canal. Diana screamed, as her whole body bore down to expel the child. The focus of her world narrowed until she saw nothing but her baby.

She asked to see him once he was born, and what she saw was a large, malformed baby that was already dead. She screamed hysterically, cursing herself, the doctor, and the nurse. The doctor gave her a strong sedative to put her into a long sleep.

The Senator waited outside to hear the joyous news. When he understood his daughter had lost her baby, he sat on the nearest seat, wishing he could say something, but words became stuck in his throat. He struggled to get to his feet, but he'd lost the partial use of his arms and legs, though he could—barely—still talk.

Diana left the hospital without a child to fill her life with joy and a crippled father in a wheelchair. He looked old and desiccated, as dry and fragile as a withered leaf.

CHAPTER FOURTEEN

The company was thirty million dollars in debt, which had to be paid. The bank representative spent long working days with Diana and the department heads, listening to their reports and demanding and receiving information.

The overall picture that emerged was grim. As the only shareholder, the bank decided to submit half the debt as stocks to the market. Since the bank didn't expect the company to show a profit, stock submission was made at discretion, lest the value decline and the bank wouldn't regain half its debt.

Simultaneously, the bank took over running the company to guarantee collecting the rest of its money. Although liquidating the company was frequently mentioned to the bank's board, the idea was found to be inadvisable, lest people read about it in the newspapers, and the company be sold for less than it was worth.

Ali summered in Simmering, enjoying nature's beauty. He went to St. Moritz and spent weeks trying to learn to ski. He chose a slope, hit the snow with his poles, and rushed down, enjoying the wind whistling in his ears. After a moment, his speed increased. When he tried to stop, he fell down. His persistent nature wouldn't admit to failure, and he tried several times without success.

A skillful woman skier stood and watched as Ali repeatedly stumbled and fell. She laughed as she approached, waiting for him to repeat his attempt. He rushed down the slope, and she went with him, keeping him in sight. He fell so hard he decided to stop and return to the hotel.

As Ali lay on the ground, he saw the woman laughing at him from above, holding her sides as if they ached. "I thought I could learn how to ski without taking lessons." He said embarrassed.

She offered a hand to help him up. "How could you attempt a dangerous sport like this without lessons?" She said still laughing.

"I thought, if I watched others, I'd learn." He glanced at her without ascertaining her features under her snow hat and dark glasses. She couldn't see his face, either, for the same reason.

"I don't mind giving you one free lesson," she said, "so you can enjoy skiing at St. Moritz."

"I was about to give up, but you give me hope."

She gave some instructions, then left, saying, "Learning how to ski has never been easier. Ski within your limits and take only the easy slopes. I'm going to a steeper slope where I usually ski."

"May I ask your name? I'm Ali."

"I'm Simone."

At the hotel restaurant, a beautiful woman with long, dark hair swirling in coquetry behind her back passed in front of Ali like a graceful deer as she looked for a seat. Her appearance provoked amused and outraged glances. She was tall with a delicate waist. Her face had the features of sociability and exultation. She quickly looked around and saw the waiter nodding to an empty seat at Ali's table.

She sat opposite him and saluted with a smile and nod before reading quickly through the menu and tossing it carelessly to the table. Her elbow on the table, she leaned her chin on her laced fingers and examined Ali with a woman's eye. Tall and elegant, dark wide eyes, melancholy looks—his beauty and athleticism were admirable. She first assumed he was from Latin America or Spain, but she soon realized he was from the Middle East.

She asked the waiter for a casual lunch and a bottle of red wine. The waiter looked at Ali.

"Exactly as Miss Simone has ordered," Ali said, "but without the wine."

"How'd you know my name?" she asked, astonished.

"From your voice." He smiled.

She burst into laughter. "You're Ali?"

"Yes."

"Where do you come from?" She studied his eyes.

"Egypt."

"I'm French."

Their lunches arrived. They ate while they talked.

"Are you here on vacation?" he asked.

"I haven't given myself a vacation for three years."

"Does that mean you work on your own account?"

"Yes. I own a perfume plant in Paris."

"That sounds interesting."

"What's so interesting about it?"

"Perfume reminds me of a beautiful melody warming one's heart."

"People differ about what perfume means to them. Some see it as temptation and enchantment. Others see it as a mystery or a ghost."

"It might also mean treachery. There's a perfume by that name."

"Some equate perfume with a snake spitting venom at people's hearts."

She stopped eating and looked at him for a long time, then said, "Perfumes have magic horizons like mystery and excitation. No one can discover the secret of a perfume vial save behind a woman's ear."

He smiled, and asked the waiter for another cup of coffee. He calmly sipped the coffee as he watched Simone pour another glass of red wine. She held the glass in both hands and tasted the wine, her eyes glowing with mischief.

"I noticed that you're inclined to excitation when you compared perfume with a snake, meaning a woman, of course. I don't see it like that. Perfume may resemble things more calm, like night in its silence and love in its mystery." He commented.

"Perfume is used only by women. It's a necessary part of a woman's beauty."

"Woman in love is a perfume in a man's heart."

She examined him carefully. "You compare perfume with love, treachery, and night. It seems that you've fallen in love, then been lonesome in the night as you search for love among the stars."

Her sharp intelligence surprised him. "It's like that if you wish."

"I don't look at the stars searching for love. I don't confine myself to one man. I move from one man to another without hurting my heart."

He arched his eyebrows. "How can you do that?"

"Each man has a special flavor. I don't confine myself to just one."

"Every beautiful woman has a special taste, but the heart loves only one."

"That's if you wish to be engaged to a particular woman. If you want to be free, you'll realize my point of view. Aren't you going to share wine with me?"

"Sorry. I don't drink."

She laughed. "You're an ideal man then. What have you also deprived yourself of?"

"We don't touch wine, and we forbid going from one love to another save with a marriage contract."

"I understand," she said sarcastically. "There are many Arabs in France. I'm familiar with their customs."

"I hope my views don't bother you."

"Not at all. To me, you're an exciting adventure I wish to explore."

"How's that?"

"I'll try living with a saint. I'll put sexual instincts aside and try to live in your idealistic world."

"My world is the world of virtue and loyalty."

"I want to see that world," she said, as if looking for a new adventure.

"It seems luminous."

"Why do you want to leave your world for mine?"

"Because you're a very good-looking man," she said simply.

He smiled. "I'm not offering anything but friendship."

She laughed. "I accept, you saint."

Ali spent weeks skiing at St. Moritz with Simone. Snow covered everything, but nature didn't stop showing its beauty in winter or summer. A rainbow, caused by sunlight reflecting off frozen ice crystals early in the morning when the sun was low on the horizon, fascinated tourists making them long to stay. There was the sense that everything was delightful—zither music, painted window decorations and wall murals, village churches, the rich mix of cream and cheese, potatoes, and noodles, foods that hadn't changed in 400 years.

Ali invited Simone to elegant restaurants and charming cafés that offered an impressive array of dining options. She accepted gladly, looking forward to his beautiful conversation, attractive smile, and strong personality. They became inseparable save for another date that might be within a few moments.

She never missed a chance to attempt to seduce his stubborn heart that lived within its ivory tower, refusing to reveal its secrets. She trifled with him through her eyes, approached him with smiles, and surrounded him with her hot emotions, but all without persistence, because she knew he'd offer only amity and friendship.

She looked grand at every meeting. Her perfumes and costumes diversified according to the time of each date and the nature of the occasion. He couldn't become accustomed to her bluntness over sexual matters and wondered if he'd ever find the key to her character. She befuddled him. She knew too much about material life, yet she was very girlish, with a merry, melodious laugh.

Sometimes, her frankness shook him, especially when she admired his looks and strong masculine body, yet there was no trace of vulgarity in her manner or suggestion of coarseness.

In a warm cozy restaurant, he asked about the diverse perfumes she used on different occasions. She replied that she chose them according to seasons, experience, and adventure. He found novelty and adventure in her, things that eased his soul, particularly because he was someone who could easily go mad from boredom.

Simone saw in him what she lacked—calmness, stability, and contemplation. It seemed as if the world wasn't big enough to contain his hopes, and that he was born to live on a luminous star, not on a world made of dust. She looked at his handsome face and reassuring smile and wanted to melt into his world and stop running after new ones.

One day, he told her that her fondness of change reminded him of the best of nature and its continous giving. He added that perfume took him to the magical, mysterious past and gave tender touches to his restless soul. She laughed when she realized, through her woman's instinct, that, by praising her perfume, he was praising her.

At dinner, he asked her about perfume composition. She answered professionally, saying it was composed of carefully selected fragrances. It was made more alluring by the addition of precious wood sap, tender Oriental elements, lily, musk, ambergris, Bulgarian flowers, and liliesofthe-valley. Sometimes, certain kinds of algae were added, long with light spices or a touch of incense.

Her description inspired his soul and took him to the places she mentioned. With dreamy words, he said, "Your talk of perfume is like a collection of exciting melodies that soothe my heart."

At another dinner, he asked why Bulgarian flowers were selected in particular to produce a good perfume.

"At the foot of the Balkan Mountains in Bulgaria," she replied, "there's a valley called Kazanlak, in which the best flowers are grown. They mature at the end of May or the first part of June. Pickers gather at dawn to collect them when they're mature. Two thousand flowers produce only one gram of essence, and perfumers strive to use it in making perfumes."

"I'd like to see that valley of flowers," he said softly. He remembered the valley of love with its blue lake, but he quickly rebuked himself for recalling the memories of the past.

Simone's vacation ended. Ali felt downhearted at her departure. Before she left, she had lunch with him at the hotel restaurant. After they finished, she rose with a look of sorrow in her eyes, but he stopped her, saying, "A small present for you."

He held up a red-velvet box. She looked at him in surprise. "Women accept gifts from men if there's something special between them. Our relationship is only a passing one."

"You gave me beautiful moments that pleased my heart. I haven't talked so much for almost six months. It's done me good to talk with a remarkable lady like you."

With a fading smile, she said, "I don't want to have anything to remind me of you. I feel that, if I stay longer with you, my heart will restrict itself to only one man. You give only friendship."

"Friendship has a beautiful meaning that gathers people's hearts."

"It's not enough for a woman who wants to be alone with you." She opened the box and found a gold watch set with diamonds and rubies.

He smiled at her astonishment, then laughed.

"It's not a watch but a flower shining with diamonds and glowing with rubies," she said.

"There you are, talking the language of flowers again. You know what I feel right now? I want to see the valley of flowers at the bottom of the Balkan Mountains."

"I'll be there in May to close some deals."

"I'll go with you," he said without thinking. "Give me your address in Paris. I might be able to meet you there in May."

She gave him her card. "Have you given all the women you've known before precious gifts like this?"

"Only those who pleased my heart."

"Are they many?"

"They don't surpass the fingers of one hand."

"I'm sorry if I'm intruding on your private life. I don't know what's happening to me. I feel I want to know all about you. You arouse deep emotions in me that might carry me to a merciless love."

He laughed. "I won't let you."

"Who can prevent a soul from loving an amiable heart?" Sadness edged her voice.

Simone stood suddenly, as if escaping. He escorted her to her elegant red Alfa Romeo sports car. She got in and looked up at his eyes. At that moment, she wished to stay with him much longer. She waved and drove off, escaping from a love she knew would make her heart bleed.

Ali felt a pang of loneliness after Simone left, so he decided to return to his house in Simmering.

One cold frosty night, Ali was in bed, reading a book. After he tired of that, he turned off the light and slept.

He dreamed he walked amid snowy mountains, with snow coming up to his knees. The cold was severe, penetrating to the bone and almost stopping the flow of blood in his veins.

Despite his heavy coat, he shivered uncontrollably and wondered where he should go. The place was strange to him. As far as he could see, there was nothing but snowy mountains surrounded by intense fog.

Suddenly, he heard a faint, distant moan. He followed the sound, hearing the moan grow clearer until he identified it as a woman weeping in the snow. He hurried to offer help.

He found a woman sitting on the ice, her hands folded on her knees, her head drooping to her chest, her eyes closed, her brows knitted as if in pain. She wore a thin undergarment that didn't offer any shelter against the frost or even cover her adequately. She was nearly naked, and her whole body quivered with cold and weeping.

He sat on his knees before her, putting his hand on her hair, but she didn't move. Lifting her head, he saw tears flowing from gray-green eyes he knew very well. In grief, he shouted, "Diana, are you all right?"

Ali awoke abruptly, feeling pain from his old chest wound. His heart pounded rapidly in his chest. The sound of her weeping made him sweat, and the words he spoke were still on his tongue.

"Diana, are you all right?"

He hadn't said those words only in a dream but also when he lay dying in her arms ten years earlier. He hadn't thought of himself at that time, only her. Did her image come to him in dreams, because she was still alive in his heart? No. That wasn't a dream. It was a nightmare.

Was she really suffering, or did his subconscious want her to suffer as he had? If so, why hadn't he had such dreams before? What was she doing alone in such a cold, solitary place?

His heart sank with horror at the thought of her in danger. How could he find out the truth? Should he fly to North Carolina to find news of her or send a letter to Susan asking about Diana's condition?

He shook his head. Long ago, he decided he'd never put himself in a position that might reveal his love for her still existed.

The following morning, Ali returned to London. From his office at the bank he called the director of his stock company and asked him to see if Stevenson and Robertson had stock for sale on the market. If not, what was the company's financial status?

Within an hour, Ali had a report on his desk showing that the company had stock on the market worth 15 million dollars. He knew immediately that meant the company was failing. Although he'd never concluded a deal at a loss before, he quickly gave orders to buy all the stock in his name.

"Do it gradually and over a period of time to ensure the stock doesn't rise above its true value," he instructed the director of his stock company.

In order for that to happen, Ali put the condition to the creditor bank that his name is not to be mentioned on any account, and that all deals and arrangements would be discussed and negotiated with Mr. Wallace, his lawyer in North Carolina.

The bank, respecting Ali's wish, sent a registered letter to Diana informing her that half the debt had been sold to another proprietor, and all arrangements concerning the debt would be discussed with the proprietor's lawyer, Mr. Wallace.

Over time, Wallace's face became familiar to Diana. She met him several times. He talked about the new proprietor's rights and the importance of paying the interest on time. He represented a proprietor who owned an equal amount of shares with the creditor bank and gave the proprietor's name as A. S. Razek.

Ali sent faxes to Wallace to inquire how the company was doing. Among his inquiries were questions about the owners' names. He learned that Diana Stevenson had taken over after her husband's death, while her father and father-in-law entrusted her with management after they left public life.

His dream hadn't been a dream, then, but reality. He felt Diana's agony even when thousands of miles away. It wasn't that strange to feel the pain of someone a person loved. Feelings weren't limited by distance or physical barriers. His dream had been a kind wind sent to him from her tortured soul, saying she was suffering and needed help.

He knew the time approached when they'd be together again. A shiver went through him at the thought that their reunion might give life to a love he buried deep within himself many years earlier.

CHAPTER FIFTEEN

In mid-May, Ali went to Paris to meet Simone at her perfume plant, located in one of the city's districts. She was happy to see him at her office door, watching her work. She looked like a first-class businesswoman. Her desk was littered with legal accounts, propositions, and contracts. Beside it was a wheeled table of precious wood carrying a large crystal boat that held many perfume vials in carved niches.

When he asked questions, she replied happily. In reply to his curiosity over perfume marketing, she said, "I work as an adornment consultant for dress houses. I have contracts with them to provide what they need from old and new perfumes. What brings you to Paris?"

"I have a date with a lady who promised to take me to the valley of flowers at the bottom of the Balkan Mountains."

Her heart pounded, and she tried to hide her feelings by appearing happy. She pulled the wooden table closer and perfumed his forehead and palms with perfume from all the vials.

He laughed. "Isn't one enough?"

"This is to remind you of certain words spoken in St. Moritz."

"What words?" he asked, surprised.

"Didn't you say that perfume is like a collection of exciting melodies that soothe your heart?"

"You remember all my words?"

"I've never met a man like you. You're someone to remember."

He smiled gratefully. "I'm staying at the Hilton. I'd appreciate it if you'd come at seven to have dinner with me."

"You've got a date."

In the famous Maxim's restaurant, they sat at a table for two. In the candlelight, a violinist came to their table and played a beautiful Russian melody.

As they ate, Simone indiscreetly asked Ali about his occupation. He stopped eating and was about to reply when he realized he couldn't give an answer. Could he say he worked in numerous fields? He laughed until his eyes became moist with tears.

She laughed with him and waited impatiently for his answer. At last, he said, "I work in several areas of trade and marketing, but this isn't the time or place to discuss it."

"Where do you live?" she asked.

He laughed again trying to wipe out tears streaming down his face. She pressed his hand persistently, insisting on an answer.

"The world is my residence. I pass my nights in hotels."

She looked at him in confusion, fearing her heart would surrender to him. His mystery captured her soul. His elegance fascinated her heart. She wanted to slip into his world and discover the magic of such mystery.

"When will you be ready to escort me to the valley of flowers?" he asked.

"Tomorrow if you like."

"I'll get you there on my magic carpet the day after tomorrow."

The following day, Ali sent Larry, his pilot, to Simone to take her passport and finish visa proceedings. The visa was ready in twenty-four hours.

Ali called Simone to tell her to prepare for traveling. Despite her prideful nature, she found herself obeying him willingly.

Ali drove her to the airport, where she soon found herself in a private jet with Larry welcoming her at the door.

She glanced at Ali. "Is this the pilot of your magic carpet?"

"Yes. He'll take you directly to the valley of flowers."

"I'm afraid I don't understand. Events are moving too fast."

He seated her before him and fastened her seat belt. "Don't bother your little head. Let's live every beautiful moment."

"Who are you?"

"A man who loves beauty and pursues it everywhere, one who carries with him an expert of beauty to turn the valley of flowers into a perfume that animates hearts."

"You're all romance, magic, and mystique."

"Those are perfume names."

"How do you see me?"

"As a spirit exuding its magic, gathering around her all who love beauty, like me."

They stayed in Sofia, the capital, for two days. On Vitosha Mountain, overlooking the city, they went about the green fields, enjoying the shade from the pine trees and the fragrance of the multicolored flowers. From Sofia, they went to the bottom of the Balkan Mountains, where Kazanlak was situated.

Flowers were everywhere. Butterflies flew in swarms, and the fragrant wind slowly crossed the area as if refusing to depart before it perfumed everyone's nostrils.

Simone watched Ali standing amid the flowers, listening to their soft talk. She called to him tenderly.

As if in a dream, he whispered, "Look at the clear water running through the rocks to vitalize the flowers. The scent ravishes my soul and fills my heart with joy. This glittering beauty shows God's admirable ability to shape the universe. Do you see what I see, or do I dream alone?"

She heard the beating of her own heart. "Beauty is in you. Your eyes see nothing else. Your feet walk on dust, and your heart lives in the light."

He looked at her tenderly, put an arm around her shoulders, and walked with her down rows of flowers, enjoying nature's beauty.

In Kazanlak, Simone made deals to buy flower essences at a fair price, after which she and Ali returned to Sofia and back to Paris.

In Paris, she insisted he stay a few days to watch an important fashion show at the famous Lafayette exhibition. After the show, she told him that fashion designers would hold meetings with the press to discuss the latest trends.

"Who knows?" she asked, laughing. "Maybe by attending, I might close a deal."

Ali went with her to the exhibition of big designers introducing their diversified dress collections. They also offered a variety of perfumes enclosed in delicate, beautiful vials.

After each show, Simone's eyes shone with competition and enthusiasm while she made deals with famous designers to purvey the perfumes they needed. All seemed like old acquaintances who responded to her views. Ali, impressed, admired her propriety and adroitness.

Before leaving for London, he called to meet her at any place she chose. Although she knew it was a farewell meeting, she proposed meeting him at the plant, because she feared a more-poetic place might excite her emotions.

She waited for him amid the extraction and distillation instruments, trying to keep busy and avoid showing her true feelings.

He held out his hand in farewell, and she took it, saying, "I wish our farewell could've been in a more-poetic place."

"There's no more poetic place than being amid the odor of perfume." He saw a sad tear in her eye and murmured, "There's nothing more beautiful than love drops glimmering in the eyes of a human being."

She stood and watched him depart. Since she met him at St. Moritz, there was something strangely mysterious about him that gave her an odd feeling. She hadn't been able to understand it at first, but finally she could.

The man who entered her life and left it like a shooting star carried a perfume of light composed of love, virtue, and loyalty. She wished he'd carry her on his magic carpet to the valley of flowers, or, rather, the valley of light.

Ali stayed in London for weeks, running his companies and enjoying his family. He had a good time with Nadia, who had graduated from the Institute of Fine Art. He admired some of her paintings and criticized others. She accused him of being unfamiliar with the technique she used. He made peace with her by offering an expensive perfume he brought from Paris, and bought three of her most-costly paintings to decorate the offices in three of his companies.

In his office at the bank, Ali found a letter in the morning mail from North Carolina University. At first, he assumed it was a letter thanking him for his donations to the university's research programs, but it was actually an invitation to attend the platinum jubilee. The university was celebrating its 100th year.

A cold shiver went down his spine. Would Diana attend the jubilee? She must've received a similar invitation. What would happen if they met again? Would love revive in his heart and become as strong as before, or would the barrier he created make it nothing but a memory that would quickly vanish? Was she still fascinating, or had time altered her beauty and affected her body?

Ali arrived in the States two days before the ceremony. As soon as he reached North Carolina, he went to the valley of love, which he replaced with Simmering, St. Moritz, and several other beautiful places in the world.

His gaze roamed the valley's sides for many minutes. Between the flowers she whispered words of love. At the lake, her laughter filled the place with joy.

Sighing, he returned to his hotel for the night.

At the jubilee ceremony, rows of tables were filled with food and drink. A band played country melodies and old popular songs, reminding him of the old days.

Between those bushes, their hands entwined, and their smiles kissed. There was the old library where they gazed at each other as if they saw the beginning and end of the world. On that day, he realized his heart would never love anyone but her.

He leaned against a tree trunk, staring at the crowd through his sunglasses. Perhaps he might see some of his old colleagues. Finally, he saw Susan shaking hands with John and Timmy. They introduced her to their wives, and she bent to kiss their children.

Ali walked up with a smile. Susan was the first to notice him. For an instant, she stared in wonder, then she gave a wide, lovely smile that illuminated her face with happiness. She ran to him with open arms to hug and kiss him.

Ali shook hands with John and Timmy and was introduced to their families. Other colleagues came over to salute the famous karate champion of the previous decade. Ali felt his youthful days returning and regretted his retirement into the world of business, where he found only satisfaction.

Susan excused herself to greet other friends and asked Ali not to wander off, promising to return in a few minutes. He promised.

He looked at the crowd, searching for Diana. She wasn't there. Perhaps she wouldn't attend. It might be better that way, because he didn't know what would happen if they met. What did he fear? She lived with another man who ruined everything he loved in her. His years of darkness were over. He learned a good deal in the past ten years and managed to heal his wounds until all that remained were faint scars. He'd gotten over his shock and crossed the barriers of agony and despair.

Suddenly, he saw her coming from afar, twinkling like a star on the horizon. How charming she was while walking between the tables, shaking hands with old friends and laughing at their jokes. She moved with lovely, flowing dignity. Well-dressed and in a good mood, she wore pale lilac silk, her long, blonde hair on her shoulders.

She looked ravishing. Her gray eyes were as clear as he remembered, while the faint lines at their corners made her eyes more expressive. Her figure had matured and became lovelier. She was more beautiful than he remembered.

At that moment, he knew nothing had changed. The years vanished in an instant, and he was as much in love with her as ever.

While laughing at a joke, Diana glanced up and saw Ali in the crowd, staring at her from behind his sunglasses. She felt paralyzed, as if the world stopped. There was no sound, light, or movement. She viewed him from top to toe and saw that he was still beautiful and lovely. No man was more handsome. He hadn't changed since they first met. He was as gorgeous as ever and still had the body of a fit, superb athlete.

She walked toward him without resistance. He moved slowly toward her until they met halfway. Taking off his sunglasses, he looked steadily into her eyes. The melancholy in that gaze took away all the words she was about to say, and she wished he'd speak and relieve her heart.

When he spoke, his words were like the lash of a whip. "I'm Ali. Do you remember?"

In a trembling voice, she asked, "How could I forget the most-beautiful days of my life?"

They shook hands. She wanted to throw herself into his arms and hide from her sadness and grief.

She wanted him to herself. Pointing to a table away from the rest of the party, she said, "Let's sit there so I can have a good look at you."

They sat opposite each other to talk.

"Do you still remember our beautiful days?" she asked. "I was happy then."

"Youth must have its fling. It was useful folly. Since then, I've aged a thousand years in wisdom and experience."

"Our lives have gone their separate ways for a long time, but you really don't think in your heart that what we had was absurd."

Smiling bitterly, he asked, "You mean the feelings we used to have? They were no more than illusions."

Feeling his bitterness, she changed the subject. "How many children do you have?"

"I never married."

Astonished, she asked, "How could a man like you not marry?"

"I'm still in the flower of my age. Beautiful women are many, but I don't find in them the glow that attracts my heart."

"What do you mean, the glow?"

"Purity and clearness. I don't know why those two are so quickly extinguished in women. Oscar Wilde once said, 'Men get married after being tired of playing around. Women get married for curiosity. All start by failure and frustration.'"

"It seems that the years have changed much of your thinking."

"Time changes people. I've learned that pain shouldn't keep me from realizing the real values of life and that work to achieve happiness is happiness itself."

"I'm happy, because you know how to enjoy your life."

"I still dream of a better world based on truth, goodness, and beauty."

"Your words remind me of the beautiful days we lived together. Can we recapture them?"

He gave her an artificial smile. "Dreams of the past are nothing but a mirage."

"There seem to be both happiness and regret in your words."

"Maybe because my life is a struggle to achieve balance between a materialistic life and my natural disposition."

"I thought you'd changed, but you're still the same old Ali who wants to save the world."

"Clean heart and pure love could change the world if they chose the righteousness upon which God created the universe."

"You say heart and love! Two words I forgot many years ago."

Feeling her misery, he tried not to let it show. Instead, he busied himself by putting a piece of cake on her dish and his. "What about you? Many years have passed since I last saw you."

Without thinking, she said, "Nothing's worth saying. I got married. My husband died from liquor. My father became paralyzed, and his political career ended. My company is sunk in debt. I'm left to face my fate alone." She lit a cigarette and exhaled smoke, then asked, "What do you do for a living?"

"I work in the areas of banking, finance, stocks and bonds, trade, industry, marketing, and several other things."

She laughed. "You're a millionaire, then."

"Say that about my father. He's been preparing me since I was a student at the university to help him manage his millions. I carry the load of his fortune and the burden of my own wealth, which I established over the years."

She was utterly astonished. "You never told me that before."

"Was it necessary?"

She stared into the distance and sank into sad silence.

Susan arrived with a big smile. Diana received her with a warm welcome, because they hadn't seen each other in years. Susan talked about the colleagues she met and how the years affected their appearance.

John's hair was thinning, and he had a wife and three kids. Timmy had grown old under a domineering wife.

While happily touching her necklace of rubies and diamonds, Susan said, "No one who has seen this hasn't expressed admiration. I'll always remember the night you gave it to me. It was like a night of a thousand and one nights."

Ali smiled. "I wish our meetings had been more frequent, but it's business. Your beautiful neck is decorating that necklace, not the opposite."

Susan laughed. "You always fascinate the ears with sweet words. How are your father, mother, and sister? I miss them very much."

"They're fine, thank you. They remember the beautiful days you spent with them. It's a small world. Perhaps we can all meet again."

Suddenly, Ali stood. "How time flies. I'm afraid too much of me is business. I have work to do before I leave for London. I must be off."

"Don't leave us before we can see you again," Susan said.

"I feel I'll see you often."

"That's what you said seven years ago, but since then, I haven't seen you."

"It won't be as long this time. I promise." He shook Susan's hand. When he pressed Diana's hand between his, he felt her unwillingness to end the meeting.

Ali returned to his suite, his mind filled with anxious thoughts. He sank into a chair and closed his eyes. Yes, he still loved Diana, but his love was mingled with justifiable cruelty. Why had love been taken from him? For what crime had he been condemned to ten years of sorrow?

She had injured him beyond forgiveness. He laid the treasure of his heart at her feet, and she cared nothing for him. He'd been near death in the hospital when she married a man she didn't love. He kept his heart clean for her all the years while she and James were busy making money.

Those days and nights of hell, his years of agony, wouldn't be without fire. He would never admit his love for her again. It would remain hidden in his soul, never mentioned.

At the party, Diana chatted with Susan. "How did you get on with Ali? It seems your relationship with him has deepened. I see that in the necklace he gave you."

"I detect a little jealousy, dear."

Diana shrugged. "What for? Our love is an old story. That time is gone."

"Come off it. The way you just looked at him, it's got to be love. It seems he got through to you again. You two looked like lovers sitting at that remote table."

"Stop imagining things."

"I'm not, dear. If love has revived in your heart, don't count on it. Ali's love for you died when you married James. His heart stopped beating as you flew to Hawaii with James for your honeymoon. When he returned to life, he was completely paralyzed for a year and a half. It wasn't a physical sickness. It was a rejection of life after you stepped on his loving heart."

"I was young and had to satisfy my sick father. You know I was forced into it. When I returned from Hawaii, I went to the hospital to see Ali. They said he was paralyzed, but at least he was still alive."

"I spent weeks at the hospital with him. I watched him go to pieces. You don't know what you did to him. You broke his heart, and I doubt he'll ever forget that. I warned you about James. I told you he was nothing but a mirage, but you didn't listen."

Diana thought back. "Ali said something like that to me when he first met James. He was right when he said James was surrounded by destructive forces."

"Everything that happened was to be expected. You rejected love, the most-beautiful thing in life, and ran after money and wealth, which are fleeting."

Diana stood. "I'd better go now."

She kissed Susan good-bye and walked away. Susan watched her go. Diana looked angelic with her hair spread over her shoulders. Her appearance was as fresh as a flower, her face still youthful.

Such a perfect appearance might restore Ali's love, but Susan assured herself that he left too soon to become too involved with Diana again.

In her room, Diana relived meeting Ali. The sight of him took her breath away. He looked impossibly handsome, just like when they first met. He was so near she could touch, taste, smell, and kiss him. His influence had been so powerful, making her memories of him sharp and clear.

She remembered their treasured past, how they met, and their meetings in the valley. Images came to her faster and faster until she saw him in her arms, covered in blood. Grief arose until she fought for breath.

Darling, she thought, *you don't know how miserable I've been. I went through my own hell. Are you still angry with me after everything I've suffered? I didn't start living again until I saw you at the jubilee. The reserve in your manner and the sadness in your eyes showed the wounds of the past.*

I wanted to say I've passed through my own bitter moments, but your sharp expression kept me silent. I wanted to tell you that being away from you was like a knife in my heart, but the cruelty in your eyes made the words die on my lips.

Do you still love me as before, or is that gone? Why try to revive hope when you left without even giving me your address?

CHAPTER SIXTEEN

The following morning, Ali saw Mr. Wallace in his office and said, "Thank you for your efforts in collecting the interest and depositing it in my account. I also thank you for representing me on the board."

"You pay generously, Mr. Razek, for my work."

"The interest is rather high nowadays. Do you think the company's financial status would allow paying the interest to the creditors?"

"I doubt it, because the company's also paying interest to the bank. The total amount of yearly interest is around five million dollars, plus they have operation, labor, maintenance, and insurance costs."

"How about the loan? The due date for payment is approaching."

"I don't think, under the present circumstances, the company will be able to pay the loan to you or the bank. The company's dying, and you know it."

"When will the board meet again?"

"In three weeks."

"It seems it's time for me to attend a board meeting."

"I've wondered for a long time when you'd do that."

"I'll attend board meetings from now on. I want you there with me."

"Of course."

As he stood, Ali said, "By the way, I'd like you to buy me a horse farm. I know of one in Virginia of 1,000 acres. The price is rather high.

Try to reach a reasonable price with the owner and contact me at my hotel. The details are in the morning papers."

After one week, Ali became the owner of the Virginia horsefarm, which consisted of a big white house overlooking a large arenasurrounded by a white, wooden fence. There were many corrals and barns. The place was calm, ideal for relaxation.

Ali made plans for further development. The excess acreage would be cultivated with vegetables and fruit trees with the purpose of marketing the produce later. The American horses would slowly be replaced by Arabians of noble birth.

From then on, Ali's residences in the States were a hotel suite in North Carolina or his new farm.

The company board meeting, headed by Diana, was held. Mr. Anderson, the bank representative, and Ali's lawyer, Mr. Wallace, attended. The department heads sat tensely around the table.

Within minutes, Diana's secretary entered the room and whispered, "The new creditor is asking permission to attend the meeting."

Diana nodded.

Ali walked in and said, "Good morning," to all those present. Mr. Wallace gave him his seat and sat beside him.

Diana was too shocked to move. Her heart throbbed, and surprise held her tongue. Sweat gathered on her forehead. She lit a cigarette and inhaled deeply, then crushed it out in an ashtray with a nervous movement. As her heart beat erratically, she tried to compose her expression.

"I'd like to introduce the new creditor, Mr. Ali Abdel Razek," Mr. Wallace told the others. "Because of his busy schedule, I've had to represent him at several board meetings. His presence with us today is a good opportunity for him to see the financial status during the critical circumstances the company faces."

"Thank you, Mr. Wallace," Ali said, "for representing me so well. I've studied the company's financial status carefully during the past months. The deterioration was due to expansion at the expense of the company's returns."

Making a supreme effort to regain her self-control, Diana found silence was the best strategy.

"Investment decisions depend primarily on the study of the cost of capital assets and the interest on the money borrowed," Ali said. "The continuous increase in the interest rate hampered the company from making progress. The old owners didn't take into account market capacity to consume production and the period within which the whole production was marketed. What is the situation of the reserve funds?"

"Mr. Razek," Mr. Anderson said, "we're in no position to criticize the company. That will lead nowhere. We, as creditors, must coordinate our efforts to protect our rights. Our main concern should be to collect the interest and the main loan on time."

"How can we do that, when the total interest is five million dollars a year?" Ali asked. "The main loan is thirty million, and the due date comes soon. How can we calculate results and chances under such circumstances? I want to find ways to support the company and allow it to continue."

"What did you have in mind?"

"We can start by retabulating the debts."

"We did that before with Mr. James Robertson."

"Retabulation of debt could be in the form of profit sharing, so the company can generate enough money for more production."

"I'm afraid I don't understand."

"The creditors would receive only half of the profits for a certain time, perhaps five years, then, with the increase of production over time, the profit share would increase. The company can repay the interest and a good portion of the loan."

"Our bank specializes in lending at interest. However, I'll submit your view to my superiors. You'll have the answer at our next meeting."

Diana looked at the other board members. "Is there anything else to discuss?"

No one spoke.

"Very well. This meeting is over."

The board members left the room, while Ali remained in his seat, examining papers.

Diana looked at him and smiled. "At least, we've met after all these years, Mr. A. S. Razek. The first letters of your name were on these papers all the time, and I didn't recognize them as yours. I can hardly catch my breath. Events are moving so quickly. First, I saw you at the jubilee. Next, you surprise me by being the owner of half our debt. Why did you invest in a project at a loss like this one?"

"I've never invested in projects at a loss before," he replied calmly.

"Why'd you come to North Carolina? I don't see any privilege in investing in my company."

"I invest in stocks and bonds. Your company offered stock on the market."

Diana walked to a small bar and prepared a drink for herself. "Would you like something to drink?"

"I don't touch alcohol."

She laughed. "Ah, I forgot. Your religion forbids it." She sipped slowly. "Nothing beats a dry martini."

He watched how she drank and realized she'd been drinking for a long time. Her hand shook as she lit a cigarette.

"Somehow, I feel you didn't come here to invest your money," she said, "but rather to recall our beautiful old days."

"Are they worth fifteen million dollars?"

"You've already paid, my dear."

"You're just imagining things, Mrs. Robertson."

Sadly, she replied, "My name's Diana, or have you forgotten?"

"That's the name on these papers."

"I remember you as tender and dreamy. Now you show a cruelty I never saw before."

"Mercy may look like cruelty to some people."

"I want to thank you for the suggestion of debt retabulation. Although you're one of the creditors, I feel you want to stand by me."

"I do what I find proper for my investments."

"How long will you be in North Carolina?"

"I'm splitting my time between here and Virginia. I bought a farm there for raising horses. You'll see me at board meetings, anyway."

"It'll be beautiful to see so much of you. I need your help."

He felt compassionate sympathy for her. Knowing his feelings were beginning to show, he steeled himself against them and stood. "Goodbye, Mrs. Robertson."

"Please call me Diana."

He smiled in regret and walked toward the door. She watched him leave. Despite his cruelty, she felt her soul going with him.

In her living room, Diana sat and thought over the day's events. She listened to Ali talk at the board meeting with a feeling of happiness flowing through her like warm wine. It was a lovely dream come true, everything she ever wanted or wished. Even though she just left him, she desperately wanted him to tell her everything would be all right. Their once-shattered relationship could be repaired, so there was hope.

She'd risk anything for that. She went to the well-stocked bar and prepared a Scotch with a splash of ginger.

The Senator, wheeled in by Mary, the governess, entered the room. Mary left the two together.

He looked at his daughter and asked, with difficulty, "What's on your mind?"

"A beautiful past I thought was over. It's returned to put life into my heart."

"What do you mean?"

"Do you remember Ali?" she asked sarcastically. "The one you deprived me of, the man James nearly killed? He has returned to put warmth into my heart and give meaning to my existence."

"I read the jubilee invitation. I suppose you met him there. That doesn't mean he's back to reawaken what died years ago."

"How enchanting he was at the jubilee. How magnificent it was when he surprised me by turning out to be my new creditor. Yes, Father. He paid fifteen million dollars to own half the debt."

"He's evil. Get away from him. His love will burn you."

"You tried to kill his love in my heart. You took me away from him, but I always knew one day, my knight would ride up on his white horse and lift me upon the saddle to take me away. When I saw him at the jubilee, I felt as if I, who had never truly lived, was finally going to taste life."

"You're drunk. Why don't you stop drinking the poison that killed your husband?"

"I don't want to hear any more of your advice. It ruined my life before."

"Is this what our relationship has become? You can't even bear to look at me."

"I don't have another life for you to ruin."

He stared at her bitterly, rang a bell, and waited for Mary to wheel him to his room.

Ali traveled to the Middle East with Mr. Edgar, whom he appointed to run his new stud farm. They went to Morocco, Egypt, and Saudi Arabia, buying Arabian horses of noble birth. Ali supervised their shipping and assured their safe arrival at his Virginia farm.

He leaned on a white wooden fence and gave Edgar instructions to release the horses so he could enjoy their beauty. They ran before him, raising dust clouds, their colors mingling. The palomino raced with the black, while the gray stallion tried to catch up to a chestnut mare. Their beauty captured his soul.

Ali murmured to Edgar, who also watched, "We have 40 mares with stallions to match. These horses will become legends in their own time. They rival those of King Solomon."

"Mr. Razek, you're a man who admires beauty."

"The Arabian horse is a noble animal," he replied as if dreaming. "He gathers strength and beauty, which endow him with dignity and honor, two characteristics that make him dear to the heart."

The board convened again. Separate reports from the department heads showed deficits in all fields.

"These reports don't add anything new to our information," Ali said. "They also lack insight on how to rescue the company from its peril. I suggest that all department heads submit one complete report identifying the least-expensive alternatives for solving the problems we face."

He glanced at Mr. Anderson. "You promised at the last meeting to discuss with your superiors debt retabulation in the form of profit sharing without collecting interest for five years. What did you decide?"

"I'd prefer to talk with you and Mrs. Robertson alone on that."

Diana dismissed the others and asked them to prepare the report Ali wanted.

Once they were alone, Mr. Anderson said, "They refused at the bank to retabulate the debt and insisted on collecting the interest when it's due. They also raised the issue of the loan, which comes due in five months. They authorized me to suggest that we sell the unproductive assets, such as the non-operating production lines. As creditors, that would enable us to regain a good portion of the loan."

"That's what I call the unfairness of the system. I invested money into this company to see it develop. There can be no development without productive assets. I want growth and advancement, not liquidation."

"I'm sorry, but we at the bank feel that liquidation would be a good solution to restore our share of the loan and debt. We feel the company has negative value."

"Is there no justice in the world? Shutting down the company would be a severe blow. You offer drastic solutions that consider only the bank's benefit, not the company's. Can't we agree on something beneficial for both sides?"

"At the bank we make decisions for the benefit of our clients."

A long silence filled the room.

"As I've noticed, you're very interested in development and growth. Why don't you buy our shares and become the sole proprietor?" Mr. Anderson suggested.

At first, the suggestion came as a surprise, but what was suggested was along the same lines of Ali's thoughts. He'd done such a thing before with declining companies. If he were the only owner, he could make the company prosperous again.

"I hope you don't mind if Mrs. Robertson and I have a few words alone," Ali said.

"Of course." Anderson left the room.

"What decision have you reached?" Diana asked worriedly.

"Let's evaluate the present situation. The true value of the company is around fourteen million dollars. The debt is thirty million, in addition to five million in yearly interest. The truth is that you own nearly nothing in the company, and you're running it on the creditors' accounts. I'll buy the bank's debt, and I'll leave you twenty-five percent of the shares. You become vice president and will receive ten percent of all excess profit."

"Ali, what are you doing? Rescuing a lady in distress?"

"It's a kind of economic reform. I hate interest. I hate usury that brings any investment to the ground. Killing such a company is almost like murder. Letting it die without every effort to save it would be a callous, cruel crime.

We're in the middle of a great tragedy that involves hundreds of lives. We have to fight to stay in existence. I want to take on that challenge."

With a shaking voice, she asked, "What would my responsibilities be?"

"I'll take the whole matter into my hands, because I'm the major shareholder. You'll be my personal assistant in charge of all other details. Wallace will check with you later today about the contract."

"How can I reach you?"

"I left my phone numbers with your secretary." He rose and walked to the door.

She stopped him by saying, "Ali? Thanks."

He shook his head. "See you later."

Diana turned away and moved to the window, watching as Ali got into his car. It was his white Ferrari, the same car they'd driven in the past, wandering the city streets. Everything she saw in him reminded her of better days, the most-beautiful moments of her life. She stared at the car until it turned a corner and disappeared.

Ali drove quickly toward Virginia. He remembered the first time Diana invited him to the company, and he told her his opinion of James. The Ferrari remained intact after all those years. Selim put the car in a private garage while Ali was in the hospital. For ten years, the garage owner received a regular check from Selim to cover the expenses of taking care of the car.

Diana discussed Ali's generous offer with the Senator, who had nothing to say but to accept. He warned her not to trust the man's intentions. Her being near Ali was like oil near a fire.

"Being burned by a man I'm enraptured by is better than being burned by one I didn't love, someone who was imposed on me through a pretext of future success," she replied.

Diana called Ali at his farm and told him that Mr. Wallace was waiting for them to sign the contract. He replied that he'd already bought out the bank's share in the company. It belonged to them now.

They met in Wallace's office and signed.

With a sigh, Ali said, "Everything is finished. We've taken a giant step. We don't have to fear those debts anymore."

"Is the company that important to you?" she asked.

"Yes. When I was a student at the university, the Stevenson name was a symbol for the state. I want it to remain that way. Your family name will be the only one listed with the company, as you've seen in the contract."

She understood that he wanted to forget all that had offended him in the past. She respected his wish and liked him for that.

"You seem to be trying to give life to the dead." She said after a pause.

As he left, he asked, "Why plunge into pessimism? Rise to the heights of optimism. Years of darkness are needed to make possible years of light."

"I remember your old words about man and nature. You told me, 'I feel that man's a part of nature. When he stretches out his hand with good to others, he becomes exactly like this lake, which waters the green plants. When he believes in truth and establishes it among people, he's like the sun when it rises on the valley and changes darkness to light.' The old days are like a beautiful dream I still recall."

"That was a long time ago. It's so far in the past that I can't remember it. See you tomorrow at the company." He nodded to Diana and Mr. Wallace as he left.

"Mrs. Robertson, you're the luckiest woman I've ever met. He paid more than thirty million dollars for a company that was already dead," Mr. Wallace said.

"I know that perfectly well. I wonder why he is doing it."

"There's only one logical explanation—he cares about the company's future rather than his own good."

In a low voice, she added, "He denies our beautiful days, though they still live in his heart."

"Pardon? I didn't hear you."

She said while heading to the door, "Nothing, Mr. Wallace. Good morning."

CHAPTER SEVENTEEN

The first thing Ali did after becoming the major shareholder was to combine the old owners' three offices into one spacious meeting room and bring in luxurious furniture. A huge oval table sat in the middle of the room, surrounded by forty chairs.

He didn't get a desk but brought in a comfortable, luxurious chair to sit at the head of the table. In the middle of the ceiling was a huge crystal chandelier. In a nearby corner, lit by a small table lamp, was a leather sofa with two big chairs of the same style.

At the other side of the vast room was a giant TV screen set into the wall. Paintings of Arabian horses hung on the walls. The furniture achieved an ideal balance between utilitarian efficiency and luxurious comfort. When Diana asked why he wanted such luxury, he said he hated narrow spaces.

At the first meeting of the board, he read the comprehensive report the department heads had prepared. None of the ideas submitted seemed good, so he called them stagnant. He asked the board to prepare a rational expenditure for each product, including the exact amount of raw material, time required, and energy needed for each stage of production. He hoped to use that to eliminate waste and extravagance.

To reduce storage to a minimum, he said production rate should be determined by true market need. He also demanded rationalization of labor use and the association of wages with production rates and level of quality needed.

Months passed as Ali supervised the daily implementation of his instructions. Some of the contractors didn't want to pay in cash, which led to the accumulation of production. The company needed a more-positive marketing program. Ali told the head of the marketing department to widen his base of circulation and deal only with contractors able to pay in cash. That enabled the company to shorten the storage period.

Ali further established a new division for advertising. With the lapse of time, cooperation between that division and the marketing department created a slight demand in the market, and products circulated better.

At first, Ali's efforts revealed only a slight increase in production return compared to wages and operating costs, something that showed his employees his willingness to sustain years of losses. In meetings with the board, Ali insisted that the company take no risk without a serious need, even when the account began to show a slight profit. His means of keeping the company afloat was to see the product of the minds he had working for him. Bringing the company back to life involved using their imagination.

His major concern was to maintain sustainable dynamics and exploit the company's potential to the maximum. His way of stating things to the board showed pointed clarity. He had a combination of firmness and tact that made the staff soon regard him as their model.

In the meeting room, Ali worked constantly. Danger stimulated him. He had to make sure everything was the way he liked. As time passed, his employees saw him as hard working without being oppressive. Whatever he did was accomplished with the bountiful cheerfulness of high, constant energy. Although he took on an enormous workload, he was always easygoing, making his employees feel like equals.

With the passage of time, the market slowly consumed more of the company's products. Consequently, the board advised Ali to increase production. He preferred to wait and told the marketing department to study real market capacity and the price of similar products. He spent hours pouring over the results of that study, realizing in the end that it was premature for the company to attempt to reach a mass market. The company still had a lot of work to do, though the basic materials were at hand.

The results of the study showed clearly that the price of raw materials and distribution was rising. Putting all production lines into full operation might not generate profits but rather raise labor and operational costs. It was too early to expose the company to market demand. He had to think far ahead and find a new idea. If the company were to rise from the ashes, its merchandise must appeal to thousands of customers wherever they were.

The fiscal year ended. Ali asked Diana to prepare the yearly budget in concert with the accounting division. He demanded she audit each budget item before submitting the final report to him.

After the budget was finished, Diana gave Ali the report and sat with him, waiting to hear his opinion. He read through it and wondered why expenditures were nearly equal to returns when the reports he received periodically from the accounting division showed a profit margin of 2-3%.

Confused, Diana couldn't think of an answer. Ali called the chief accountant and ordered him to revise the budget and get it ready in an hour. Diana went to her office, anxious to see the result.

Ali's expectations were right. The revised budget reflected a 3% profit margin. Ali rebuked the chief accountant and demanded that he give Diana a copy of the corrected budget.

Diana went to Ali and apologized, but he said tenderly, "You should've expected the partial success in marketing that occurred over the last months. Why wasn't it in the budget?"

She tried to apologize again, but he cut her short.

"The error has been contained."

In her office, she relived her moments with Ali, which had been filled with embarrassment, not delight. He invested millions into the company to keep it afloat, and she was making mistakes. He worked day and night, while she escaped into wine, because she sensed that her future didn't include him.

After they signed the contract and became partners, she assumed she'd see more of him. Instead, she saw less. She wanted to be near him and discuss everything in the world. He simply talked about his plans to upgrade the company and make it prosper. He cared only for business and apparently had lost interest in her. He never seemed happy with her, either.

She remembered his depths. His unemotional exterior sheltered a tender, romantic, idealistic soul. She wanted nothing more than to see it. Her love for him grew into an obsession, an emotion akin to worship. He became the center of her life. Losing him would be to lose her purpose for existence. When would she be able to ask him if they could repair the shattered pieces of their lives? How could she when he hardly looked at her and confined all conversation to business?

If he understood even a little, he'd never have neglected her until she became melancholy and angry. If he continued to ignore her, she might destroy herself. She wanted to blot out his memory with drink, but even that failed. She'd been drinking, because she couldn't keep her mind on her work, and she feared that would slow Ali down.

She refuses to slow him down. She wouldn't make any of his work be in vain or surrender to any depressing influences. She would show him she was capable of working with him as an equal.

Ali spent endless days shut up in his room, thinking of a smashing success for the company. Such a challenge lit up his nature and reawakened his spirit. He had faith in his own creativity to produce such hoped-for profits, but, to achieve success, all departments needed to work together with devotion, competence, and skill.

He straightened out the situation to achieve that. All departments worked in harmony except the accounting division, which needed restructuring until it was harmonious with the others. It had to work with the spirit of a team, perhaps even friendship.

Then he thought of Susan. *Aren't you working as an accountant for Bektel in San Francisco?* He wondered. *Would you agree to work for me here? I won't send a cable or a phone call. I'll fly to you. Your reassuring smile, happy words, and confident affection have always delighted my soul. I'll travel to you, because you've entwined yourself around my heart.*

Ali called his secretary and told her to tell Larry, his pilot, to have the jet ready by the following day. He summoned Diana to his room and told her that, through careful organization, he reorganized his obligations to give him a few days' liberty.

"It would be good for me to take a breath of fresh air after being busy for several months," he added.

Her heart seemed to stop, and she felt ready to faint. She trembled like a leaf while exercising careful self-control. She didn't dare ask where he intended going. All she could do was insist on driving him to the airport.

He sat calmly beside Diana in his white Ferrari. They both recalled the many times they cheerfully drove through the city together. It was a major part of their love story that had witnessed their grand days.

His glances at her as she drove were sad and sorrowful. She felt his passion, though his heart tried not to be touched.

"How long will you be away?" she asked.

"Two weeks."

The words swam in her head until she fought back tears. She stared straight ahead so he couldn't see the moisture in her eyes.

They rode in sad silence until they reached the airport. They left the car and proceeded to the gate. With a calm smile, he shook her hand, but his smile faded when he saw her eyes were filled with tears that she didn't bother trying to wipe away.

"By leaving," she said softly, "you put death in my heart."

As he walked toward the gate, his soul shouted: *Don't cry! My heart, too, has been wrecked on the shore of life. Bidding you farewell is like bidding life farewell, though my heart still bleeds from past wounds.*

In San Francisco, Ali surprised Susan by walking into her office. She whooped in delight. "Darling! How nice to see you!" She hugged him joyfully.

Touched, he hugged her in return. She seated him in a comfortable chair and sat before him.

"How sweet of you to come," she said, looking at him.

"I came to restore the beautiful memories of golden days."

"Those were grand days."

"How about getting back the dream of youth and the glow of hilarity?"

"How can we do that?" she asked, astonished.

"Come to North Carolina and work for me."

"Wait a minute. I don't understand."

"I'm the major shareholder in the Stevenson Company. I need a good accountant like you."

She stared into his eyes. "Are you still in love with her?"

"I'm not ready to rush into a love affair of any kind."

She lapsed into silence.

"Are you happy here?"

"I have a good salary. I know how to spend it, but that's nothing, because I'm always sad. I've been sitting here doing nothing but feel sorry for myself. At times, I look back and long for the old days."

"The flowers of youth can be restored if we call them back."

"You're unforgettable. I can't stop thinking about you."

"I always think of you when I long for something beautiful."

"Why'd you return to the States? For Diana, of course."

"To reestablish a failing company. I always do that with broken firms."

She laughed to hide her despair. "You're deceiving yourself. You still love her."

"You'll leave with me. I don't accept refusals."

"I'll go with you to search for our happier days, though they've faded over the years." She laughed when joy filled his face, and his eyes flashed.

Over the following days, Ali and Susan found endless things to tell each other. They went sightseeing in California and spent beautiful moments at the Pacific shore, talking about their college days. Happiness filled her, because she knew he was the only man who could warm her heart and make her feel secure. Hadn't he crossed the United States from East to West to see her?

She didn't care whether his love for her was that of the heart or of friendship. What mattered was that he needed her, and she'd see more of him in the future. Hadn't he said she was the big heart that comforted his soul? She had no real friends in San Francisco, spending most of her free time in her room, living a life as still as the grave.

The friendship and loyalty she and Ali had for each other was a thing of great beauty, a fantastic and unusual love. She felt, by accompanying Ali to North Carolina, she'd leave behind the unwholesome atmosphere in which she lived.

Without hesitation, Susan resigned her job and flew to North Carolina with Ali. His jet fascinated her, and she accused him of exorbitant wealth. She laughed a lot, making him wonder why.

"I wonder how Diana will accept my return?" She asked.

"Surely she'll welcome you."

"No, Darling. We're two women struggling to win the heart of one man." She laughed again.

He stared sullenly ahead. "I don't look at it that way," he muttered.

Diana was surprised to see Susan at her office door, smiling at her. She received her with a warm welcome and asked, "What brings you to North Carolina?"

"Ali flew to San Francisco to spend a few marvelous days with me, as beautiful as the days we spent in London. He insisted I leave my job and come work for him here as the new head of the accounting division. He offered me a salary that's nearly as big as the one I had at Bektel." She watched Diana carefully, waiting for a reaction, and saw fidgeting, annoyance, and disappointment.

Diana entered Ali's room and welcomed him back, then tenderly reproached him for assigning Susan without her knowledge.

"She's a competent accountant and is quite capable of organizing the accounting division," he replied. "She also has a big heart that'll put smiles on frowning faces and add some merriment to desperate souls. I like to see those things where I work."

Diana looked at him regretfully, then rushed nervously from the room.

CHAPTER EIGHTEEN

Weeks passed, and Susan showed a profound ability to run the accounting division. She even cooperated nicely with the former head of the division, who became her direct assistant. She skillfully adjusted the accounts and adequately organized a detailed budget.

Ali admired her work and demanded she conduct a study emphasizing ways for upgrading the company and cost needs. The results matched his thoughts—more investment for the production of new dress fashions appealing to consumers, hence the quick circulation of merchandise in the market, leading to production increase. Ali was relieved. He finally found another mind to support his ideas and fulfill his wish that work in the company should be a team spirit.

He summoned the board to his room and explained that the company must consider the fierce competition it faced each month for its share in the market. "In order for us to win in the market, it's necessary to design new clothes for men and women, because too many of the current styles are old-fashioned." He looked at the head of the production department. "What's your opinion on ways we could develop?"

The man suggested several ideas that didn't strike Ali's fancy, so he turned to Diana to ask her opinion.

"We should contact European dress designers," she said. "I'd say Gerar the French for women's dresses and Roberto the Italian for men's clothing."

Ali liked that idea and ordered the head of the production department to travel there immediately and see if the company could sign a contract with those two designers.

The head of the production division traveled to France and Rome and managed to sign the necessary contracts. The designers came to North

Carolina to meet with the board, and Ali expressed his view that a blend of European and American fashions would keep the company prosperous. A novel fashion that matched the American manner, style, and character, would stimulate their customers' sense of what was harmonious, beautiful, and socially proper.

He also asked them to design novel clothes for children that were inspired by the designs for adults. "If these designs are successful and accrue profits, I'll renew your contracts and add three percent of the profits."

The designers were surprised and delighted.

The board members left the room, all except Diana, who looked at Ali in love and admiration.

"New designs can easily be seen in collections of ready-made clothes," he said enthusiastically. "Ready-made clothes are the link between designers and consumers. If novel designs match the consumers' taste, they become attractive fashions that last for years."

"You've given me hope for the future of this company. You need release from all the pressure, though. How about having dinner someplace quiet, away from here?"

"I'm afraid I have a lot of work to do." He said hearing his heart beats pounding loudly in his chest.

"As you wish." Her heart broken, she left the room.

Ali charged Diana with supervising Gerar, because she was an elegant woman who specialized in women's fashions. Ali supervised Roberto, so he could express his own views on men's fashions. Soon, the two designers were totally absorbed in their work. Their skill became obvious when Gerar mixed raw materials with happy colors, producing poetic designs admired by all who saw them. Roberto produced attractive collections of morning, evening, and sport clothing for American and European taste. As for children's designs, they created many new ideas, taking children to an elegant kingdom that matched their innocent thoughts. The new designs synchronized with a child's simple, unsophisticated world.

Ali ordered the advertising division to hire models of both sexes to present the new fashions at the exhibition hall. He admired the designs from both designers and wanted the show recorded on video for national advertising on TV.

Ali decided to stop producing traditional clothes and replace them with Gerar and Roberto's designs. Release of the new lines was preceded by an intense TV advertising campaign. The new dresses soon became familiar in several American states and appealed to the public. Sales figures climbed. Within weeks, the results were clearly outstanding, and the company had a backlog of orders.

Ali convened the board and said, "We are on the verge of success. The new fashion lines created by Gerar and Roberto have opened enormous possibilities. This business has become successful enough that we can now afford not only to appeal to a mass market but to keep all production lines working at full capacity."

New production quickly reached the market and filled the enormous demand. The company flourished and achieved eight million dollars' net profit. Ali generously gave bonuses to his employees and kept his word to give Gerar and Roberto three percent of net profit.

Diana watched Ali work ceaselessly, totally giving himself to his work. Sometimes, he went twenty-four hours without sleep. There was something ageless about him. Time was his friend. He smoothed out difficulties with boundless care and did it easily, willingly, and with a good nature. Because of his work, people requested the privilege of purchasing a Stevenson dress.

For the first time in her wretched life, Diana glimpsed happiness, but why did he evade her when he knew that love for him still burned in her heart?

Ali sat alone in his room, thinking of his life, which was filled with money and success but devoid of love and sympathy. Diana's love was like a flame that raged in his bosom. To whom could he complain about his loneliness and ardent love? Pride wouldn't allow him to admit it, so he would leave to love her somewhere else—in nature's grandeur at the bottoms of valleys and amid radiant flowers. There, he would melt into love drops that would visit her with the morning dew and fill her heart with all the love he held for her.

He decided to take a long trip to London and announced his departure would be Christmas Eve.

Hours before he left, Ali stood in his room, shaking hands with the board members and thanking them for their contribution.

"I'll miss you a lot," Susan said.

"I feel the same."

Diana shook his hand, her smile hiding her grief.

Ali spent the first hours of Christmas Eve on the sofa, trying to relax. A light knock came, and he went to open the door. Diana was there to see him before his departure. She was dazzling in metallic-blue silk, her blonde hair piled atop her head.

Welcoming her, he sat on the sofa. She sat close enough to him that the warmth of her body crept into his heart. Her sad smile made his pulse hammer. She was glad to find herself alone with him.

For a while, they sat in perfect silence.

She broke it by saying, "I hope you don't mind my coming to see you."

"Not at all. Please make yourself comfortable."

"Who wants to spend the night shut up in a cold room? Are you sure you wouldn't want to celebrate Christmas with the others?"

"I have to visit London and several other places in Europe to make sure things are prospering as well as can be expected. I also want to see my parents. I haven't visited them in a long time."

"Your business must be pressing."

"I crisscross the ocean several times a year."

"Will you be away long?"

"I expect it'll be two months."

Her heart sank, and tears came to her eyes. Silence filled the room, broken by her deep sighs.

"When do you leave?" she asked finally.

"In two hours."

"I'll stay with you for those two hours, then."

"Don't bother with me. Go enjoy Christmas with the others."

"I find the happiness of my soul is with you."

A shiver went through him. He stood and walked to the large table, covered in papers, busying himself reading a few. "I worked hard to make sure everything would run smoothly without me with only a little effort from you. I'd like to make sure you'll be able to run the company in my absence. If you have any trouble, don't hesitate to get in touch with me through my London bank. I'll straighten out any difficulties."

She looked at him in regret. He hadn't shown any sign of interest in her. Instead, he gave orders to make sure the company would be all right during his absence. Panic seized her at the thought of his sudden departure.

"Why are you leaving at night?" she asked.

"Sometimes, I feel so lonely, I take darkness as my companion."

"Don't you have someone to comfort your heart?"

He returned to the sofa and sat beside her. After a pause, he said, "My heart is a good companion. Talking with it enables me to understand the wisdom of my existence."

"What conclusions have you reached from such talk?"

"The human soul may go to the lowest degree of despair if it doesn't wholly engage in useful work."

"It seems that nothing is more important to you than your work."

"Sometimes, I spend endless days in winter and summer places without work."

"Alone?"

"Most of the time."

"You travel abroad frequently. I thought you must see several women to entertain your heart."

"I'm accustomed to silent company. In my bosom, a sweet spring waters my soul."

"It seems you have strong relations with Susan."

"She stood by me when darkness drowned my heart. Well, I must start for London." He rose suddenly and pulled on a well-tailored camelhair coat.

"I'll take you to the airport," she replied, rising with him.

"I don't want to burden you."

"I'd love to do it."

As she drove him to the airport, memories surfaced. She wanted to shout in his face that she loved him, but she feared being repulsed would destroy her pride. She wanted to give him love, but, whenever she approached him, he remained aloof. Had his love for her died?

Ali glanced at her sad face and trembling lips and realized how much his departure hurt her. His tormented soul exclaimed in silence, *Oh, ornament of the world and utmost object of desire, when will the fire now kindled by separation be quenched by your approach? When shall we remain as we once were? Who can keep from enjoying the beauty of your face? Your image is within my eyelids, and I think of you when my heart throbs or is quiet. To whatever part of the world I go, my footsteps always lead back to you. I wish my tongue would become free to utter words of love, but the pain in my heart makes such words never cross my lips.*

At the airport, he bade her farewell. With a sad look and wave, he strode away. She watched with weeping eyes, waving from afar. Instead of saying good-bye, she murmured, "I love you."

He boarded his private jet and settled into a lounge chair. Larry took off and flew across a clear, starry sky.

"Would you care for anything, Sir, before we cross the Atlantic?" Larry asked.

Ali sighed and stared out the window. "Fly above the clouds, near the stars. Maybe, we can find a moon I left there years ago."

Ali needed that height and distance to utter the words that no one but he understood.

Diana shut herself in her room, crying bitterly. All her friends celebrated Christmas Eve, while she sat alone with a crushed spirit. "What's to become of me now? I wish I were dead."

Panic crushed her soul. She felt immensely alone and already missed Ali frightfully.

She reached for a bottle of Scotch and poured some into a glass, then drank it as if it were water. She looked at the mirror, seeing a shadow, a stranger. Her knees buckling, she sank down to hug herself and rock in tight misery.

Unsteadily, she rose to her feet again, leaning against the wall, feeling her head spin. She laughed and cried, though her laugh was hard and bitter.

Mary, hearing her groaning, came to see what was wrong. She found Diana beside herself with grief and tears. Mary held her and tenderly patted her hair.

Diana trembled in her arms. "Mary, he's gone. I won't see him for months. Go fetch him. I want him to know he's the only man I ever loved. I can't take this anymore. You have to talk to him for me."

"Put all worry from your head, child. He still loves you, but he won't admit it until the right moment. Do you know why he returned? To help you through your great distress. He reorganized the company and made it prosper just for you. He wanted to clean you up and settle you down, to rescue you from your sordid condition."

"He's left, and I'll be empty again. Look at what I've become. I feel sorry for myself," she said mournfully.

"The day will come when he realizes the extent of your love for him. Now, my child, don't drink yourself to the edge of death. You gave up alcohol before, and you can do it again. It's over. You're safe now."

As Mary put her to bed, Diana cried like a little girl. Filled with anxiety, Mary walked down the stairs to her room. It was clear that Ali rescued Diana from destruction, but he destroyed her soul in the process.

Weeks passed, and Diana sank into sullen apathy. Mary tried to comfort her, but Diana refused comfort. All joy had fled her life. The cold wind whistling past her window maximized the feeling that she was a lifeless land, without shadow or fruit. She washed away her fears with sips of wine, increasing her longing and confusion.

Two months after Ali left, he sent a cable from Simmering announcing the date of his return. Diana was waiting for him at the airport. Tremendous joy overwhelmed her when she saw him. A sweet smile came to her face, and she laughed with delight, following his movements with eyes filled with joyful tears.

Seeing her waiting, he smiled. She ran to meet him and held onto him passionately, gazing at him with eyes misty from tears. His love for her overflowed to reach its climax. Gathering his courage, he inquired about her health. Unable to answer, she let her eyes fill with the sight of him. He noticed that her passion had a shade of sadness and a touch of bitterness.

As she drove, he watched her carefully. He realized she hadn't slept well and had been drinking. Shadows were visible under her fine eyes, and tiny crows feet appeared for the first time. Nothing could've given more-ample proof of her dependence on alcohol than that little scene, and his heart sank.

Collecting his courage again, he asked, "Why do your hands shake? Why is your face so pale?"

She laughed. "When I knew you were returning, I had trouble sleeping, and that sapped my energy."

Ali realized she was losing the battle with alcohol. She knew it, too, because grief showed clearly in her eyes. She was breaking down in front of him, and he had to be prepared for any emergency. He prepared to watch over her and circle her cautiously.

Employees welcomed him enthusiastically. Susan walked in with a broad smile and held him affectionately. He was happy to see her and asked her to stay.

They sat near each other alone, chatting about how the company did during his absence. He surprised her by handing her a letter from Nadia. Susan read it in delight and inquired after his parents.

"They're well and long to see you again," he replied.

They talked of the lovely days they spent together in London and San Francisco.

Diana entered the room to find Ali and Susan sitting there, chatting and laughing. She knew she had no right to be jealous, but the idea of his having a relationship with Susan tortured her.

"Am I in the way?" she asked from the doorway.

"Not at all. Come in," Ali said.

Diana joined them.

"Where'd you spent your vacation?" Susan asked. "Don't say you spent it all in London."

"I spent one month there, another in Simmering."

"Simmering at that time of year? Ice covers everything!"

"That's where I find the solitude I seek after months of hard work."

"Don't say you sat alone in the snow without a companion."

"I'm accustomed to loneliness. It's my privacy. My occupation is tourism."

"It's common for a young man like you to have ladies escort him on such trips."

"Susan, you're imagining things."

Susan, smiling wickedly, put a handful of letters on the table. "Your mail was put on my desk by mistake. There were a lot of Christmas cards sent to you by British ladies."

"Those are from my old acquaintances in London. Do you ever stop doubting my good intentions?"

"How could that be, when a French lady sent you a letter from Paris?"

"Simone! Did she really write a letter? How nice of her."

"Who's Simone, or is she a secret?"

"A French lady who rescued me from the snow of St. Moritz. She escorted me to the valley of flowers at the bottom of the Balkan Mountains."

"It seems you know very well how to enjoy your time," Diana said.

"Coincidence may sometimes play a part in people's acquaintance."

Diana excused herself to return to her office. She bitterly wondered, was he still loyal to her? Seeing him alone with Susan alarmed her. Was he hanging around with a French woman somewhere? She adored him. Why drag in other women?

Susan excused herself to return to work. Once alone, Ali picked up Simone's letter and opened it.

> I, the perfume maker, have longed for a special perfume, not made of wood extract or flower nectar, but of the light inhabiting your heart and flooding with love all those who surround you.
> Merry Christmas

He replied with a few words.

> The effect of your words was like magic to my soul and perfume to my heart. I keep thinking of them, for they soothe my heart.
> Merry Christmas

CHAPTER NINETEEN

After the success of the Stevenson dresses on the market, Ali decided to upgrade cosmetics in the same manner—through more investment to produce new varieties that would better compete in the market. During long board meetings, he understood that the cosmetics the company currently produced had been designed ten years earlier under the supervision of specialized experts.

He inquired about the possibility of contracting new experts acquainted with recent developments in cosmetics. The head of the production department said that Davidson laboratories were the best in the field.

"Prepare a detailed report about the kinds of cosmetics produced in the company and the distribution of each," Ali said.

When he received the report, he read it over thoroughly until he became certain of investment feasibility, then he asked Diana to escort him to the laboratories.

The head of the laboratories took them on a tour and explained recent developments in cosmetic research. Ali and Diana chose a selection of cosmetics and a cream that soothed minor burns, removed eye makeup, and helped prevent diaper rash. They chose another that provided continuous, cumulative, visible relief of dry skin and lips when used regularly. They also decided that the new makeup should be novel and suit women's natural beauty in all seasons.

"We have immense capability in our laboratories," the man said. "Those formulae can be easily produced."

Ali signed a contract with the head of the laboratories, adding a condition that production would occur at the Stevenson company. Davidson experts would supervise the installation of the new equipment after disposing of the old. They would also supervise the blending of the ingredients in proper proportions in the mixing tanks.

The new instruments were installed, and the Davidson experts tested the new production to quality specifications established in their own laboratories. These steps were accompanied by intelligent advertising on TV and in magazines focusing on women's elegance and beauty. When the new products were released, they were completely sold out in a few weeks.

Ali knew there was no major demand in the cities where there was a market for everything, but he changed the market to his benefit when he flooded it with quality products at fair prices. What he needed all along was the quality of the merchandise. If such points were made, he could steer his ideas through the tedious stages from production to completion, then get the products to the market on time. It was fantastic to plant such things and watch them grow.

In *Time* magazine, Ali read an article criticizing certain kinds of commercial soap. The article mentioned that the chemical reaction that occurred between alkaline soap and acidic human skin usually irritated the consumer. The writer suggested the production of a new soap that achieved a natural acidic balance with that of skin. In addition, it would have to contain lipids and wetting agents sufficient to preserve skin softness while being equally effective on oily or dry skin.

Ali decided to produce the new soap in collaboration with Davidson laboratories. After several experiments, researchers produced a new soap. Ali added it to his collection, gaining more profit in the market.

The situation was going well. Success bred success, and the company prospered. Through his companies working in trade and marketing worldwide, Ali opened new markets for his novel products in the Middle East, Asia, Africa, and Latin America.

After a few months, he made up for his losses and had enough left over, so Diana's share amounted to millions.

Ali was performing afternoon prayers when Diana entered his room. She sat to contemplate him. He wore a rich camelhair cloak as he bowed in worship. Why would a wealthy young man show such reverence and submission? Rich men usually ran after pleasure and bestial passion, forgetting God until calamity arrived.

She remembered that the past was the father of the present. Hadn't she seen Ali pray in the valley twelve years earlier? She remembered the tiny bird that sat on his shoulder in peace as he prayed, as well as the strong shiver that went through her when she thought the whole universe prayed with him.

After he finished his prayers, she said, "I smell the odor of a beautiful perfume. Is it from the East?"

"It's a perfume whose ingredients I mixed myself. It contains flower extract, ambergris, and musk."

"I didn't know you liked perfumes."

"I perfume my hands and face before I pray."

"I appreciate your being religious."

"Living without faith is like walking in the desert without landmarks or sailing the sea without a sail."

When he said that, James' last words, spoke in the agony of death, returned to her. *I prepared for everything, but I didn't prepare for...for....* What had he meant? Maybe it was that man's effort and skill in running things were useless unless God supported him and directed his steps onto the right path. Maybe he realized in those last, critical moments that he hadn't considered being resigned to God or thanking Him for His blessing.

The prayers she'd just seen made her realize that the rich could be content, and money could bring poverty. She realized that money could deceive its owner, and glory was to submit to God in solemnity. That was how foreheads could rise and souls withstand.

"Is there something on your mind?" Ali asked.

"I just wanted to see you before I leave."

He rose from his oratory, put the cloak on a nearby chair, and sat down.

With the perfume odor penetrating her intuition, she said, "A little thought came to me while you prayed. How about adding a perfume to our collection?"

His eyes glowed with satisfaction. It was as if he heard the voice of her soul and the current of thought arising within her. "That's a splendid idea. I'll let you know when I find a way." He smiled.

After a few days, Ali told Diana about the advantage of using the French experience in making perfume.

She agreed. "You know I trust your judgment."

Ali decided to go to Paris for a few days, but Diana became extremely upset. She had the courage to tell him that being away from him was, one way or another, the end of her world.

He assured her it wouldn't be for long.

He insisted on going to the airport alone to spare her the grief their separation might cause. He knew she dreaded thinking of the future when he was away. Her collapse hung by a hair, and he wanted to do something but didn't know how. How could he pull her from the shadows when the thick barrier around his heart prevented him from interfering in her private life and advising her not to drink? Moreover, seeing her surrender to alcohol reminded him of her bitter life with another man, a life that turned him into a living dead imprisoned in a wheelchair for eighteen months. He wondered how immense pain could make the heart stop expressing its true feelings.

In Paris, he met Simone at her perfume plant. Pleased to see him, she asked why he came.

"I'm searching for a special perfume that reveals the odor of paradise," he said.

She laughed. "How could I know the odor of paradise when I haven't been there?"

"How many times has my imagination taken me to the gardens of paradise, where I explored its roads and filled my eyes with its beauty. When we visited the valley of flowers, the sweet fragrance, emanating from everywhere, made me ask what the odor of paradise might be. At that moment, I thought you were the only one who might answer my question."

She laughed again. "What would you do with a perfume inspired by the odor of paradise?"

"I'd perfume every heart to pulsate purity and beauty."

She was fascinated. "How much I've missed your sweet words."

He told her he was investing money in an American company that manufactured cosmetics and clothes for both sexes. He needed a perfume for women and an eau de cologne for men to complete the company's collection in the market.

"Why don't you come to the States to prepare the two perfumes in our laboratories?" he suggested. "If you accept, I'll pay you a good salary and also three percent of the net profits during the first three years of mass production, after which all profits go to the company."

She accepted on the condition that she becomes his agent for marketing the perfumes in France and Europe after three years.

"When can you come to the States?" he asked.

"I must remain in France for a month until I finish certain commitments with my clients. How long can you be in Paris?"

"I'm here for only a few hours. I have important obligations to the company."

Ali returned to the States and told Diana about his agreement with Simone. She agreed immediately. When he saw her trembling hands and red eyes, his heart sank, and he became even more determined to rescue her.

In his hotel suite, Ali heard a soft knock on his door and opened it to see an old woman with a kind face asking to see him. When she introduced herself as Diana's governess, he welcomed her, offered her a seat, and sat before her.

"Diana spoke about you often when we were at the university. That made me love you more than what I knew about her parents," Ali said.

"I've looked after her since she was a baby. I watched over her like a mother. I came to thank you for what you've done for her."

"All I did was investing some money. That's it."

"No. You came to rescue a heart from drowning. I appreciate very much the favor you did for her and her family, but I must warn you that unless you give her love and sympathy, she'll collapse."

"What have I done? Has she complained of something I did wrong?"

"No, but don't make the situation worse for her. Your withdrawal from her life has set her back. She's drinking herself to the edge of death."

"You talk about her despair as if it were my fault. You blame me for every problem she encountered with her late husband. I had nothing to do with her misery and fears. She must face that for herself."

"When Diana was a young woman at the university, I watched your love grow strong in her heart. When they forced her to marry James, her love didn't die. On the contrary, she resorted to drink to tolerate the pain she had with James. He degraded her by torturing her soul into sadness. He pushed her to drink after he killed every beautiful feeling she had.

"When you returned into her life, she didn't regret the past, because she loved you during it. Now your love burns her being, yet she receives nothing from you but desertion and deprivation. You know what you've done to her? You've pushed her to liquor again."

"I've done all I could to help her by not digging up a past I've completely buried. I wanted, as I still do, to help everyone."

"Maybe you have restored her pride in herself as a working woman and eased the terrible, hard coldness that possessed her. Maybe she wouldn't be in business today without you, but unless you give her your love, all your efforts will be in vain. Diana needs love to warm her heart, and you have plenty of that."

"I gave her my heart once. She slaughtered it and threw it away, then went to live with another man who gave her nothing but pain and loss."

"Don't take revenge from a loving, suffering heart that has been faithful to you all these years."

"She didn't suffer like I did."

"For that reason, she loves you more, hoping you can forget a past she was forced into against her will. With a mother's heart, I ask you to take care of her. Try to warm her heart with love and affection. Now, will you excuse me? I must leave."

He walked her to the door. She opened it, then stopped as if remembering something. "After her husband died, and she lost her baby, the Senator was paralyzed, and her business had collapsed, I went to her room at midnight to make sure she slept in peace. She wasn't in her bed or anywhere else in the house. Terrified, I wondered where she might be on such a cold, icy night. Rain lashed the panes, and the wind was howling.

"You know where I found her? She was in the garden sitting in the snow, wearing nothing but a short nightgown. She was trembling and crying in the cold. She said through her tears words you once said to her, 'Remember always that my love will surround you with peace and security. Even when I'm away, I leave my heart and soul behind to protect you from life's iniquities. Where are you now? Did you really mean what you said, or were those just words said by a loving heart?'

"I'm sure you heard her call, or you wouldn't be here, talking to me, right now. Please don't tell her I came to see you."

Mary turned to go, but Ali stopped her.

"These are my telephone numbers," he said. "A call will bring me immediately."

He stood alone in the vestibule, thinking over her words. His heart throbbed strongly. Diana still remembered his words to her verbatim. His memory was engraved on her heart and would never be erased by passing time. Oh, God, her groan on that cold night was her soliloquy to him to come to her rescue!

That miraculous dream told him of her suffering. That didn't surprise him, for he often felt their two souls were as one. He helped reorganize her company and made it prosper, but that was all he could do for her. He'd do anything to save her but one—offer his heart again. How could he surrender to her love after his blood had been mixed with pavement dust and stepped on by passersby? She married a man she didn't even care for!

Yes, he offered her millions, but he'd never offer his heart twice. That was the most-precious thing he owned. As long as his heart carried that blast from hell, burning the memory of his days with her, he would never love her again.

CHAPTER TWENTY

*S*teps of loyalty aren't wasted even if they walk on sand or the waves of the sea. Mary's visit to Ali wasn't in vain. Ali watched Diana carefully. It was clear she was breaking down before his eyes, though at work, she tried not to look as bad as she felt.

The best way to help her, he thought, was to visit the city hospital and see if they had an addiction ward. He was relieved to find one and met the director, who was pleased to hear that Ali was willing to make a donation to the hospital. The director was shocked when Ali handed him a check for five million one hundred thousand dollars.

"I'm accustomed to donating funds to organizations that look after human rights and health," Ali said.

No one knew that amount of money was the interest on his loan to the company for two years. It was usury forbidden by God, and it was time to donate it all to the hospital.

Their conversations extended to the number of hospital departments, their specializations, and the department of addiction. The director explained that the latter worked with the psychotherapy department, because usually addicted patients suffered from depression.

Ali thanked the doctor and took his direct phone number in case he needed the hospital for an urgent matter. As he looked for the elevator door, he couldn't find it and descended two floors, hoping to locate it.

All the doors looked similar. Suddenly, a door opened, and a nurse came out carrying solution bottles. Ali glanced in and was stunned to see Susan on a bed with IV tubes in her arms. A plastic bag of blood hung on a rack, feeding into her arm.

Tongue-tied, he stood in the doorway. Her eyes were closed, as if she were at peace. Ali quietly walked to the bed and stared down at her in wonder.

Susan opened her eyes and saw him gazing at her in confusion. A faint smile came to her lips.

"What are you doing here?" Ali asked.

With laughter that sounded like weeping, she said, "As you see, I replace my blood with another's."

"What for?"

She shook her shoulder as if making light of the matter. "That's what they do for blood cancer."

Her words struck like a thunderbolt. He sank into a chair, his elbows on his knees, his face in his hands in pain.

"Don't feel so miserable. Life is still worth living," she said.

"You're my dearest friend. My gratitude to you is fixed in my innermost soul."

"I didn't do anything that deserves such appreciation."

"You're the most-loyal heart I've ever met. I'll always be with you. We'll cure the pains of the present with the dreams of the future."

She was silent.

"Since when have you been ill?" he asked.

"More than a year."

"Since you were in San Francisco?" he shouted.

"Yes."

"Why didn't you tell me?"

"I didn't want to bother you with my problems. It's a little secret I keep to myself. You're the only one who knows. How'd you know I was here?"

"It was a coincidence. I donate to charities regularly."

"You always feel other people's pain and appear when you're needed. You know what's beautiful in you? Your pure temperament. The beauty and nobility in you are the fruits of such a temperament."

"I always remember how you infused my soul with goodness when I gave up on life."

"How beautiful it was to see you today. I was thinking of you, then I saw you standing there."

He took her empty hand in his palms, pressed it gently, and went into deep thought. Susan was very special, she was ill from a terrible disease but she kept it hidden from him and all her friends. Those who passed through similar situations usually wanted to share their grief with others. They feared to be left alone with loneliness and suffering.

Susan, however, filled the air around her with laughter and mirth. She considered her affliction to be a little secret she kept to herself. She wanted to live with her pain in peace without disturbing others.

How noble was her heart when filled with purity even though death approached. *No, balm of my soul, I won't let you leave in silence like this, he thought. I'll transform tears of separation into a string of pearls to give you. I'll change my sorrow into a perfume to fill your heart. The love you have longed for, which my heart has withheld, will become compassion to heal your broken heart.*

"I don't want to bother you with my problems," She said. "You're a very busy person."

He stared at her with a sad smile, pressing her hand against his chest before touching it to his cheek. Tears ran from his eyes. He gently kissed her hand.

Feeling his agony, she murmured, "I'll remember you until I breathe my last."

The nurse came in and was surprised to find Ali with her patient. "Please leave, Sir. My patient's taken a sedative that will send her into a long sleep soon."

Ali kissed Susan's forehead and walked to the door with heavy steps. At the door, he stopped and asked, "When do you leave here?"

"In a week," Susan replied.

"The company will cover all expenses."

She smiled and nodded.

"I'll visit you every day."

"I look forward to it."

Ali left to find the doctor in charge. He told Ali that Susan suffered from acute anemia caused by blood cancer. One year earlier, she'd been having a transfusion every six months. Then it changed to every three months.

Although the doctor assured him that medicine had made fantastic advances on treating cancer, making it less serious than before, Ali knew that Susan was dying. Realizing his dearest friend was slipping away made him feel lost and terrified.

Ali visited Susan every day. She was surprised when she saw him sit with her for hours, as if he had nothing else to do. If sedatives made her sleep, he sat on a chair and watched her for hours. When she awoke, he rushed to her, taking her hand in his and talking to her. He told her delicate and beautiful fairytales, like the ones his mother told when he was a boy. He flooded Susan with sympathy and tenderness, until she wanted to stay in bed forever just to have him to herself.

When she left the hospital, she saw Ali waiting for her with a large smile. She laughed at seeing him bow and point to get into an elegant Honda. When she sat behind the steering wheel, he said, "A small gift for you."

She drove away feeling abundant happiness. His presence satisfied her pride and made her feel he was her man. He guided her to a two-story house with a private garage, white wooden fence, and flower garden in front.

"Another gift for you," he said.

She glanced at him in surprise, but he didn't give her time to think. He got out, opened her door for her, and took her hand to help her out of the car. He walked her to the front door, opened it with a key, and gave it to her.

"Rose, where are you?" he called.

A middle-aged woman hurried out to welcome Susan.

"Rose is here to serve you," Ali said merrily, taking Susan's hand to pull her inside and give her a tour of the house. "Here's the living room, with a view of the garden. This is the dining room, and this is the kitchen. The bedroom's in the best part of the house. The sun shines on it until noon. In your closet are the most-recent clothes available, and, at your mirror, are the latest perfumes and makeup items."

They walked through a sliding-glass door to the garden, where he showed her the beautiful flowers, surrounded by white acacias.

Trying to catch her breath, she said, "Wait. I can't catch up."

"I'm sorry to give you so much trouble."

"I can't accept all this luxury. I want to live the rest of my life in peace."

"You need a change of scene. All this beautiful nature will make it easier for us to enjoy our endless friendship. It's my right to live beautiful days with you."

"Live with me?" she asked ecstatically. "Will I see you frequently?"

"Yes." He said holding her in his arms. With a tormented heart he whispered in his depths, *"How little have I offered you – just a little money. I wish I could give you what you long for – my heart.*

Ali stopped spending his nights alone at his suite. Instead, he and Susan dined by candlelight. He wished he could give her more happiness. Nothing would impair their friendship.

Susan wanted to give him her whole body, but she knew his spirit was too delicate. His character was too noble to descend to earthly passion. On weekends, he took her on outdoor pleasure excursions, sharing

good meals he brought. Although the disease moved through her blood, she felt the best moments of her life were with him. At work, he surrounded her with care and compassion, visiting her office frequently and begging her not to exhaust herself. He charged her employees with difficult tasks.

At the end of the workday, he escorted her home, then visited her each evening for dinner.

Diana watched all that with a broken heart.

In the midst of Ali's despair, Simone cabled him to inform him she was coming to the States. Ali suggested that Diana accompany him to the airport to meet her.

Diana was surprised when Simone hugged Ali affectionately. "Simone and I are old acquaintances," Ali explained.

Diana put on an empty smile and gave Simone a cold welcome, watching her with a woman's eye. She was beautiful, luxuriant, and showed the bloom of youth. For the first time, Diana felt that liquor rendered her unable to compete with other women to win the heart of her beloved.

Ali reserved a beautiful suite for Simone to do justice to her own beauty. He also gave her a car and driver.

"Why all this luxury when she's getting a huge salary and percentage of the profits?" Diana asked.

"That's how I like to be with my guests," he replied, filling her with sorrow and regret.

Simone didn't waste any time. The moment she arrived at the company, she examined the laboratories and existing instruments, then requested new extraction and distillation equipment for perfume making. Ali bought whatever she wanted. Nothing remained but for Simone to begin work.

Simone sat in her elegant office, thinking of the ingredients that would compose the perfume and the eau de cologne. There were many of them, and each had various sources. For the first time, she felt the weight of her new responsibility. Hadn't he asked her in Paris to produce a perfume that would reveal the odor of paradise, one with which he would perfume every heart pulsating with beauty and purity?

Simone decided to speak with Ali and Diana to negotiate contracts with dealers of perfume ingredients.

"I've settled on the ingredients for the perfume and eau de cologne," she said. "I have to travel to several countries to get the contracts. The perfume will be composed of jasmine and lilies from the Nile valley, famous Bulgarian flowers, lemon flowers from Morocco, and Asian flowers from China. The eau de cologne will bring together flowers from Virginia, Guatemala, Indonesia, Madagascar, and southern France."

"Here's my checkbook with my signature," Ali said. "Use it for your deals. My private jet and pilot, Larry, are at your service."

Remembering the beautiful days she spent with him, she said, "I'll go to the valley of flowers at the bottom of the Balkan Mountains. Aren't you coming with me?"

"Not this time. I have many things to do."

"I thought we'd travel around the world on your magic carpet to collect the ingredients for the paradise perfume."

"I'll wait until you mix the components."

"Simone, remember to submit to Susan an explanatory report about the costs of your deals," Diana added.

Simone looked at her carelessly, stood, and turned her back on her. At the door, she stopped. "You're talking about something very obvious, my dear. All the costs will be recorded in the contracts between the company and the purveyors. I'm the one who'll conclude the contracts, because most of the purveyors are my clients. Of course, all the contracts will be owned by the company."

Simone left.

"Why'd you alienate her like that?" Ali asked Diana.

"I don't like her," she said nervously. "She's a flirt who likes to show off. You've filled the company with women you've had affairs with— Susan and now Simone."

"You talk about my affairs with women?" he asked quietly. "You consider them many?"

"How about the house and car for Susan?" she asked sharply. "Her colleagues wonder about the high standard she suddenly attained. You're the reason for that. As for that French woman from Paris, she was practically flirting with you before my eyes. She doesn't mind inviting you to go with her to anywhere she wants."

"Susan needs my care. It satisfies me to offer her anything that can make her happy. As for Simone, she's a good deal that'll bring us millions. Those are the two women you're talking about."

Diana tried to light a cigarette with a match, but her hand shook too hard. He held it firmly until it stabilized. "The trembling's worse," he commented. "Is it alcohol?"

As she walked toward the door, she said nervously, "I'm free to do whatever I like. No one can interfere with my private life, not even you."

Simone traveled to the capitals of the world to get the contracts and deals she needed. In two weeks, she was able to collect the necessary items for the two perfumes.

After she returned to the States, she stood in her laboratory, admiring the materials. She told her associates to send the flowers and wood to the cutting machines, then pass them through the processes of extraction and clean up. The pure extracts would then be placed in containers before mixing them in the required concentrations.

Simone conducted several experiments on the proportions of the ingredients for the perfume and eau de cologne. When she had the final formulae, she called Ali in the meeting room and told him that the perfume of paradise and the eau de cologne were ready. She wanted him to come over and breathe their fragrance.

Diana and Susan were with Ali, showing him the previous year's budget. He suggested they all go to watch the birth of the new perfume and eau de cologne.

At the laboratory, Simone moved around her visitors with pots of perfumes, asking them to smell and give their opinion.

"It's warm, refreshing, and exciting," Susan said.

Diana admired Simone's skill. "I never imagined you were so proficient. It reflects a poetic, tender soul."

Simone looked at Ali. "What do you think?"

"It emphasizes the idea of eternal love that makes life peaceful and delightful."

"I kept my promise," Simone said. "I produced a perfume for you with which you can fill every heart pulsating with beauty and purity. What will you call it?"

He thought for a moment. "Paradise."

Simone smiled as if expecting him to say that. She offered the eau de cologne and asked their opinion. They all liked it.

"It reminds me of the magic and mystery of the East," Diana said. "How about calling it East?"

"A poignant name that reminds me of my homeland. Let's call it East."

"There's one other matter—a suitable vial for each perfume. We need a vial designer," Simone said.

"Who do you think?" Ali asked.

"Marcel of Paris."

"Call him and ask him to design two vials." "I'd prefer to go to France and see him."

Simone went to France to meet Marcel, who showed her an album of vials he recently designed. She chose the two that were the most beautiful and sent the photos to Ali and Diana, who admired them. Ali suggested Simone sign a contract with Marcel right away to produce a large quantity of the vials.

The perfume and eau de cologne were manufactured in the Stevenson laboratories, then placed in attractive vials. With intelligent TV advertising, marketing of the perfumes went well. Over time, profits began to come in.

CHAPTER TWENTY ONE

One afternoon, Ali sat alone in the meeting room, thinking of Susan's unique way of resisting illness. She knew she was dying, yet she filled the world around her with joy and hilarity. During work, she always joked with employees. She even invited them to lunch or dinner at her new house. She was like a godmother who solved all their problems. They loved her, though none knew the pain she bravely endured or the agony she lived with every day. Pain was something that belonged to her, something she slept with and woke up to. Death might crush her soon, but she kept desperation from her life.

Susan's way of accepting reality helped Ali understand many things. When he watched her at dinner discuss her dreams of the future, or at the hospital getting a transfusion while smiling optimistically, he felt he was a pupil sitting in reverence before a teacher, learning how to surrender to God's will and accept his fate. Man was strong when he defied death, the defeater of life.

With Susan, Ali didn't just feel sociability, friendship, and compassion, but also strength and the desire for more success. Man was a strange creature. He found weakness in strength or strength in weakness. His strength could also become patience, long-suffering, or wisdom.

Ali called Susan at her house, and Rose answered the phone. "Please tell Susan I'll come to dinner tonight."

"She's away for a few days," Rose said, "but she left you a message. 'I want to hang onto life, because it has a beautiful taste with you.'"

He didn't feel sorry for her, because she was greater than life and stronger than death. He drove quickly to the hospital and found her in bed, receiving another transfusion. Her eyes were closed as she slept.

He sat beside her bed throughout the night, watching over her. She awoke and looked at him. He smiled back.

"Did you get my message?" she asked.

"Yes. I came to enjoy life with you."

His words sent warmth to her heart. She closed her eyes, and the sedative took her back into deep sleep.

After an hour, Susan awoke. "Have you been here the whole time?" she asked drowsily when she saw how much time had passed."

"Yes."

"Don't you find it lonesome to sit in that chair?"

"Being with you delights my heart and enlightens my mind. Your way of accepting fate supports me with strength and stimulates valor and intrepidity in me."

"How do you mean?"

"You'll know at the next board meeting."

The meeting came, and Susan was there. Ali gave a demonstration, his voice filling the room.

"In the past, this company has been exposed to whirlwinds and earthquakes. When efforts were made to protect it against loss and strengthen its ability for production, the company showed profits, and we witnessed a revival that places a heavy load on our shoulders.

"As more consumers have confidence in us, our efforts must be doubled. Now that we're on the right track, it's only a question of time before the company prospers. Let's move forward even harder. I've decided to give a fashion parade at Lafayette exhibition, a big show of all our production lines for clothes, cosmetics, and perfumes. We'll conquer Paris, the city of arts, fashion, and perfumes, with our novel production. Paris attracts the world's excellence."

He glanced at Gerar. "The show is next fall. Your designs must look like beautiful, attractive paintings. Women's clothes must match all seasons."

He looked at Roberto. "I want to see designs for men who rush toward life and don't wait for its gifts."

Turning to Diana, he said, "Diana, you and the head of the production department will be responsible for organizing and presenting our new cosmetic collection, as well as commenting on our exhibits in English.

"Simone, make arrangements with the Lafayette director. I want to rent the place for one day during November."

"Have you carefully estimated the results of this risk?" Simone asked. "Critics might lower the value of your products."

"Go there and tell them that the Stevenson fashion house is coming to compete in the heart of your homeland," he said earnestly.

She laughed. "I just want you to be prepared for unexpected results."

Ali glanced at the head of the advertising section, then pointed at the giant TV screen set into the wall behind him. "I want to see Gerar and Roberto's designs on video tape."

Looking tenderly at Susan, he said, "You, of course, will come with us to take care of all the expenses."

Before Ali ended the meeting, he looked at Gerar and Roberto as if he'd almost forgotten something. "Remember designs for children's clothes. The women who attend such shows are mothers."

People in all departments worked like bees in a hive. With a woman's sense, Diana guided Gerar to select the proper textiles, with bright colors that appealed to the eye. Roberto did his best to design the most-elegant clothes for men.

Alone in the spacious meeting room, Ali watched the large TV screen. The exhibits of the new production lines were new and appealing. He liked what he saw, and his eyes glowed with satisfaction. He remembered Simone's warning about the risk, but her words merely filled him with a sense of challenge and competition.

He also remembered Susan's way of accepting faith. She was no dying woman. It had been growing on him for some time that there was a feeling of impermanence about her, not a threatening vision of death, but a brave, peaceful acceptance of fate. Her strength filled him with enthusiasm, and he couldn't wait until it was time to go to Paris.

Diana entered the room to find Ali watching TV alone. She sat quietly beside him, and he welcomed her with a nod before watching Gerar and Roberto's designs on the screen again.

After a moment of silence, she said, "You've kept the company safe and made it prosper. For that, I'm grateful."

Dumbfounded, he replied, "After the show at Lafayette, I'll consider my job here done."

She couldn't tell by his tone what he meant, and the grief and sadness she felt inside kept her from speaking.

Autumn arrived. Larry gunned the jet engine, and, moments later, they were airborne for Paris. The plane looked like a council chamber. Diana and Simone revised their comments on the exhibits in English and French. Gerar and Roberto perused fashion catalogues. Susan studied checkbooks and lists of hotel room numbers, which the American team and the models on the other plane would occupy.

During the three days before the show, there were several rehearsals to ensure everything would go according to plan. Finally, the promised night arrived. Ali and his people felt tense. The whole team counted on that evening.

Guests began arriving at Lafayette's doors. At each door stood a hostess in one of Gerar's gowns, presenting each woman who arrived with Paradise perfume in a superb green vial. The main passages of the building were decorated with photographs showing the originality of Stevenson in the world of fashion, style, and cosmetics. Under the dome of the famous Lafayette, a huge, illuminated vial of Paradise perfume twinkled in the air as if it were a giant pyramid.

Guests took positions around the platform. At a special table sat Ali, the famous young billionaire. Men in dark suits and women in their best dresses watched him admiringly.

The stage lights dimmed, and the audience watched attentively as the show began. It was the start of a successful story, displaying dress fashions for autumn, winter, spring, and summer. It was highly unique that a fashion house would present clothes for all seasons together.

Simone opened the show with an introduction in French, followed by Diana, who gave the introduction in English.

"The plaid taffeta skirt and tiny Cashmere sweater," Simone began. "It's covered up enough for a business event, yet it's fun and makes me feel like having breakfast with a sweetheart in a cozy place."

"Only nature could inspire a fragrance as perfect as Paradise, a new perfume for women," Diana said. "This warmhearted, wonderfully feminine fragrance is a marriage of Oriental and Western flowers."

An image of the perfume vial appeared on a giant TV screen.

"The poetic blouse," she continued, "vest, and sheer-at-the-bottom skirt. The pieces are very sexy but not too revealing."

"The ankle-skimming velvet skirt and long, lacy vest are a little offbeat and eclectic," Simone said. "It's the one-of-a-kind look that you prefer. You don't want to see ten other women on the street wearing what you're wearing."

"Now's the time to think about festive dressing," Diana said. "Romantic dresses that follow fall's long, lean silhouette are one way to go for an evening out, but you can also revitalize a short dress by teaming it with long, natural linen jackets. A simple black dress, whether short or long, is always right for holiday affairs."

Stevenson cosmetics appeared on the screen.

"Now your skin doesn't have to act its age," Simone announced. "Stevenson presents the renewal night cream concentrate. It carries away flakes, dead surface cells, and discoloration. What's revealed is fresher skin with a new glow, less –visible damage, and fewer fine, dry lines and wrinkles. Stevenson has discovered a new miraculous soap that contains the essential lipids found in healthy young skin. After a bath, the texture feels like velvet. The look is younger, and the results are dramatic."

"Now for a refreshing change," Diana said. "Makeup that does more than cover up. It actually cares for your skin. Colors for all seasons are in the makeup kit by Stevenson. This ideal traveling companion contains eight eye shadows and two blushers in today's most-fashionable shades—red, pink, and apricot."

That was followed by a show of men's clothing.

"Sport coats and blazers," Diana said, "classic and contemporary styles from Stevenson. You can get the best colors. Chose from Stevenson's single- and double-breasted suits in traditional or updated styles. Athletic or regular fit, in different sizes. Ask any man who ever owned one, and he'll tell you it's the best jacket he ever had."

East eau de cologne appeared on the screen.

"East, a new perfume for men," Simone said. "As classic as its noble namesake. A masterpiece of masculinity and romance. A blend of flowers with spicy sandalwood."

Diana terminated the show by commenting on children's fashions.

"We're a big hit with little kids. Entire stocks of children's outerwear are available, including jackets, parkas, snowsuits, and dress coats. Then there's an entire line of playwear, made of all-cotton or cotton blends, and all by Stevenson."

Nonstop applause indicated the show was a smash hit. The lights came on, and Diana, Susan, and Simone glanced at Ali's table only to see it vacant. When they walked to it, they found letters addressed to them. One was addressed to all in general, while they also found letters addressed to them in particular.

Susan opened the general letter and read it.

> I offer my sincere thanks to all of you for the tender touches I saw this evening. I've asked Larry to fly me to the sky to look at you from above and see you as twinkling stars smoothing every difficulty and making the impossible easy to achieve. See you in the spring.

Susan opened her personal letter next.

> Owner of the big heart, how much I've learned from you. Tonight's success was inspired from my sitting with you. Your refined acceptance of the realities of life makes me bow in esteem. I arise to the sky, for, maybe, God will grant me some of your characteristics.

Susan smiled regretfully and sat at the table. "He sent a love bouquet that will fade over the winter until spring arrives to restore its bloom." Simone opened her letter and found a large check and a few words.

> Perfume maker, you filled the parade with joy and perfumed it with the odor of paradise. I wonder what man could wish for more?

She smiled and said in sorrow, "This check reminds me of a winter frost. I was hoping to spend the night with him." She immediately corrected herself. "I mean, that we'd all spend time with him."

Diana took her letter but decided to open it in her room. When she returned there, she found a fox fur on her bed—possibly the most-expensive fur in Paris—purchased by Ali the previous day.

She turned the letter over in her hand, then tore it open and found a few lines of writing.

A piece of warm fur to protect you from the winter cold.

Her hand trembled. She looked at his admirable present, held it, and brushed its softness against her face. Going to the window, she looked at the brilliant stars in the dark vault of the sky and murmured, "Words of love are warmer than any fur."

Fear rose, pressing against her. She left her room for the bar and bought a bottle of whiskey.

After their big success, the American team returned home. Diana sat trembling in her office, fearing what the future would bring. Susan kept busy with her work, hastening the days until Ali returned from his vacation. Simone was a mass of energy, running after perfume markets inside and outside the United States after the outstanding success at Lafayette.

Winter arrived, bringing cold days. Diana inclined to silence, contemplating her love for Ali. It was a strange, painful love. She knew he loved her as much as she loved him, yet he insisted on wounding her by his departure. Was his heart still bleeding with sorrow after so many years? She knew he was tender and compassionate, so why couldn't he forgive the past?

What counted was having him back beside her. Loving him, knowing his warmth and giving him hers were the only things that could save her from liquor.

"Ali, where are you now, for heaven's sake? She murmured in pain. "Wine is ruining my health."

Spring arrived with its charming green and bright flowers. One day, the employees were surprised to see Ali sitting in his regular chair in the meeting room, and they received him gladly. Ali asked his secretary to call

Diana, but she said that Diana hadn't been in the office for two weeks, though Mary called for Ali several times.

Worried, Ali went to Susan in her office. She was delighted to see him. They chatted for a while, then he asked about Diana.

"I haven't seen her in a while," Susan said. "I tried calling her the previous couple of days, but Mary denies that she's at home."

Ali, returning to the meeting room, sat beside the phone. After a brief hesitation, he dialed Diana's number.

As soon as Mary recognized his voice, she said, "I did everything I could to keep liquor from her, but my efforts were in vain. She's locked herself in for three days, and I think she's collapsed. Please come and do something."

Ali was there within minutes. Mary, waiting at the door, escorted him in. The Senator sat in his wheelchair, shaking in fear for his daughter.

"Who's that?" the Senator asked Mary, speaking with difficulty. "Diana's partner."

"Your presence has complicated her life." The Senator shouted angrily.

Ali ignored him. Mary pointed to Diana's room on the first floor, and Ali took the steps two at a time. He knocked but received no answer, so he shouted, "Diana, open up! It's me, Ali."

He tried the handle but found it locked. Finally, he broke open the door and went in. Diana lay on a chaise longue with a glass full of wine in her stiffened hand. She wore a nightgown, her hair shining like burnished gold. She stared at him as if he were a ghost.

"Diana, are you all right?"

"The elegant billionaire come at last," she said sarcastically. "What do you want? How dare you force your way into my room? You have a lot of nerve coming in here. How dare you invade my privacy?"

Her face was so white, her eyes stared so hard, he feared she would faint. She stood and put her hands to her throat as if suffocating. Her knees gave way, and she uttered harsh cries, hurling her glass at a mirror. It shattered, leaving whiskey stains on the carpet.

Her knees buckled, and she collapsed. He lifted her in his arms and carried her downstairs to place her on the sofa. His heart ached for her. She looked like a flower that had been drained of its freshness. Instead of anger, he felt pity and love. Diana had gone through so much.

He called the director at the city hospital, reminded him of who he was, and asked for an ambulance. The Senator and Mary cried, but Ali assured them the hospital would take care of everything, and Diana would be all right.

Soon, the ambulance took Diana to the hospital. Ali escorted her and didn't leave until he made certain she was under a doctor's care.

He visited her at the hospital every day but she was heavily sedated, unaware of what was going on around her. Ali spent many hours discussing her care with the director. The director sent for the doctor in charge, who said that Diana's condition was critical as she went through withdrawal. Minor withdrawal symptoms could include anorexia, insomnia, general weakness, tremors, mild disorientation, hallucination, and convulsions. Those would peak within 10-30 hours after she stopped drinking and would last for 40-50 hours.

Major withdrawal symptoms would have their onset between 60-80 hours after she stopped drinking. They were characterized by extreme autonomic hyperactivity, tremors, fever, hallucination, and global confusion.

Diana's early minor signs were treated with strong sedatives to prevent the onset of the major withdrawal symptoms. Once those occurred, it was doubtful if further therapy would be able to alter the final result. Antagonists were helpful in the attenuation of autonomic hyperactivity, especially tremors and anxiety.

Days passed. Diana slowly responded to treatment. Her agitated paroxysms became less frequent. Her pulse became regular, and strong sedatives took her into a deep stupor. The doctor felt that psychoanalysis would cure her of sullenness, but the truth was, she'd lost all desire to live due to her desperation for Ali's love. The doctor finally decided that physical and psychotherapy should proceed simultaneously and asked the psychotherapist to join him.

Although the treatments ran in parallel, the patient fell into an agony of despair that pushed her to frustration. She was driven by a strong desire to end her life. She refused to talk to the psychiatrist, staring straight ahead with sad, downcast eyes.

Sedatives didn't help much in preventing her from surrendering to nothingness. When a paroxysm struck, her body trembled, then she curled up into a ball and went into a coma.

The psychiatrist informed Ali that Diana wasn't responding to psychotherapy. Liquor appeared to have ruined her life and destroyed any desire to live.

"She and I are intimate friends," Ali said. "I'd like to see her."

"It might help, but you can't stay any longer than ten minutes." Ali entered the room. Diana sat silently on a chair, her eyes closed, her head hanging down to her chest. She looked exhausted.

"Diana?" he called softly.

She slowly lifted her head to look at him with suffering eyes. He sat beside her and tenderly held her palms in his. She felt his love flowing in her depths, but there was also misery tearing her apart.

"Diana, everything will come out right in the end," he said. "You mustn't take it too hard. Discharge your mind of any worry. Try to understand the wisdom of calamity. God has put you to the test."

She turned away regretfully. He came to pay her a special visit. Didn't he know he was the one who brought her here in the first place? He dragged her down and destroyed her soul. *Spare me your advice and utter the words I long to hear,* she thought.

"One has to accept the rough with the smooth. Look upon the bright side of things. We can bear what we must bear if we keep up our strength. Don't surrender to despair."

"You talk about despair," she murmured in her depths, *"You put despair into my heart, and only you can remove it. Medicine won't heal my wounds, nor will the doctors. Just one small word from you will, though. I'll leave the hospital if you but say the word. If you say, 'I love you,' I'll recover and fly with you to your beautiful, bright world."*

She waited, hoping to hear the words she longed for. She felt them in his heart and on his lips, but he didn't speak them, so she stared miserably at him. Her mouth felt so numb, she wasn't able to speak.

She wanted to say, "I love you. I want you to myself for whatever time we have left. I want you to take me in the arms that heal as nothing else can," but her weak voice was lost in the wave of a strong shiver.

She realized an agitation paroxysm was coming on. She didn't want it to happen in his presence. A terrible sense of shame swept over her, making her feel unclean. The pain would strip her of all dignity and courage before him. Why didn't he leave and let her face her agony alone? Seeing her like that would erase the love he might still have for her. That would be the final indignity.

As she began trembling, she asked, "Please leave the room."

He saw her panic and felt the tremors going through her. Although he appeared calm, inside he felt no quiet. Feeling her hands shaking in his, he decided to stay until the first shock wore off.

The paroxysm came like a raging sea, washing away her soul, body, and dignity. She clung to him, clenching her hands tightly on his. "Give me one hope that might make me feel that life is worth living."

"You must not despair. It's not like you to surrender. Hold on tight."

She shook her head, rejecting his words. "Say something else I want to hear. Say, 'Diana, I love you.'"

Looking at her in misery, he didn't reply.

She shook him. "Just say, 'Diana, I love you.' Say that to ease my heartache."

Bitterness in his soul prevented him from admitting his love.

"You're so cruel." she shouted. "You can't utter a small word to save a soul from ruin? Say something modest then. Say, 'Diana, keep up your strength for me.'"

Crying, she threw herself into his arms. "You're my whole world. My love for you is the only thing still standing."

With a bleeding heart, he said, "Diana, keep up your strength for me."

"Take me to bed and call the doctor."

He lifted her and put her in bed. She curled up, trying to end the strong quivering that shook her. Ali rushed from the room to summon the doctor. Grabbing the man's arm, he pointed to Diana's room without a word.

Ali sank into a chair and covered his face with his hands. With tearful eyes, he prayed to God to remove the bitterness from his soul, so he could give hope to Diana's dying heart.

The doctor returned after giving Diana a subcutaneous injection that would knock her out. "You can't visit her again until she's completely cured. Your presence has complicated her condition and made her liable to such attacks. They should be less frequent now, not more, under her present treatment."

Ali left feeling melancholy. He came to the United States to make Diana's fortune and spent millions on that purpose, but he seemed to have animated her heart only to put it to death. How strange was man. Money couldn't make him happy, but words of love could do that, or perhaps the smile of an innocent child. Hadn't that happened to him?

Every day, he sent Diana a flower bouquet with a card containing a few words. In one he wrote, *When I first visited you, I was led by grief and anguish. Did I commit something wrong by accustoming myself to your society?* In another, he wrote, *Don't back out now. Most of our lives are still ahead of us.* In a third, he wrote, *Sorry if I've deserted exultation. I've lost the glow of happiness in loneliness.* In a fourth, he wrote, *It's no time for clouds. Can't you look on the bright side? I know it's there. Misfortunes don't last. You'll get over it.*

She became anxious to receive his morning bouquets and read the tenor of his words. She wanted the days to pass quickly, so she could receive more flowers and read new words. A strange tipsiness flooded her when she read those notes. They expressed his hidden love and the desert where he lived alone.

The psychiatrist noticed Diana's spirits revived with Ali's words. He kept emphasizing their meaning, insinuating there were loving, caring people outside to surround her with love, overwhelm her with sympathy, and push her toward success.

Diana's treatment finally ended. On the day she left the hospital, Ali sent a bouquet with a card that read, *I'll wait outside to carry you to a more-beautiful world.*

When she left the building, she felt she might not be able to face life again. A tremor of fear passed through her thin frame despite the warm spring day. She quickly shook off such notions when she saw him waiting for her beside his car—the car that witnessed the best days of their lives. She slid in the passenger seat, feeling her romance would continue somehow after all.

"Thank you for everything," she said.

"Thank you, because you've seen that life is worth living."

He told her, as he drove, the importance of continuing therapy outside the hospital. She must stay away from everything that reminded her of liquor. He suggested she spend a few days at his Virginia horse farm, where she could see his superb collection of mares and stallions. She agreed, saying a change of scene was what she needed, and she didn't mind going anywhere he wanted as long as they were together.

The Senator and Mary awaited Diana at the mansion door. She invited Ali inside, but he excused himself, saying he had to make arrangements at the farm before her visit.

The Senator watched him go and wished he could have thanked him personally. Diana bent over his head and kissed it, then she held out her arms to Mary and hugged her tenderly. All three of them cried.

Diana ascended the staircase to her room, but the Senator, speaking with great difficulty, stopped her, "Diana, that man loves you."

She looked at him with a sad smile. "How much I wish he'd utter those words of love." She continued going upstairs, entered her room, and closed the door behind her.

The Senator stared at her closed door. "How can love still burn in her heart after all these years?"

"That's not so strange," Mary replied. "With him, life is peaceful and admirable. The point is, he loves her the same way but won't admit his love."

"Nothing can keep them apart now."

"His heart is more precious than the millions he possesses. He offered her his heart once, but she refused it. He won't offer it again, and who can blame him? That man, of whom you deprived her, felt her suffering thousands of miles away and reappeared from God knows where to make her fortune and rescue her from liquor and loss. Astonishingly enough, he did it quietly and persistently. He loves her in silence without showing his emotions. He looks like a mother showing her love to her baby by feeding it and fulfilling all its needs without being able to take it in her arms and kiss it.

"The beauty in his heart is enough to attract any woman, let alone Diana, whose heart has been opened to his love since her youth. Now she feels his eager desire to regain her as clean and pure as she was at the university. Nothing in the world has ever been as sweet to her as his return into her life.

"Although he's generous and helpful, the force of his love frightens me, because it might hurt Diana. His love shakes her soul, and she'll keep running after him to her last breath until she gets him back or falls into destruction and failure. She'll never be safe until he unchains his heart and lets it rest in her bosom."

"Shut up, Woman," the Senator said angrily. "You filled my heart with worry."

Mary walked from the room, saying, "Sometimes, they seem like one soul wandering astray, looking for something embedded in its profoundness."

CHAPTER TWENTY TWO

Selim sent ali a cable informing him that Safia, Nadia, and he would be coming to the States, because Selim had to attend a business conference in New York. Ali was happy to receive his family in North Carolina. He reserved a suite for them in his hotel and made arrangements for them to tour the state.

After they arrived, Selim told Ali he'd be there for only two days, then he'd fly to New York for the conference.

"How is Susan?" Nadia asked.

"She's fine," Ali replied. "I'll make sure you meet soon."

Safia filled her eyes with the sight of her son and smiled. "All that remains is for you to get a wife who can please your eyes and rejoice your heart."

Ali smiled. "That time hasn't come yet."

When Selim had a moment alone with Ali, he said, "Your North Carolina projects keep you busy. We don't see you as often as before."

"I invested a lot of money here. I can't just disappear until I'm sure the company is doing well."

"Why'd you invest in this company? To be near her! Don't think I don't know what's going on when you're away from me, especially with her. This state may remind you of the beautiful memories of the past, but it also witnessed your downfall over a girl who married another man. Despite that, you returned after all these years to make her fortune. Do you still love her?"

"I love her more than my life, as unbelievable as that may seem, yet I find myself unable to admit it to her."

"Even when you know she was a drunkard? You've seen her clothed in nothing but misery and pain."

"That made me love her even more. You know why she suffers? Because she loves me and I can't make her feel the same."

"What keeps you from admitting your love?"

"Bitterness that has accumulated over the years. When she was suffering in the hospital, she clung to me, pleading for words of love, and I couldn't say them."

"Listen to me carefully. You've performed your duty toward her beautifully. Her company has recovered, and you made her benefit from your investments in it. It's about time to sell your share and find another project somewhere else."

"Who knows? I might do that someday."

"This woman might hurt you again. Your inability to admit love is good proof of the uselessness of any relationship with her. Liquidate your work and leave this state before you're hurt."

"Don't rush me, Father. Darkness in my heart fades when I see her countenance."

"You love her that much? Can't you get her out of your life and marry your cousin? She's beautiful, educated, and moves in your social sphere."

"It's not in my hands, Father. What I felt for Diana in the past, what I still feel for her now, I can't feel for another woman. Her service is my duty, her pain my suffering, her regard my reward."

"I wonder about you. What kind of love hides in the depths and refuses to surface to make both of you happy? You seem to be taking revenge because of something she didn't do on purpose, something that was forced on her."

"I don't look at it that way. I always thought she could have chosen me if she wished. She didn't feel my suffering when I fought death and disability because of her."

"I wonder what the future of your love will be. It might destroy you both," Selim said sullenly.

Selim and Safia went to New York, while Nadia remained in North Carolina for a few weeks before joining her parents in London. Ali was pleased that Nadia would host Diana at the farm.

One evening, Ali called Susan and asked her to consider another guest for dinner.

"Who is it?" Susan asked.

"Wait until you see for yourself."

Susan was pleasantly surprised when Ali arrived with Nadia and received her warmly. During dinner, they chatted about their happy days in London, Nadia's interest in painting, and Susan's devotion to her work.

Nadia, watching her friend carefully, saw sadness in her eyes, which stimulated Nadia's drawing talent. "Could we meet frequently enough for me to draw your portrait?"

"I'd love that."

"I'll be going to Virginia to rest awhile on my farm," Ali said. "That would make a good opportunity for me to draw some of your fine horses, whose reputation has already reached London."

A few days later, Nadia finished Susan's portrait and gave it to her. Susan delightedly hung it in her living room. During the following days, Susan took Nadia to the beautiful forests and fields of North Carolina. She even invited her to her office and introduced her to her associates, showing her various aspects and activities in the company.

Ali called Diana and reminded her of the importance of spending time recovering on his farm.

"I look forward to it," she said.

"I'll come by at ten in the morning to pick you up."

Ali went to the company early that morning and convened the board, telling each department and division head to prepare a detailed report about what they'd do during his absence. He asked Susan to evaluate those achievements and to motivate the various branches of the company. He also asked for a list showing the rate of perfume sales, so he could give Simone her percentage of the profits. That would keep his employees busy while he was away at his farm.

Before he left for Virginia, Susan asked how long he'd be away.

"Two weeks," he replied, "then I'm going to Africa for a long trip I make each year."

"Why hasn't Diana come in to work for so long?"

"She's been in the hospital, being treated for alcoholism. The doctors want her to spend some quiet time away from all tension and anxiety. My horse farm is suitable for that."

Susan smiled sadly. "I hope to see you every night for dinner."

"I'll always be with you. Where's Simone? I'd like to say farewell to her."

"She's not in her office. She left a message saying she went to watch the performance of the perfume sales in the markets."

Ali laughed. Simone was a businesswoman who knew how to use her ability to make a profit, as well as enjoy life's pleasures.

Ali went to Diana's house at ten. While driving back to his hotel, he surprised her by saying, "I'll pick up Nadia, too, and take her to the horse farm with us."

Nadia sat in the back seat, while Ali introduced the two women. Diana saw the close resemblance between brother and sister and admired Nadia for being so slim and elegant. Her wide, black eyes with long lashes cast radiant shadows on her beauty. Her mouth was full and rosy, and her skin was dazzlingly white with a hint of red. Her elegant dress and expensive perfume filled the air around her, showing her elegance and the luxurious life she lived.

Although Diana's attitude was that of a woman in love, Nadia watched her doubtfully. Wasn't she the sweetheart Ali mentioned in London? How could he continue a relationship with her after what she did to him? Nadia feared that Diana's love might have bewitched her brother. Whatever the cost, Nadia was determined to know the nature of that love.

After driving for hours, they arrived in Virginia and found the farmhouse neat and welcoming. Diana wanted to see it all. Apparently, the pleasant site and elegant interior surpassed her expectations. The graceful house had a tiled roof and airy rooms, with large, deep windows. White walls and a polished wooden floor gave it quiet dignity. Bowls of fresh-cut flowers stood on small, round, wooden corner tables. Paintings of horses from superb collections hung on the walls. A few Oriental rugs lay on the floor, adding color and warmth. The large, well-lit kitchen seemed a comfortable place to work.

From the house, the view of the farm was spectacular, making Diana recall Ali's words he spoke in the hospital. *I'll wait outside to carry you to a more-beautiful world.*

In the evening, Edgar's wife prepared a delicious dinner for the guests. Afterward, they sat to talk.

"Early in the morning," Nadia said, "I want to start painting the horses."

"Don't you want to wait until I give you information about their quality?" Ali asked.

"I prefer to discover that with an artistic eye."

"She's right," Diana said. "The eye of an artist is more accurate and comprehensive."

"The horse world is filled with wonders," Ali said. "It needs a guide to explain its classic beauty."

"You give me a difficult task, but I'm sure I'll pass the test," Nadia said, "especially when you understand I'm painting horses for the first time."

"The results are what count," he said, laughing. "I'm anxious to see what you do."

"Wait until tomorrow. Then you'll see," she replied in a challenging tone.

In the morning, Diana stood in her room, looking out the window at the flowers in the front garden that ranged in color from white, yellow, blue, to red. Joy filled her heart. She couldn't stay in her room any longer and went down to the garden, touching the flowers and leaves.

Nadia wasn't at breakfast, because she was up at dawn to look for horses to paint. Ali ate breakfast with Diana.

Afterward, he helped her up and said, "Come. I want to show you around."

He took her to the stalls and explained his plans for the farm. "I'm gradually turning the farm into a supremely productive operation. We have horses to sell without touching the breeding stock, and we have vegetables and other fresh produce to market at good prices."

He opened the windows of several box stalls. Beautiful horse heads of noble appearance came out to gaze at them. He told Diana where he bought each horse and about its sire, dam, and bloodlines. He petted their foreheads and necks as he gave them sugar cubes.

"These horses inherited their size, slender grace, wide-set eyes, and shapely heads from the blood of fine Arabians. More and more are trained and sold each year. The purebred horse has a noble character.

"Horses are of two kinds—purebred and crossbred. Purebred means their parents are Arabian. The crossbred is one whose father is crossbred, and its mother is Arabian. You can see the character of the purebred horse in its splendor, bearing, affection, and loyalty to its owner. One characteristic, indicating its dignity and contempt for certain things, is that it won't eat the leftovers of another horse's fodder."

Seeing how fond he was of the horses, she asked, "What do they mean to you?"

"Courage, endurance, and intelligence. The Arabian horse is unsurpassed by any other breed for its beauty, harmony, and high breeding. Due to its outstanding prepotency, it is used to improve nearly all hot-blooded and native breeds."

"Raising horses is expensive."

"One who spends money on horses is like a man stretching his hand with charity and alms never taking it back. Stinginess never finds its way to him.

"The broodmares are kept loose in two large stables, each with a wide yard with their offspring until weaning time, which is at five months. Then they're transferred to another stable.

"At one year of age, colts and fillies are separated. Stallions live in box stalls. Mares commence their breeding careers at three to four years. Fine, strong stallions are chosen. An improved breeding program is followed every year to reach the top level of beauty, conformation, and other necessary Arabian characteristics. The rest of the horses are sold at auction every two years here on the farm."

The tour ended. Diana felt so occupied with Ali that all thoughts of alcohol vanished. She felt renewed intimacy with him. "I thought the undulation of color and the interweaving of petal colors within the flower were enough to please the heart, but after seeing the colors of the horses moving around you, I felt like I was watching an exhibition of color beyond the skill of any artist."

He smiled at her lovingly. The transparency he once loved in her was returning.

Nadia worked on several paintings of Ali's Arabian horses. She also made paintings of the mechanics of their movement at walk, trot, and canter.

Being at the farm gave Diana the chance to rediscover the path to joy she once knew with Ali. The beauty of the horses and the cool peace of the place filled her with hope, encouragement, and heart's ease.

One evening, Nadia took the opportunity to be alone with Diana and chat. "How long have you known Ali?"

"Since we were students at the university."

"You know Susan, then?"

"Of course. We were colleagues. She works with us at the company."

"What's your position there?"

"My father, with another partner, were the owners before Ali became the major shareholder. I own one-fourth of the shares." "Are you the girl he loved at the university?"

"Yes," Diana said worriedly.

"Do you still love him?"

"I never stopped."

"How about him?"

"I don't know."

"You think he'd admit his love to you after all that happened?"

"I hope so. I hope he can forget the bitter moments of the past."

"I don't think that'll be easy for him."

"I was young then. I fought hard to protect our love, but I couldn't stand up to my father. I passed through bitter moments, too, which eventually led to worry and depression."

"Did you admit your love to him after all these years?"

"Yes, when I was in the hospital, clinging to the hope that would give life to my dying heart."

"What were you doing in the hospital?"

"Being treated for alcoholism. Ali brought me here for my recovery period."

"Did he admit his love to you?"

"No, but I hope he will."

"That's what I expected. The wound of the past is still deep inside.

The tenderness he shows you hides a fire burning in his heart. Those of us from the East are sensitive to such matters."

"I can see that in the sadness of his eyes and his long silence. I'm terrified by the thought of living a desperate love."

Ali suddenly entered the living room, interrupting their conversation. "The horse auction will be at the farm in two days. I saved the best horses for this occasion, I'm sure they'll bring a good price."

Diana admired him for turning even beauty into gold.

Auction day arrived. Folding chairs were set up in rows opposite the horse arena. People watched attentively, studying the conformation of the horses. Bidders competed eagerly. One horse sold for $100,000, another for $200,000, and a third for $1,000,000. Diana wondered at the difference in prices, because all the horses were of noble origin.

Ali explained it to her. "The features of the horse that sold for one million closely approached the breed's basic qualities. That horse had an extraordinarily strong constitution; a light, chiseled head with a broad forehead; pointed ears that almost meet at the tips; large, protruding, fiery eyes; a dished nose; a curved, fine, graceful neck; a relatively deep chest; sharp, high withers; short, compact rump; short, round croup with beautiful tail set high; well-developed legs and joints; long fetlocks; small, round, tough hooves; and a mane and tail that are exceptionally fine and silky without being too thick."

After the auction, Ali invited his guests to lunch in the open air. Diana leaned against a tree, watching the guests eat lunch with him. She was tired of sharing him. She wanted him for herself. When the guests had their lunch and were finally ready to leave, Diana was glad for a chance to be alone with Ali.

During the coming days, Ali was frequently silent, staring at the horizon as if searching for something. One day, Diana went looking for him and found him performing prayers in the middle of the horse arena. The sun sank toward the distant blue horizon in a blaze of glittering golden light.

She leaned against the fence and watched in tender silence. His prayers eased her soul, making her feel at peace with the world.

It was time to exercise the horses, and Edgar released them into the arena without noticing Ali was already there. Diana became terrified and shouted a warning, worried the horses might trample him.

The horses ran toward Ali but stopped as they neared. Slowly, they formed a big circle and watched him. Ali finished his prayers, stood, and smiled at them. How beautiful to see such elegant horses of high breeding after finishing prayers. They gleamed in the fading sunlight, pushing one another, each wanting its share of Ali's compassion. He stroked their necks and foreheads with love and joy.

Diana walked between the horses until she reached Ali. "I feared they'd trample you while you prayed."

"How could that be, when they know a man's prayers?" He looked at her face. The sunlight was gold on her skin, casting a web of light on her blonde hair. "You're twinkling beauty."

His words penetrated deeply, subduing her heart and sending a rush of emotion to her eyes. Ali looked around and chose a delicately built pearly white mare, a three-year-old with dark eyes and a perfect flaxen mane and tail. "This young mare has been well-trained. I offer her to you as a present."

"A gift for me? That's too much!" she said, surprised.

"With your slender frame, there's something fitting about horse and rider."

Without warning, Diana's love for him washed over her as it often did, and she fought back tears. She wished to hear the words of love she so desired.

She loved that mare and exercised her twice a day.

Diana noticed during the following days that Ali often sought solitude. Even when they rode together, he was silent most of the time, as if something occupied his mind.

They sat at the supper table, eating, when Diana saw a twinkle in Ali's eyes she held her breath. She'd seen that before when she put her arms around his neck and drew him close, or when he saw a beautiful view. Was he about to admit his love for her?

After dinner, Ali went to the balcony to sit alone in a far corner. Diana calmly approached and sat beside him.

"What's up?" she asked. "You seem worried."

He took a deep breath. "Verily, God has smoothed all my affairs for me. We ought to be benevolent and pay alms."

"That's what you call Zakat in your religion, I suppose. I remember your speaking of it in that seminar years ago."

"You still remember?"

"My moments with you are unforgettable."

He returned to deep silence.

"How much is your almsgiving?" she asked.

"Millions each year."

"Millions!" she said, surprised. "You could invest that in profitable projects. Why waste it?"

"Our religion prompts us to spend money in goodness and charity. It's a profitable trade with God."

"I still don't understand the wisdom of spending all that money without any return."

"May God protect me. I trade with Him by paying charity and almsgiving. In return, I'm blessed with livelihood, health, and wealth."

"Where will you spend all that money?"

"On starving people in Africa."

"Don't you think they're the reason for the famine? They don't work to earn a living."

"To us, people are of two kinds—either a brother in religion or an equal in creation. Both deserve almsgiving or charity. That's God's instruction to us to earn His blessing."

"Is that what has made you worried these past few days?"

"Yes."

"How will you spend those millions in Africa?"

"By departing to areas afflicted with calamities. I make a trip like this every year to approach God."

"It seems these trips are encompassed with toil and pain."

"They are, indeed. Nonetheless, there you can feel the strangest of all impressions. It's like a blur of light, in the midst of which you can see the real value of life that fits the facts of existence."

"It sounds heavenly. When will you leave?"

"I gave orders to some of my companies to ship foodstuffs to Sudan, which is already suffering from drought and starvation. I'll leave as soon as I receive permission from the Sudanese authorities to enter the affected areas."

"How long will you stay there?"

"One or two months."

Her face paled at the thought of being deprived of all that happiness. She feared, after his departure, she might resort to liquor again.

CHAPTER TWENTY THREE

On a beautiful Sunny day, Ali, Diana, and Nadia sat in the garden, eating breakfast. Edgar came to the table and placed a telegram before Ali. Diana, looking at Ali's beaming eyes, realized his departure for Africa was near.

"Everything is set," Ali announced.

Diana stopped eating and felt hysteria rising in her. Ali saw her shivering with hopeless fury, then she bolted toward the house.

Ali went after her and found her sitting alone in the lobby, her eyes wet with tears. Sitting beside her, he asked, "Diana, what's wrong?"

She broke into hysterical sobbing. Away from him, all her beauty would gradually fade, and the promise of her womanhood would bear no fruit. During the silence that followed, her face grew paler and paler.

She shook her head in rejection. "Don't fly away. Don't tear out my heart with your departure. I don't want to be burned again. It's a joy to live in the world when one has someone to love. You're all I could've hoped for. I see nothing but you."

Looking at her tenderly, he knew what she felt.

She smiled through her tears and whispered, "Say the words of love." "Gone is the time when you and I were lovers. That was ages ago." "What do you want of me? I've never stopped loving you." Her voice died in a sob.

His heart softened. He took her hand. "For God's sake, don't make this any harder."

"I want you to talk about your feelings. I'm sure there's a chance we can begin again."

Tense silence fell.

Trying to pull herself together, she said, "I won't beg love from you again. I'll wait until you realize how much I love you. I'll bury the pain in my heart and won't complain about being forsaken and repulsed. The days will prove to you that your soul inhabits mine, and my love burns in your heart."

He released her hand, his black eyes blazing with fury. He said shaking, "My life is a desert of confusion. I travel through its quick sand searching for a flower that once perfumed my heart but there's nothing but a mirage."

She smiled through her tears. "How beautiful are your words. Do you love me that much?"

"I didn't admit anything," he said quickly.

"No, my beloved. You did, but your love is joined with pain. I'll give you compassion that will rejoice your heart and love that will heal your wound until you whisper the words I long to hear."

Trying to escape his weakness, he said, "I leave for Africa now." "I'll go with you," she said confidently.

"Don't press me too far."

"I don't think you like the idea of leaving me by myself for too long."

"My trip won't be about fun. It's hard there."

"Nothing would induce me to stay behind."

A beautiful smile dawned on her lovely face when she detected tacit consent in his long silence.

The days of merriment ended. Ali asked Edgar to prepare the station wagon. On the road to North Carolina, Ali reopened the subject of Diana's traveling to Africa, emphasizing she might not be able to withstand the hardships of such a trip.

She insisted she had nothing to fear, because she would be traveling under his protection.

Nadia, listening, surprised them both by saying, "I'd definitely find fertile nature there that I could draw."

Ali laughed at the unexpected surprise and agreed to take her if their parents allowed. Deep in the bottom of his heart, he was glad to have Diana accompany him to Africa, because that would keep her away from liquor and would also show her another side of the world.

When the Senator learned of Diana's plans, he felt the trip was an essential part of her treatment against alcoholism. Mary hugged Diana and said, "The trip will be a good opportunity to see something of the world and discover the secrets of your soul."

Ali also had dinner with Susan, as if apologizing for traveling away. Seeing the fragile appearance of her face, his heart ached for her.

Noticing his worry, she laughed. "They take good care of me at the hospital. There's nothing to worry about." She didn't admit she was getting transfusions every ten days.

After dinner, Ali excused himself early so he could rest before departing. He hugged Susan hard, and she held onto him tearfully. When he wiped away her tears with his fingertips, she smiled. It was impossible to do otherwise.

As Susan watched him go, she had a moment of overwhelming fear.

Ali's private jet touched down at Khartoum airport just before 2:00 PM local time. The passengers disembarked to find a representative of the Sudanese government waiting. He conveyed his government's thanks for the sincere effort Ali devoted to help the hungry.

"I have also given orders to the authorities to help you in any way they can. They are to place no obstacles in your way," he added.

"I hope they can help me locate fifteen drivers and twenty carriers to bear provisions to affected areas," Ali said.

"Your group of companies has already sent a representative to take care of everything. He's waiting with the fleet of trucks."

Ali told Larry to stay with the plane in Khartoum until the mission ended.

The government representative took Ali and his companions to the waiting trucks. Ali thanked the man for getting things ready for him.

The man, handing Ali a pass to cross the Sudanese territories, wished him a successful trip.

Ali, Diana, and Nadia spent the night in Khartoum trying to adjust to the time difference.

With dawn, the stream of lorries started their journey to Darfour in the far west, hundreds of miles away.

After several hundred miles, the fleet of trucks reached Wadi Madany, the capital of the middle region of Kordofan. They refueled and continued for another 300 miles until they stopped near Costy city for the night. Ali gave orders to set up tents, and the drivers and carriers set to work. In an hour, everything was prepared.

The sun had already sunk behind the horizon, casting a faint, trembling light on the sandy earth. Ali sat before his tent, staring ahead. Heat and glare from the sun were replaced by the coolness of night. After a while, the moon rose.

The still night made silence fall upon the camp. Suddenly, a black driver stood and called to prayer. Ali and all men gathered in rows to pray. Diana saw them bow as one in adoration of God. They looked equal, casting off differences in color, language, and wealth. Her heart was filled with respect and reverence.

After prayers, Ali left the crowd and sat on a sandy hill, watching the moon's soft light.

Diana sat beside him. "I see signs of contentment on your face." "I feel close to God."

"Can you describe that feeling?"

"It puts happiness into my heart and reassurance into my soul."

"While you prayed, you looked as if you were embracing the earth. I felt the power of giving flooding out of you to water this land."

He glanced at her with affectionate eyes. Looking at her countenance delighted his soul. She looked luminous, elegant, and comely.

"The prayers you've seen purify man's soul from showy civilization and materialistic extravagance. This barren land isn't as it seems. It keeps its treasures in its interior until man is matured by belief, his heart purified with love and his will for reconstruction is strengthened."

"I'm puzzled. In the past, you were very romantic. Then you became realistic. Now you look at things spiritually."

"The worship of God isn't just restricted to performing prayers. It also extends to all other aspects of life. In that manner, both material and spiritual lives join in believers' hearts. God created the universe based on truth, justice, and mercy. Those are the characteristics of perfection, which believers strive to adhere to and pursue through life."

She was silent, thinking that over. His words took her to a world of light. At the bottom of her heart was a melody of gladness. Her soul, which had been as black as night, became pure and white like newly fallen snow.

Early the following morning, the fleet continued moving toward Elabiad city in the Kordofan region. The lorries had great difficulty getting through. The air was so warm and still, it seemed as if not a blade of grass or single cloud moved.

In the afternoon, they reached a spot near Elabiad city that the guides assured them offered good camping for the night. Ali removed his European clothes and put on a gown and light cloak. He advised Nadia and Diana to wear flowing outer garments to protect themselves from the unbearable heat.

In the morning, the trucks proceeded to Elfasher city in the far west of the Darfour region, near the border with Chad. Their last settlement was six miles from Elfasher city. After many long hours of difficult driving, they reached their destination.

Tents were set up, and sheets were placed on the ground with foodstuffs on them. Ali sent scouts north, south, and east of the camp to look for the hungry and guide them to the place of food and drink. The day was waning, and in the deep desert, it was growing dark.

The following noon, masses of the hungry began appearing. Ali watched them through binoculars and gave orders to the carriers to prepare to distribute the food. Nadia and Diana looked ahead, trying to locate them, but all they saw was burning sand.

Ali loaned them his binoculars, and they took turns looking through them, seeing emaciated bodies dressed in rags, some so weak they could scarcely drag their bare, bruised feet along. They were exhausted from the strain of their long walk.

Diana was silent and motionless for a moment. Her gray eyes drenched in tears, she felt her heart in her throat.

Ali couldn't wait. He ran toward the hungry, and Diana kept up on the hot, bright sand. The sun beat on them fiercely. Her heart raced at double speed, and her hand instinctively sought Ali's arm. He raised his cloak over her head to protect her from the heat.

They ran until they reached the hungry. They stood amazed and astounded. Waves of bony bodies slowly passed them, looking painfully ahead. They seemed hardly human. All were hungry, famished, and in pain. Lips and knuckles were split and bleeding, and their hair was as dry as straw. Some of the men with bent backs leaned on sticks and dragged their legs painfully along, often breaking down. Diana's heart beat so violently, she thought it might break.

Ali, speaking to them in Arabic, pointed at the camp, where the food was.

Back at camp, Ali asked Diana to supervise food distribution for women and instructed Nadia to take care of their drink. Women with linen kerchiefs on their heads glared at Diana with piercing eyes, frightening her until she complained to Ali. He calmed her down by saying, "The signs of cruelty and grief on their faces will turn into love and appreciation after their starved bellies are full of food and their tired bodies take shelter under the trees."

Ali gave orders to put food and water in two separate places, one for women and children, the other for men. Diana stood amid the women, giving them food and seeing that their needs were fulfilled until she put them at ease. Nadia went around the women with pots of water. They ate and drank, then took shelter under the trees.

Diana looked at them in compassion. She realized by helping them, she was helping herself. In those moments, she clearly saw her own position. She saw herself in the people she cared for. The heavy layer separating her from the world fell away, and dread fell from her face.

Tired and exhausted, she stretched out on the ground under a shady tree and slept.

Ali moved among the exhausted bodies. Men sat in circles, staring at him sullenly. They couldn't ask for food, because their tongues were too dry to talk, and terrible thirst tormented them. Some fell to their knees from exhaustion while waiting for food. Others pushed and shoved to get water. Since they came from different parts of Africa, they didn't know each other, but there was a strange likeness among them. Their bodies were cast in the mold of hunger and drought. Ali offered them food and water, then sat in a remote place to watch them with tear-filled eyes.

Diana awoke and looked around. The women, who previously looked at her sternly, became warm and affectionate. One old woman, who felt motherly toward Diana, sat before her with a smile. With a trembling hand, she plaited Diana's hair into one long braid behind her back. Diana looked at the long braid and smiled her thanks to the old woman.

Other women came and dyed Diana's hands with henna. She stared at their faces—thankful, simple, calm African faces that were pleasant to look upon. With food in their stomachs, the women smiled until their faces were as bright as day.

"Thank you," Diana murmured gratefully, then burst into tears.

She needed to see Ali and found him sitting among small children. Within minutes, they ate from his hands. She remembered how he compassionately petted his horses and fed them sugar cubes. She stood behind him a long time, watching him at his work.

After the children were satisfied, Ali stretched his hand to a piece of bread and was about to put it in his mouth when a small boy came out of nowhere, snatched it, and swallowed it. Ali kept feeding the boy until he was full.

Diana put her hand on Ali's shoulder. He lifted his sad eyes to hers and asked, "What were we doing on the other side of the world while people were starving here?"

She sat shoulder-to-shoulder beside him. "Your submissive sadness makes me feel that life is small and vapid. Love is the only source of goodness as long as life remains."

"I always pray that God will put life in my hand, not in my heart. Life in the hand of believers means charity, almsgiving, fidelity, and mercy. If people knew that, on the day of resurrection, God will differentiate between them according to fear of God and not wealth, they'd take the road of piety and godliness as a path to Him. Only here will God send His blessings. Then dearth and famine will turn into abundance and fruitfulness."

"I find my own happiness here while living a hermit's life."

"The rough life we live is our safeguard against the destruction of our souls. Here, we tame our souls to become content with giving and feeling other people's pain."

The day drifted away. It was fearfully hot, without even a faint breeze to ruffle the leaves. Nadia chose a spot overlooking the hungry and painted pictures expressing the sights of misery. Her hands were always busy, painting or drawing. Her eye for color and line was amazingly fine. The dark colors she used in her paintings clearly showed how the bodies before her were tortured by thirst and fatigue. The images were dimmed by famine.

Days passed, and more of the hungry came to the camp. They looked to Ali like dry tree trunks. He didn't wonder at that, because man was created from dust, and to dust he would return. What was truly agonizing was the children.

Ali watched them with a bleeding heart. Their bony bodies moved slowly with hollow eyes and swollen bellies. Ali received them with compassion and fed them from his own hands. They had confidence in him and broke into his tent, seeking more of his care. The echo of their laughter filled his heart with joy.

Ali liked most the boy who snatched the piece of bread from his hand. That boy followed Ali everywhere, as if he felt Ali would give him the parental love he lost after the death of his parents in the desert. Ali grew fond of the boy whose smile shone like sunrise.

The constant work Diana gave to the women was like nourishment to her parched soul. Ali saw her blossoming every day. He watched her for weeks, stepping among the hungry with food and water. She did everything with great simplicity. Whenever she felt exhausted or filled with fear, she continued working with fresh energy and persistence.

After a full day of work, Diana was very tired. Her body ached and twitched with fatigue. She tried to sleep in her tent, but she couldn't.

"Are you awake, Diana?" Ali whispered outside her tent.

"Is anything wrong?" she asked, glad to hear his voice.

"I just wanted to invite you to a cup of tea."

She came out of the tent with a radiant face reflecting her love for him. He'd never seen her more beautiful, nor as soft and young.

"Your face is as bright as an angel's from heaven," he said.

His words gave her strength. She needed every bit of that. Her insistence on coming negated her right to complain, and she was determined not to, even though her task severely tested her endurance. His tender, encouraging words made her fully aware of the importance of her mission. A mission representing the graces to people starving.

She smiled when he escorted her to a fire before his tent. They sat on the sand, which glittered white under the soft moonlight, while the dark sky was lit by a million points of starlight. It was very romantic and peaceful.

He gave her a cup of tea that she sipped slowly while looking into his strangely beautiful eyes. Did he know about his eyes?

He looked deep into her eyes and saw love and compassion. She looked at him a long time, seeing light and brightness in his face.

Yes, Lord, she thought, *almsgiving puts light in the face and affection in people's hearts.*

"How beautiful to sit in the desert and enjoy the moonlight," she said.

"Beauty is a prominent feature of the universe. Discovering beauty and enjoying it is one of the ways to worship God. God made the universe open to man's reflection to see signs of His existence and oneness."

"You talk about the universe as if it were a living being."

"It was created to obey God and praises Him."

"Is that how your religion looks at the universe?"

"It's not only that. In Communism, nature is exploited for the benefit of the ruling class. In capitalism, it's exploited for the benefit of the individual. As for us, we forbid what's prohibited, and we allow what's lawful."

Nadia joined them, and Ali offered her a cup of tea. She drank it down thirstily. From under her garment, she took out a painting of the boy Ali liked most. Ali was pleased by the resemblance.

"This is the best work you've ever done," he told Nadia. "I'll pay you a fair price for it."

"No. It's a present. I didn't know you loved children so much."

As they sat and drank tea, a guide came up and said, "We have discovered groups of hungry men and women wandering six kilometers from our camp. We showed them the way here, but they haven't arrived."

Ali feared they might die before they reached the camp and gave orders to the drivers to start searching for the missing people at dawn.

As the day drew toward dawn, Ali and his scouts searched for the hungry. It didn't take long to find them. Their withered, bony bodies lay on the hot sand, groaning in pain.

Ali, looking around in dismay, said, "We must save them at any cost. Carry them back to camp."

At the camp, under a large umbrella, a doctor examined the patients as the bearers brought in more and more dying men. The doctor's face was tense. He shook his head at Ali to tell him many would die.

Diana, looking at the dying, felt terrible grief. They looked like drowning men clutching at a straw. Nadia stood near her and watched, too. She shrank from their suffering but was thrilled by their courage at the moment of death.

"This is how the world will end," Nadia muttered.

Diana sought Ali to take refuge and found him standing on a hill with his men, digging graves for the dead. There was nothing but days of frightful suffering and death. There wasn't even time to wash the bodies before burying them. The feverish breathing of hundreds of men and women filled the air with death. Groans, sighs, and sharp screams filled the air. The angel of death hovered over them ceaselessly. Seeing people die day by day without end was intolerable.

Ali spent days at the edge of the graves, burying the dead and offering funeral prayers. Diana came near in silence. Ali stared at her gravely and said, with the faint odor of decomposing bodies in the air, "It's God's will. We shall all come to it someday. They were undone by heat and famine. It makes no difference now. They rest in the arms of death. Six feet from their heads to their heels was all they needed. They need not bow to anyone now."

Ali met more and more corpses carried on stretchers. With difficulty, he pushed his way through the corpses until he reached his tent, then he sat on the ground and held his face in his hands. Diana listened to his sobbing and saw his shoulders shaking with grief.

He took refuge in his tent for hours. It seemed as if he became so absorbed in thought that he didn't notice the passage of time. Diana, becoming worried, asked Nadia to check her brother.

Nadia found Ali lying on the ground, eyes shut, breathing with difficulty and perspiring heavily. "Diana!" she called.

Diana ran into the tent and watched with eyes that glistened with fear as she knelt. "You'll be fine," she murmured, smoothing the hair back from his forehead.

Nadia called the bearers to put Ali in bed, then she sent for the doctor. After a careful examination, the doctor said Ali suffered from malaria. He took tablets from his bag and showed Diana how to treat Ali.

Nadia couldn't bear to be away from her brother more than a few minutes at a time, but she was able to sleep deeply at times, because she trusted Diana to be a competent nurse. Diana was like a tigress, hovering over Ali and letting Nadia help only when she was ready to drop from exhaustion. In a far corner of the tent sat Ali's new friend, the little boy, waiting impatiently for him to recover.

Diana sat beside Ali's bed for hours, sponging his face with a cool cloth. Ali, feeling his strength leaving, knew he was almost finished. Diana softly said his name. He tried to focus on her with sore eyes. Diana feared he would pass out. Burning waves of fever made him rave:

"Calamity befell them. How cruel man is when satiation blinds him from seeing the other side of his face."

When Ali's fever was at its height, he shivered and swallowed desperately, and beads of sweat broke out on his forehead.

Outside the tent, guides and carriers walked by, carrying dying men, women, and children on stretchers. Men were still starving and dying in the camp. Under the influence of tired nerves and restlessness from lack of sleep, Diana worked harder than before. Ali was alive, so she, too, was alive.

Ali, struggling up through layers of pain, saw Diana's face swim into focus. He smiled when he recognized her during such episodes. He said with difficulty, "Go take care of the women."

A wave of tenderness washed through her. She held him and muttered assurances.

"I have confidence in God." He said while another wave of nausea swept through him.

Diana's heart pounded painfully when Ali began raving again, "They've got me. I'm done. Let me die in peace. Death is better than being alone, decrying our separation."

She remembered those words. He said them when he was stabbed many years earlier, and collapsed in her arms with his blood running like a river. Did he still remember those dark days? Why couldn't he forget the wounds of the past? She was free, and he could have her anytime he wanted.

After a while, his raving voice sank to a whisper. "No, I won't surrender to death. I'll cling to life, but what's the use of being alive when all I have loved in you has been extinguished by another man? What are you doing with my body? I don't want to live."

Diana shuddered and sobbed. His disjointed phrases gave a terribly clear picture of what he felt in his subconscious. She leaned down to kiss his chest and buried her face against his neck, her tears warm against his skin.

Her voice threatened to fail, so she spoke barely above a whisper.

"Stop blaming me. Your words are like a fire in my heart. Don't say all that I've loved in you has been extinguished. Your eyes say that you love me. I love you, because you're the dream of my youth and the support of my life. I'd risk my life for love of you."

Quickly straightening up, she lifted her head as if fearing he would feel her tears.

Ali's recovery was slow and painful. He became more his normal self, and he regained his mobility. Diana's heart melted when he opened his eyes and smiled at her. She felt as if her life drained into him. Tenderness flooded through her, filling her eyes with tears.

"You'll be all right," she whispered, "because I love you best in the world."

"I feel better now," he said terribly exhausted.

Nothing could lessen the boy's joy when Ali opened his eyes and told Diana he felt better. The boy noticed Ali didn't fade from consciousness again but remained alert. A large smile came to the boy's face.

Ali stared at the boy, who ran to him. Ali wrapped his arms around him tightly. Diana took the child in her arms and cradled him right and left while joyful tears ran down her face as she cried and laughed simultaneously.

CHAPTER TWENTY FOUR

Days drifted past while Ali recovered completely. Diana watched from her tent as he walked around the hungry, feeding them and offering drink.

"People will be pressed together hungry and thirsty at judgment day," he told them. "Those who feed others and give them drink on earth, God feeds them and gives them drink on judgment day."

Nearly two months passed since their mission began in Sudan. Finally, their journey was near its end. Ali and his companions prepared to leave. He left the fleet of trucks, tents, and food as a gesture of personal friendship with the Sudanese government.

Before he left the camp with Diana and Nadia in a wagon full of provisions, Ali prayed to God, raising his hands to the sky. "God, You're rich, and we're poor. People want water, but they don't find it. They need food, but it's not enough. Misery shows in their eyes, and pain grinds their hearts. Have mercy upon us. Wipe out their pain and send your rain."

On the day of their departure, Ali stood on a hill and spoke to the people, pointing to the nearby graves. "Their life was agony, their fittest place a burial ground. No soul can die except by Allah's wish and at the appointed time. Nothing can befall us save that which Allah has decreed for us.

"Every nation has its term. When that term comes, it can't be delayed even an hour. These corpses are, in fact, alive. Allah placed their souls in the bellies of green birds that will drink from the streams of paradise, eat of its fruit, and resort to lamps of gold in the shade of the throne.

"When they see such good drink, food, and a warm welcome, they say, 'We wish that our brothers knew what Allah has done with us, so they might not abstain from accepting faith or shrink from fighting against infidels.'

"Allah Almighty said, 'I shall make it known to them for you.' Then Allah revealed unto His Messenger Mohammed—Allah's peace and blessing be upon him—these verses: 'Think not of those who are slain in the way of Allah as dead. Nay, they are living. With their Lord they have provision. Jubilant are they because of that which Allah hath bestowed upon them of His bounty, rejoicing for the sake of those who have not joined them but are left behind, that there shall no fear come upon them, neither shall they grieve.'

"I have prayed to God to turn desert into green. Maybe my prayers shall be answered. I bid you all farewell. Peace, mercy, and the blessing of Allah upon you."

His sincere words filled their hearts. They shouted, "God is great!"

Diana was overwhelmed by the spell Ali seemed to have cast over them. The strange impression remained with her that she'd died and been reborn. It seemed to her that she was Ali, and Ali was she. Her fears, doubts, and painful anxieties dissolved. He let her see the golden fruit that shone from afar. The quest wasn't the world. The concern and the quest were Allah. No one shall turn away from Allah, but he will be humiliated, and no one shall cling to him, but he'll become dear. A mysterious sense of servitude, submission, and tractability to Allah washed over her.

The women came to bid Diana and Nadia farewell, offering baskets made of palm leaves. They cried as they said farewell to the women, then the wagon moved off, heading to Khartoum.

Crying, the little boy ran after the wagon. Ali stopped the wagon, went to the boy, and held him tenderly.

"The blessing of God is coming," Ali told him. "I want you to be the first to receive it. You're deeply rooted in this land, so stay and don't leave. We can't reap what we don't sow. This desert looks bare now, but soon, there'll be plants again. It's hard to believe in fruitfulness when drought covers the land, but abundance always comes whether we believe it or not."

The boy didn't understand Ali's words, but a sense of calm filled him, and he released the wagon without further weeping.

The wagon took four days to reach Khartoum. When they approached the city, they stopped to rest. Suddenly, they saw slashes of lightning, heard the explosions of thunder, and watched huge cloud masses gather. Rain fell onto the dry earth, and the rich, damp smell was like the sweetest perfume.

It rained on and off for hours. The drought was broken. Their prayers had been answered. Overwhelmed by God's power, they stared at the sky.

Ali prayed, knowing he witnessed proof that life was coming out of death. He felt God had accepted his alms. The well of giving and love was renewed in Diana, so she felt it overflowing endlessly. She watched Ali pray and saw God's presence in him.

They spent a few days in Larry's hotel in Khartoum, then they flew to the other side of the world.

In Ali's private jet, Nadia sat in the back, busily rearranging her paintings. Some were finished. Others were still just sketches, waiting to be completed later.

Ali and Diana sat together. He stared out the window as the African continent was getting smaller and smaller below.

"I appreciate your loyalty for the continent from which you came," she said.

"It's a land of prophets and religions. From it I receive my inheritance and personal traits. The south is still the conservative portion of the world."

"I've never been so grateful to you as I am right now. I was on the verge of exhaustion each day, but I felt my body growing stronger and reaccustoming itself to long hours while serving the hungry. I see light where there was only darkness."

"The world of giving is full of bright glamour that never dims. To my relief, you were strong enough for almost anything. You feel satisfaction even during fatigue."

"You're the cause of all the good things that happened to me."

He smiled without comment.

Her memory wandered through the beautiful past, seeking joy and happiness, and a question suddenly came to mind. "How'd you know of my tribulations with the bank?"

He gazed at her thoughtfully for a while. "I saw you in a dream, sitting amid snowy mountains on a cold, frosty night. Your naked body quivered with cold and shook with weeping."

Seized with astonishment, she lifted his hand to her lips and kissed it. He looked passionately into her eyes and saw her tears as purer than pearls and more radiant than moonlight. He smoothed her hair back from her forehead.

Her face softened and shone. His care for her soothed and relieved her. She put her head on his shoulder and slept peacefully.

When they landed in London, Ali decided to remain with his parents awhile. Diana continued to the States after two days she spent relaxing in a hotel in London. On the day of her departure, Ali and Nadia bade her farewell at the airport. They waved until she disappeared among the crowd boarding an American airline.

Nadia turned to gaze at Ali. "She waited on you hand and foot. She tore herself away for you. She sat by your bed for hours, sponging you during your fever, watching over you with anxious love."

Staring at the gate, he muttered, "When fever ate into my body, she softly cried my name. I opened my eyes and saw damp tears on her eyelashes. I fear I said something that hurt her."

After her long absence, Diana sat in her office, working. She called her secretary and asked her to get Susan on the phone. Diana didn't know why, but she felt deep appreciation toward Susan after the dramatic events she experienced in Africa.

"Susan's been in the hospital for three weeks," her secretary replied. "She's receiving treatment for blood cancer. She kept it a secret for a long time, but she realized, once she knew the disease was incurable, it would be better to have her doctor call us and explain, so work in the accounting division would continue smoothly without her."

Diana felt as if a vise squeezed her head.

Simone came into the office to congratulate Diana on her safe arrival. "As soon as Ali's back from London, I'll leave for Paris. I've done all that you need. My share in the profits from perfume sales will be sent to my bank in Paris."

"Why this sudden desire to leave?" Diana asked.

"Susan and I have become intimate friends these past months. I don't want to stay here and shed tears while seeing her to her grave."

A telegram reached Ali in London. *Susan very ill. Please come. Diana.*

Ali felt that Susan was dying.

In the hospital, Diana saw Susan had become terribly emaciated. Her shoulder and chest bones stood out through her transparent skin. With tears in her eyes, Diana hugged her.

"The whole matter is in God's hands now," Susan said. "Thank God you came to see me. I always wondered when I'd be able to see you. Listen carefully. I don't have much time left.

"I don't want you to think for one moment that Ali and I had an affair. I wanted to give him my body and soul, but he never asked for anything. I still remember his words. 'I don't want to hurt your feelings, but my heart could never love someone else.'

"It's you he meant, of course. I stood by him in times of distress, not only because we were friends, but because I loved him with all my heart. Because he couldn't love me the same way, he offered an everlasting friendship that lit the darkness in my soul.

"In San Francisco, I lived alone in a desolate apartment. I hated men because of the incident I experienced at the university. I felt bored with my monotonous life and prayed God would send me a glimpse of hope, something to make my life joyful.

"Ali felt my grief and came to offer happiness. His sudden appearance didn't astonish me, because, several times before that, I saw him in my dreams, coming to me from afar with a fascinating smile on his face and his hand out. That smile eased my restless soul and put hope into my dying heart.

"I left everything behind without thinking and went with him to the land of dreams where there was no misery or pain. I kept my illness to myself in order not to trouble him with my pain, but he felt my agony again, and one day, I found him innocently standing at my hospital bed asking what brought me there. When he knew of my illness, he gave me beautiful moments that enabled me to face my destiny and accept my fate.

"I received strength from him to live, but he left, and now death threatens me at any moment. Diana, I thought you could send for him, so I could see him before I die, but there's no need for that now. I see him coming from afar, crossing the distance with his hands outstretched and a reassuring smile on his face.

"Open that drawer. Inside is a precious necklace he once gave me. Put it around my neck, so he can see me as beautiful as I can be."

Tears flowing from her eyes, Diana obeyed. Susan touched the necklace in admiration, then asked Diana to comb her hair back from her forehead. Before she was swept into a deep sleep, Susan murmured, "The last thing I want before I die is to look into his eyes. I've always seen purity and giving in them. How I miss their love, compassion, truth, and beauty."

Susan slept most of the time. Drugs helped her sleep, but even during sleep, pain came to her. Diana sat at her bedside, crying silently. She didn't know why, but Ali's words returned to her. *I saw you in a dream sitting amid snowy mountains on a cold, frosty night. Your naked body quivered with cold and shook with tearful weeping.*

Susan awoke in an hour, her eyes open and focused on the door. "It's time," she whispered.

The door opened, and Ali walked in. Diana left them alone.

At sight of his dearest friend, Ali knew it was over. Something had died in her. Her softness was gone. Her lips were thin and blue, and the only life left to her was in her dark eyes. He was helpless to do more than hold her and stroke her hair back from her damp cheeks.

She looked into his eyes for a long time, seeing only love and purity. "The necklace is for you after I'm gone. I have no family but you." She touched it with a frail hand.

He nodded, tears falling constantly from his eyes.

"You infused my soul with care and love. I'll always remember your kindness in times of grief."

"It's you who gave without return. You've been a dear friend and guide to me through life."

"I feel a huge relief at having said those words. Now I can die in peace."

"Gently, my love. You'll be fine. I'm sure."

"You said, 'my love!' I've waited so long to hear those words."

"I have loved you without doubt."

"Put your pitying hand on my face and wipe away tears of deprivation."

He wiped tears from her eyes.

"Hold me tightly."

He hugged her gently, feeling she was nothing but skin and bone. "How wonderful to die in the arms of those whom you love. Now

I release you from loving me. I'll sleep a little. Don't be sad." Peacefully, she closed her eyes. Her last breath fluttered from her like a falling autumn leaf. He studied her dead face and felt his heart turn to stone, never to feel emotion ever again. After he released her onto the bed, he burst into tears. When he pulled himself together

again, he gently removed the necklace and put it in his pocket.

Diana entered the room, seeing immediately that Susan was dead.

She put a compassionate hand on Ali's shoulder to console him.

He lifted tearful eyes to hers. "I thought I stopped burying the dead, but here I am, burying part of my soul."

Black limousines slowly filed to the cemetery. The coffin was gently lowered into the grave. Ali, Diana, Simone, and the company staff stood holding flowers and listening to the priest's prayers. After he finished, they threw their flowers onto the coffin.

Ali stared at the coffin with all the sadness in the world in his eyes. "There'll always be much of you left." He tossed in his bouquet. "The sparkle in your eyes, your gay smile, our endless friendship, the loyalty we shared—all those decorate a necklace I once offered to you. I put it in the bouquet I just tossed to you."

Ali took refuge in his suite afterward. Susan died, but sorrow wasn't over. She couldn't be dead. He'd seen too much death recently. His grief wasn't just for Susan passing from his life but for all those he buried in Sudan. What was the use of life when it became empty of pitying hands and sincere friendship? There was nothing left for him to do in the States. He would ask Larry to take him into the sky. Maybe there, he'd hear the echo of Susan's laughter.

Ali sat in the meeting room, sullenly staring at the table before him. Simone walked in to see him sitting alone with eyes deeply sad. Respecting his silence, she didn't speak.

He looked at the chandelier overhead, then asked, "What's up, Simone?"

"I came to offer my condolences for Susan."

"Thank you."

"I don't find North Carolina as beautiful as before. I wish to return to Paris."

"What are you escaping from?"

"I don't like sadness. I hesitated a long time before attending the funeral, but Diana insisted."

"I see what you mean. Sadness might be tolerable without confrontation."

"I've already discussed my wish to leave with Diana. We agreed she'd send my share of the perfume sales to my bank in Paris."

"As you wish."

As she stood to go, Ali walked her to the door, and she hugged him dearly. "I'll be gone in a few hours. I'll definitely see you again."

Dumbfounded, he said, "It's a small world."

He returned to his seat and stared at the crystal chandelier shining in the sunlight.

Diana came in calmly and sat beside him. Something melted painfully inside her when she saw the sparkle in his eyes.

"I've done a lot of thinking recently," he said. "The company's making a handsome profit. Our balance sheet and profit-and-loss statement are healthy. I want to sell my business to you on terms to be arranged. My job's done. I'm going home."

The idea that he'd leave aroused anxiety in her. She wasn't prepared to face not seeing him again. Her face white with grief, she leaped to her feet. "How dare you say that?"

Rage shook her from head to foot. She looked as if someone clubbed her, or perhaps she'd been hit by a train. Her heart paused as she felt her world crumbling. He thought of consoling her, but she never gave him the chance as she ran from the room. A moment later, he heard her car start, then the sound of tires screeching as the car careened down the driveway.

Diana raced toward the highway, pressing down hard on the gas pedal until she was doing 100 miles per hour. Pain drove her beyond the limit of endurance. She looked blindly ahead with eyes filled with tears of suffering and pain.

Atop a small rise, the car struck the shoulder and shot into the air like a bullet before it rolled several times across a field. Passersby pulled Diana's unconscious body from the car and called an ambulance. Not seriously injured, she had only minor cuts and bruises. The doctor ordered her to stay in the hospital for three days.

Ali received a phone call in his office. It was Mary, Diana's governess speaking in alarm, "Mr. Ali, Diana was in a car accident a few minutes ago. She's in the hospital."

Panicked, Ali dropped the receiver and ran from the room to the street. The bad news diverted his thoughts from taking his own car. He ran down the street like a madman, fighting the throngs of rush-hour people. Strolling groups turned their heads in astonishment as he raced past. He never heard the squeal of brakes and the angry shouts of drivers as he crossed city streets.

Outrageous thoughts raced through his mind. His instincts told him she had died. He had buried the dead in Africa, then Susan, and now his soul. He was the cause of her death. His words of separation killed her.

"Awkward brute that I am," he shouted while running like a mad man, "I ought to have admitted my love to you. How could I be so unkind to you? Wait, my love! Don't go now. I adore you as much as ever. I see nothing but you. I can't bear having you out of my sight. If you die, I die with you. I'll ask them to bury my body with yours."

He reached the hospital totally out of breath. At the information desk, they gave him Diana's room number. He fought back tears as he rushed to her room. Opening the door, he stood abashed and motionless in the center of the room, staring at her with grave, wondering eyes. Dear God, she was alive!

She sat in bed with her golden hair falling down her back. She looked at him regretfully before turning away in pain. She remembered her despairing hopelessness when he always left her to despair, and her conviction she'd never see him again.

He walked to her and sat beside her on the bed, looking at the woman he once loved and never stopped loving. His body quivered, and his face was pale. He ran trembling fingertips over her forehead, beautiful eyes, delicate nose, and tender lips. He brushed back the silky, golden strands of her hair. His fingers went down her neck and clung to a large golden heart he once gave her.

Waves of weeping pushed up from within his depths to become abundant tears as strong sobs shook him. Suddenly, he took her in his arms and burst into tears.

Her mind was paralyzed, and she fell through vast, endless space. Was it true she was in his arms, or was it a dream? Was she really alive, or had she died? Was her spirit wandering the universe, dreaming of his embrace? He continued weeping as he held tightly onto her.

He said still crying, "I thought you were dead. I felt dead inside. What on earth did you do it for?"

"You're selfish, caring only for yourself. Nothing moves you except news of my death."

"You're my heart. No one can steal that from me, not even you."

"I didn't think, when I admitted my love for you, that you'd treat me with such alienation. Your heart's made of stone. The supposition that I died was what made you come here."

There was a supreme instant, during which a wish to see his tears burned within her. "Let me be. I want to see your tears."

Trying hard to stop weeping he said, "Stop that."

She insisted, and he tenderly released her. She looked into his tearful, loving eyes, crying in anguish for her, and ran her fingers through the dampness covering his face. "You shed tears for me?"

"I love you."

She couldn't believe it. "What did you say? I didn't hear you."

He hugged her hard while still crying. "I never stopped loving you. You're my costliest flower, the air I breathe."

"You kept your love hidden in your heart. You even denied it, though it made me suffer."

"The wound in my heart was deep. The passage of time didn't heal it."

"For a long time, I wanted to make you happy, but you refused. You ruined our youth."

She released herself tenderly from his arms. "I'm afraid of you."

"Don't fear a loving heart," he replied with compassion.

"I've always asked myself who you were. Sometimes, I see you as a dreamy man. Other times, you seem very realistic. Your love and compassion flow endlessly when you feel the groans of the needy, yet you refuse to admit love to a heart that never stopped loving you. Who are you? This persistent question always confuses me."

"I'm a man who loves you."

"You put hope into my heart, but, when I long for you, you fly away."

"Forgive me for the pain I've caused you."

"Your love is joined with pain. My heart can't endure that anymore." He lifted her hands to his lips and kissed them, wetting them with his tears. She put her arms around his neck and hugged him. Staring into space, she said, "I'll give up the struggle. I'll leave you."

"Leave me?" he asked, grieved. "I can't live without you."

"How many times have you left me alone? I won't let you play with my feelings again."

"I travel around the world to think of you."

"I won't let pain hurt my heart again. I won't follow you just to be burned." She said determinedly.

"How do you want me to correct myself? I beg you, don't go away."

"I'll tour the States for a change of air and to regain a sense of calmness away from you."

"Who knows?" he asked. "Maybe, when you're away, you'll understand facts you don't see now."

"I want to be by myself. I want to be left alone." She said tenderly.

With difficulty, he stood and walked to the door feeling completely dispirited. She watched him with regretful eyes until he was gone. She hadn't wept yet.

She looked at her hands and saw they were still wet with his hot tears. Lifting them to her lips, she kissed them, then cried her heart out.

CHAPTER TWENTY FIVE

In a flight heading toward New Orleans, Diana sat with an idea fixed in her mind. She looked forward eagerly to an independent life away from Ali. She couldn't do anything more for their love. She did the utmost already. She would never be his slave and let him be her master. She surrendered herself completely to his love, and had forgotten all about dignity.

Her willingness to accept more help from him went against her pride and self-respect. She had enough. He went too far. She would dispense with his assistance and would end their association. From New Orleans, she'd go wherever she wished.

She spent two days in Baton Rouge, then went to New Orleans, where she found a room in a fancy hotel. The receptionist, when he heard the last name of Stevenson, explained the many advantages of the luxurious suites they offered. A black man and his wife and child came in, and the receptionist carelessly said all the rooms were booked. Downhearted, the black family left.

Diana, extremely annoyed, couldn't argue with the receptionist, because racism was common in the South. Taking a key, she went to her room and sat in a big, comfortable chair to close her eyes and relax her tired body.

Ali rose in her imagination. She saw him feeding and watering black, withered bodies. Cups of water in his hands were like glasses filled from rivers in paradise. His words rang in her ears. "People are of two kinds—either a brother in religion or an equal in creation." Wasn't that equality in its perfect form? Taking her to Sudan had been an awakening for her. It brought her to herself. Their life there had a completeness that gave it beauty.

Suddenly, she opened her eyes as if blaming herself for letting her thoughts turn to him. She went to the window, opened it, and leaned out to look down. Light wind ran through the flowers, shaking them. She found herself whispering, "Your body was shivering with fever in my arms exactly like those flowers shake on the breeze."

Diana, feeling bored, decided to travel to a distant state. She flew to Nevada and stayed in Las Vegas for a few days, hoping to entertain herself and forget the memories that haunted her.

She entered a casino, planning to try roulette first. She bought chips from a cashier and placed a bet in seventeen. The wheel spun and stopped. Diana lost a few thousands.

She sat down to play cards and lost a few more thousands. She didn't care about recovering her losses. She walked carelessly among the intent gamblers, her nostrils assailed by cigarette smoke and whiskey fumes.

Ali's words came to her again. "We forbid what is prohibited and allow what is lawful."

Looking around, she saw money being thrown away on the spin of a wheel or the turn of a card when there were hungry people dying around the world. She felt sick of the false glitter of Las Vegas and its showy civilization and materialistic extravagance.

Ali turned her into something terrific. He made her recognize the real value of life even when it led her from a luxurious life to the world of the poor. He was a man of the earth, as rooted in it as the great pyramids, as steady and dependable as night following day. He had a deep knowledge and appreciation for his religious heritage. The self-denying, self-sacrificing part of his religion commanded the homage of his soul.

She'd seen the light of God in his face when he spent alms on the needy. Because of her, he returned and saved her more than once. The many things he did came to her. Finally, she was able to see and speak of them.

What was happening to her? Whenever she traveled, she found herself attracted to him like a moth attracted to light. She felt a strong need to escape to the Sahara, where she could find sanity and reality. She looked at the miles of desert around her, with palm trees rising high into the air in their passionate quest for the sun. Even the barren desert produced its best at his invocation.

How she longed for Ali's tent in the middle of the Sahara, it was like a star twinkling in the sky. His words flowed over her. "I travel around the world to think of you." She had to stop thinking of him. She still had her pride.

In her room, she sat in burning silence. With worry and boredom hovering nearby, she talked to herself. "God, where can I escape from him? His memory besieges my soul everywhere I go. I've become frightened of him. The tears in his eyes haunt me. They stab my heart."

She recalled him saying, "Don't fear a loving heart."

Suddenly, she realized her journey of sadness began when she left him.

From Nevada, she flew to Washington to spend a few days in Seattle and enjoy the beauty of its famous lakes. She remembered the valley of love and its blue lake. She wondered when he would take her there to drink again from the pure wells of his love.

She refused to surrender to his spell. She is now full of confidence, ready for anything. In the famous Olympia garden, she walked and tried to enjoy nature's beauty. Why did she see it deserted and devoid of beauty? Every beauty she felt was only through Ali's love, the love that had opened her eyes in her teens on every thing beautiful, and which she still dreamed of and lived for. She found real beauty in his kind heart and his power to give without expecting anything in return. God granted him magnanimity, wealth, and youth, and he kept his heart clean for her all those years. What else could've been so overwhelming?

From Washington, she went to California. In San Francisco, she walked the city looking at shops and the attractive trams going up and down the hills. On the hanging bridge with its golden gate, she watched boats sailing into San Francisco Bay.

"Who do you think you're kidding?" a voice asked. "You sail away from him searching for security while you know he carries with him a circle of timeless peace and reassurance."

On horseback, she rode for miles in a desert bare of everything except rocky mountains. She remembered Ali standing on a hill delivering his farewell speech, and the watchers replied, "God is great." At that moment, she saw him on a haughty peak rising to the highest sky.

Days passed, and every minute reminded her of him. Tired and bored with travel, she locked herself in her room and sank into deep silence, gazing into the dark for hours.

One question occupied her mind. *"Who are you?"*

Moments with him flitted through her memory.

When she called him from the darkness, he came with a wounded heart to stand by her and liberate her from the torture she went through. He set up a broken company and kept its name so she'd feel her family name was still there, something worth working for.

Who are you?

You give this a sense of your manners and that a brand of your knowledge. While life slaps at us from all sides, you proceed without hesitation down the road of love, giving, and truthfulness. You aren't limited by time or space, for in your hands the past meets the future.

Are you the good moving in creation since eternity or a torch giving guidance to those who are astray? Each time I seek light to disperse the darkness, I see you praying. Thus, my heart shows submission, and I feel at peace with the world. Who are you? A man whose pleasure is to bring back to sad faces their happiness, dreams, and to erase worry around the eyes, or are you a man ingenuously confronting the world with candor and a pure spirit?

The ideas and manners derived from your tradition remain fixed. They don't change over time. You have a touch of mysticism that makes you above the people among whom you live. That combination makes your summing up of complex facts a mixture of clarity, precision, and wisdom. You have a thousand years of civilization behind you.

There's no doubt that the way you understand civilization is the way God wishes it to be, one of truth, love, goodness, and beauty. Civilization isn't technology, power, or wealth. Those things could be owned by people seeking their own benefit. True civilization is a loving heart capable of spreading good on earth and harvesting love in the hearts of people. You, my love, have done that.

I haven't known compassion since my mother died. My father raised me, giving me care but not compassion. I always ask myself, "What are the most-beautiful kinds of compassion?" Is it that of the mother I lost so early? Is it that of the father under whose protection I lived most of my life?

I don't know why I realized the meaning of compassion when you shed tears of love, and your body shook convulsively in my arms. Why do I love you more when you cry? Maybe because weeping is a true expression of the heart's compassion when the tongue can't reveal love. Overwhelming happiness encompassed my soul when you admitted love, weeping in my arms.

At last I know who you are! You're a man God has endowed with compassion of the heart and a love of goodness and beauty. You're the man I love, but who am I? In terms of money, I'll always be a debtor to you for the thirty million dollars you paid willingly to make my fortune. In terms of words, you saved yourself from saying words that might bring back the wounds of the past. In terms of sacrifice, I lived my life like millions of women, but you kept your heart clean for me all these years. You even ignored yourself to the extent of not telling me about the dream that made you come to my rescue.

I was your dream, and you were all I hoped for in life. What am I doing here without you? Wait, don't go away! I'm coming to you. Walking along the road of life without you is an extravagance of time. Being away from you is nothing but loss and emptiness.

She collected her possessions and flew back to North Carolina. She didn't feel the passage of time on her way back, because she was lost in thought. Was he still at the company, or had he left for London? If he wasn't at the company, she'd chase him around the world.

She reached home and went to her room, walking in her closet to find the most-beautiful dress she owned, one that would suit the occasion. Finally, she found the white dress she wore years earlier when she first met Ali in the valley. To her surprise, it still fit like new.

She dressed quickly and brushed her hair. She didn't bother with makeup. Her reflection was satisfactory when she studied herself in the mirror. She looked as if she were still eighteen.

She arrived at the company and went to the meeting room. When she opened the door and walked in, she saw Ali convening with the board. Surprised, he stared at her as ardent longing filled his heart with love.

Without taking his eyes off her, he said, "Gentlemen, we'll continue this meeting later."

The board members looked at each other in surprise, then left.

"You want to sell me your shares?" she asked. "You want me to sign the contract for your departure from me? How can that be when I'm the heart beating in your chest and the eyes with which you look at the world? Don't you ever stop wasting precious time?"

His eyes twinkled. He rushed to her and took her hand firmly, pulling her close. She closed her eyes and smiled, because she knew without doubt where he was leading her.

They reached his white Ferrari. She sat beside him as he drove, her loose hair flowing around her. He took her to the valley of love that witnessed the most-beautiful days of their lives.

They left the car and stood on the hill looking at the lake which sparkled down below reflecting the afternoon sun. Removing their shoes, they ran toward the lake with the sweetness of love flooding their hearts.

Rose scent engulfed them. Cool water lapped at their ankles. She glanced at his eyes and saw the sparkle that always captured her heart, and she surrendered completely. He took her hand, and they waded in to their waists. With his palms, he wiped her hair and face with water that looked like beads of pure pearl. She felt a deeper, stronger love reborn in her heart and delightfully surrendered to his touches, feeling his feelings and existing through his existence.

He said, "With water of love, I put clarity in your soul and love in your heart that raises you above the wounds of the years. I'm the arm you lean on while crossing the bridge of life. I'm the boat you sail with across the vicissitudes of times. I'm the man in your life. I'm hope, I am love. I see you as I first saw you, a pure heart that knew no one but me. Now, you can see that I love you with all the power of my soul."

A last wave of clarity broke through her. She put her arms around his neck and drew him close, looking enthusiastically into his eyes she said with love overflowing, "For a long time, I asked myself who you were. I thought you were the man I loved, but only now do I understand who you are—a man from the East."

www.ingramcontent.com/pod-product-compliance
Lightning Source LLC
LaVergne TN
LVHW040138080526
838202LV00042B/2948